Dolores J. Wilson's

Big Hair and Flying Cows

Platinum Imprint
Medallion Press, Inc.
Florida, USA

Published 2004 by Medallion Press, Inc.
225 Seabreeze Ave.
Palm Beach, FL 33480

The MEDALLION PRESS LOGO is a registered tradmark of Medallion Press, Inc.

Printed in the United States of America

Library of Congress Cataloging-in-Publication Data

Wilson, Dolores J.
  Big hair and flying cows / Dolores J. Wilson.
    p. cm.
  ISBN 1-932815-17-1
  1. Women truck drivers--Fiction. 2. Automobile mechanics--Fiction. 3. Eccentrics and eccentricities--Fiction. 4. Women television personalities--Fiction. 5. Georgia--Fiction. I. Title.
  PS3623.I5784B54 2004
  813'.6--dc22
                        2004024622

Dedication,
For my cousin, Sandy Bair, who always
brings happiness into my life and makes me laugh.

Acknowledgments

My thanks to:

Jeannie Dickson, my dear friend, for being the first to tell me I should write a book and for encouraging me along the way.

The Plot Queens, Vickie King, Marge Smith, Heather Waters, and Laura Barone for your friendship and mountains of guidance and support.

Helen Rosburg and Leslie Burbank for believing in my work and helping my long-time dream come true.

Last, but definitely not least, my husband Richard. Thank you for supporting my quest to be a writer. I couldn't have done it without you.

Chapter 1

"Bertie," my father yelled from the doorway between his office and the hot garage. Roberta Byrd is my name, but everyone calls me Bertie. That's right. Bertie Byrd. Please don't ask what my parents were thinking. It's pretty obvious . . . they weren't.

"Bertie?"

"Yeah, Pop?" I slid out from under the Lincoln Continental I'd been working on, struggled to a sitting position, then pulled a rag from my coverall pocket. A twinge of old age crawled across my shoulder blades. Rolling my head from side to side, I hoped to relieve some of the ache.

When I lay under a car, flat on my back on a creeper, as opposed to flat on my back with a creep, I tend to feel much older than my thirty-two years.

"Were you sleeping under there again?" Pop had left the sanctum of his air-conditioned office to see what I was doing.

"Only for a few minutes," I lied. By the pain in my back, it must have been quite a while. "I didn't get much sleep last night. I worked that big wreck out on Turner Highway, and Martin Griffin drove off the culvert in his driveway about three this morning."

"Well, you got a call now too. Ethel Winchell's out of fuel, again. She's in front of the Dew Drop Inn and Tavern. She wants you to get her away from that 'heathen breeding place.' You better get out there before she develops a case of apoplexy."

"I'm sure it's not the first case she's had today." Or the last. I had to smile thinking of the snit she'd be in worrying that someone might see her out there and report her to the Sweet Meadow Garden Club. They might put her on one of their lists. Trust me. You don't want to be on their list. I know I try to stay in their good graces at all times.

Every Sunday morning, when anyone enters the back of the First Baptist Church over on Liberty Street, the whole Garden Club turns in unison to see who came in. As people enter, the ladies mark that person's name off the list. At the end of services, they check to see which infidels didn't show up.

The Garden Club is easy to spot from the back of the church. They're the group of women who have two hair styles-high and higher. The colors span about three shades of blue.

They're a powerful group. I go to church every Sunday, as much for the Garden Club as for the Lord.

Pulling into the parking lot, I didn't see Mrs. Winchell. I backed my wrecker up to her 1982 Mercedes. You couldn't ask for a finer running machine, if Ethel Winchell would quit letting the diesel engine run out of fuel. However, Mrs. Winchell felt that pulling into a filling station was beneath her. I thought that having to be towed about six times a year was stupid. Of course, I make more money with her way of thinking.

I hooked the chains to the undercarriage, then winched the wheels off the ground. As I walked toward the Dew Drop Inn to find her, I caught a glimpse of Mrs. Winchell scrunched down in the front seat. I walked to her car, then tapped on the window. With dark eyes she looked up at me. The driver's window eased down. Mrs. Winchell whispered something I couldn't make out.

I leaned closer. "What'd you say?"

"Get me out of here before someone sees me." The old woman ground her words through her teeth and stared at me like I'd sucked all the fuel from her car and left her stranded at the devil's doorstep.

"Yes, ma'am. Come on up in the truck with me." I opened her

door. She snatched it shut so fast, I almost got my hand caught.

"I'm not setting foot on this parking lot. Now, get me out of here."

"If you didn't get out, how did you call for a tow truck?"

She reached to the seat next to her, then waved a cell phone in my face. "I'm electronically connected to the world. I have a computer too. I even do e-mail. I instant message Millie Keats every day."

"Millie only lives three blocks from you. You could holler out the window at her."

"It's the thought that counts, Bertie. You'd do good to get your-self a computer. Might find you a husband on the Internet."

I shook my head and walked back to my truck. As I pulled out of the parking lot, I glanced at my rear-view mirror. Barely sticking above the steering wheel of Mrs. Winchell's Mercedes, I could see the cutest wisps of blue hair.

I guess the world advanced for everyone, regardless of age. Imagine Mrs. Winchell being electronically connected. Now, if she'd learn to keep fuel in her car, that would be a real advancement.

I dropped her and her car at our shop-Thomas Byrd and Sons' Garage. Of course, Sons' chose to move to other towns leaving me, Pop's only daughter, to fulfill his dream of sharing his business with his children.

He'd had the sign painted when Billy and Bobby were in high school. They joined the Marines and Navy, respectively, and never came back to Sweet Meadow to live. Pop never had the heart to re-paint the sign. I think he still hopes they'll change their minds and come back. Personally, I've been real tempted to climb up on the old tin roof with my trusty spray paint and turn Pop's sons into a daughter.

The phone rang, its shrill jangle magnified through the of-fice, garage, and probably as far away as the Chow Pal Diner down the street. Before the phone could wail again, I plucked it from its cradle. "Byrd and Sons."

"Bertie?" A weak voice floated through the receiver.

"Who is this?" I asked.

"It's Carrie Sue. Please come get me."

"Oh, good Lord. Have you been in an accident? Where are you?"

"I'm at home. Yes, there's been an accident. Please come get me." She sounded on the verge of tears.

"Where's your car?" I hoped no one had been hurt.

"My car's in my garage. Why do you ask?"

"If you need a tow truck, Carrie Sue, I need to know where the car is."

"I don't need a tow truck. I need a ride," she announced.

"A ride? I drive a wrecker. Not a taxi cab."

"Please."

I hate it when people beg. "Okay, I'll be right there." The day kept getting stranger.

Carrie Sue Macmillan had graduated with my brother Bill, the Marine. I think she actually auditioned for the village idiot, but got turned down. Whatever she wanted me to do surely would be interesting. Of this, I was certain, but I had two cars I had to finish putting back together before five o'clock. I really didn't have time to play games with Carrie Sue.

I arrived at her house in about five minutes. Pulling into the drive, I blew the horn. She didn't come out. After waiting a few minutes, I climbed out of the truck and made my way along a path lined with various flower containers-tires turned inside out, plastic swans, and my favorite, a commode overflowing with petunias.

"Psst!" The shrub with the pink flamingo in front of it hissed at me. I walked around it and found Carrie Sue stooping behind it. Her head sported a bright yellow knit cap pulled down over her ears. A purple pom-pom danced on top of it. I glanced first at her, then up at the sky where the bright sunshine caused the thermometer to teeter somewhere between 92 and 93 degrees.

"Your head cold, Carrie Sue?"

"No," she snapped, glaring at me.

I waited for her to explain. Explain anything. Why she'd called me to her house? Why she hid behind a yard shrub? Why she wore a wool-knit cap on a stifling day?

Finally, she stood erect, then pulled the hat from her head. It looked like it was sucking her hair from her scalp. When it popped free, I realized something really had removed her hair.

"What happened?" I asked, shock vibrating my voice.

"I was babysitting Donna's kids. I just dozed off for a minute. When I woke up, this is what they'd done to me."

"Looks like they tried to scalp you. What do you want me to do, drag them behind the tow truck?" I visualized Carrie Sue's two nephews and one niece bouncing along behind the wrecker like tin cans tied to a wedding bumper.

"No. I want you to take me to Bonnie Boo's Curl Up and Dye. I can't drive downtown looking like this. You gotta sneak me in her back door."

"I don't gotta do anything, Carrie Sue. I drive a big, old truck with beacon lights on top. I can't sneak anywhere. Besides, I'm not a taxi driver."

"Oh, come on, Bertie. You can do this for an old friend."

"You've never been my friend. Especially after you threw me into the boys' locker room."

"I gave you your first glance at a naked man." She smiled.

"Yes, but it was fat old Coach Henderson, for crying out loud."

She started laughing. I did, too. I gave her a ride to Bonnie Boo's Curl Up and Dye. Although bald Carrie Sue never realized it, my beacon lights flashed all the way there.

On my way back to the shop, Pop dispatched me to Sweet Meadow Elementary School. Ida Josevedo, first-grade teacher and bus monitor, needed to be towed to Wal-Mart in Shafer. Her car's battery thought it was a good day to die.

Everybody who climbs inside my tow truck has a story to tell. Most of the time, I'm as interested in listening to them as I am performing my own root canal. At those times, I take a deep breath and let the gas fumes carry me away to a tropical isle. But, when Mrs. J. talks, I listen.

Her students call her Mrs. J. because they can't say Josevedo. Until she went on vacation a few years ago, she was plain Ida Mae Wells. In Mexico she met her own personal, generic Antonio Banderas. Within two days of her arrival at the Ritz Carolino, she became Señorita Duarte Josevedo.

At the end of her two weeks, she returned home. She called me to pick her up at the airport. I objected due to the fact that I'm not a taxi driver, then I picked her up at the baggage claim. She climbed into the truck and proceeded to tell me about her vacation. I zoned out shortly after she told me about the bumpy flight there.

When I came back to earth, she'd given all the details about her marriage which ended with something to do with a voodoo curse and chicken's feet. She was going to keep his name because it was more romantic than Wells.

I had missed it all. I swore right then and there I'd never miss another word Mrs. J. had to say.

"This has been one bloodsucking, backbreaking, migraine kind of day. Ever had one of those?" Okay, I could miss some of her words.

"Must be something in the air. It's been one of those for me too." I hadn't really thought of it in those terms, but now that she mentioned it, it was exactly that kind of day.

"My kids got kicked out of art class this morning. Some people have no sense of humor. That woman from the museum brought a bunch of books with Renaissance pictures of naked women in it. She freely passed the pictures among six-year-olds, then had the nerve to get all flustered at their interpretation of the finer arts." Fire seemed to shoot from her eyes. "What did she expect?" Mrs. J. demanded.

"I . . . I haven't a clue." I tried to appease her, but she appeared very distracted with her bloodsucking, etc. "What did your little darlings do?" I scooted closer to my door.

"One boy looked at the naked women and announced that he could see their boobies. The next one hollered, 'Oh, he said

Boobies.' Then the next, 'He said boobies.' 'Boobies,' 'boobies.' It went through the crowd like the wave at a football game." She floated her hands through the air and raised her backside from the seat to mimic the wave.

I tried not to smile. Really I did.

"I don't know what that curator was so uptight about. I was just thrilled the kids didn't start a wave with the "F" word like they normally do."

I lost it. I laughed so hard I had tears in my eyes. Mrs. J. just stared at me. I guess the voodoo curse she'd told me about when she returned from Mexico, which I never did get to hear about again, had something to do with her being stripped of her sense of humor.

By the time I got back to the shop, it was after five o'clock. The two cars still needed repairing. I'd have to work pretty late to get them finished, and, since I didn't have them done when the owners got off work, I'd have to deliver the cars to the people's houses.

With the long hours I put in every day and well into the night, it's a good thing I don't have anyone or e-mail waiting at home for me. Although a husband could bring me dinner and, if I had e-mail, I could let people know how much I love them.

I guess I am just an old-fashioned gal. I have to do things the old-fashioned way. I picked up the phone, then punched in the numbers.

"Hi, Mom. I love you. Can you bring me dinner?"

Friday has always been my favorite day of the week. If I could survive until five o'clock in the afternoon, then Pop took over my duties as an on-call mechanic/tow truck driver until eight Monday morning. I looked forward to my Friday nights at the Dew Drop Inn where I could enjoy a few glasses of Sweet Meadow champagne, better known as draft beer, and dance with some of the local cowboys. Yee haw!!

Tonight would be a little more interesting than usual. My best friend, Mary Lou, planned to introduce me to her cousin from Atlanta. A fine specimen of mankind, according to Mary Lou. She just knew for sure we'd hit it off.

Only time would tell.

I glanced at the tire-shaped clock which hung on Pop's office wall. Eight-fifteen. I tapped on the face, hoping it had stopped. No such luck.

Just then the phone shrilled. Lordy, I wish Pop would get a different bell. I swear to high heaven that sound could shatter glass.

"Byrd and Sons."

"Hi, Bertie," Millie Keats sang through the receiver. The woman had to be a hundred years old, but still lived an active life that I could only dream of, including an on-again, off-again romance with Coach Henderson.

Let me make this point perfectly clear-I dream of romance, not Coach Henderson. That thought sends chills through my entire body. I saw him naked once . . . Never mind, it's a long story.

"Good morning, Millie. What can I do for you this beautiful, sunny day?" Darn, I must be in a better mood than I thought, probably the Mary Lou's cousin thing.

"I want to reserve a ride to my doctor's appointment at ten. I have to take him a urine specimen."

"I'm not a limo service, and I've told you a hundred times, unless you can tell me you have a car in the ditch, don't call me for a ride. Good-bye, Millie." I hung up the phone.

Guilt washed through me. I hoped Millie needed to see the doctor for maintenance reasons and not some life-threatening condition. Time would tell that too, I figured.

Later, I'd just pulled the fuel filter from a Honda Accord when the phone rang. After wiping the grease from my hands, I answered it.

"My car's in the ditch." Millie Keats' voice sounded rushed. I checked the time. Ten o'clock.

"You don't have a car." I tried to hold my temper to a slow simmer.

"No, but I do have a doctor's appointment, and you're not here."

"I told you I can't take you to the doctor." Feeling a tad guilty, I asked, "Why do they need a urine specimen?"

"To see if I'm pregnant." Hysterical laughter zinged its way through the phone to my unappreciative ears.

I gave myself a mental head slap. "Miss Smart Aleck, you'll have to find another ride."

"But Bertie. I'm all dressed in my brightest pink dress to go see Dr. James."

I wondered if Millie realized, no matter what dress she wore to the doctor, he'd never see her in it. That thought would probably be wasted on the old woman.

"I can't take you. Good-bye, Millie. I have a date with a fuel filter."

"Well, I hope you two have a grand old time." She snorted into the phone. Then the line went dead.

Thirty minutes later, Chief of Police Bob Kramer phoned. "I need a wrecker in the two-hundred block of Laurel Street. There's been an accident."

While I washed my hands in the garage sink, I jostled the phone against my neck. "Anyone hurt?" I asked.

"No. It's a man from Shafer. He just seems a little confused. He said some lady stood in the middle of the road, raised her skirt, and flashed him. It startled him so bad, he ran into the ditch. Gotta go." It took the Chief a few seconds to actually hang up.

Before the connection ended, I heard someone in the background yelling, "I tell you, it was a shocking pink dress."

I hung up the phone, then stared at it for a few seconds. Surely, Millie wouldn't do something like that. I'd almost convinced myself when the phone startled me from my wishful thinking.

"Byrd and Sons." I held my breath.

"Bertie, now there's a for-real car in the ditch. I'll be waiting for you," Millie Keats announced, then hung up the phone.

After I winched the wrecked car out of the ditch and found no damage, the owner drove away, still mumbling to himself. Inside the truck, I found Millie Keats, wearing a pink dress, waiting for me.

"That could have all been avoided, Bertie." She stared straight ahead, nodding.

"You're a fruitcake, and I should turn you in to the Chief." I nodded too, knowing full well I'd never tell anyone. Millie and I rode toward the doctor's office, both of us nodding like those toy doggies in the rear windows.

If my luck held out, Millie would buy me a cap with the words "Millie's Limo Driver" embroidered on it.

At five o'clock sharp, Mary Lou picked me up in front of the garage. Her mission centered around making me beautiful so she could present me to her cousin from Atlanta. When she talks about him, she never uses his proper name. She only refers to him as her Cousin from Atlanta with the same reverence you would use if talking about the Duke of Windsor.

By the number of shoe boxes filled with cosmetics stacked in Mary Lou's backseat, she planned to do major renovation on me. I shuddered. Flipping down the visor for a glimpse into the vanity mirror, I could see she had her work cut out for her.

Wild, runaway auburn curls sprouted from under my Braves baseball cap. The parts of my face that weren't covered with grease sported freckles galore. Poor Mary Lou. She might need therapy after this.

I slapped the visor up, then slumped back against the seat.

"I can't wait for you to meet my Cousin from Atlanta." Mary Lou made a two-wheeled turn onto my street.

"Does his majesty have a name?" With jealousy, I admired the well-manicured lawns of the three yards we passed before pulling into my driveway.

"Rupert Haines." Mary Lou shut off the car.

"Rupert? That's interesting."

"You two will make a perfect match." She started pulling boxes from the back seat. I wished I shared her enthusiasm. However, I think I am a descendant of Doubting Thomas.

I picked up the last shoe box, then traipsed through my grass, brown and crisp as a paper bag. I could at least water the lawn and turn it green. But what good would that do? I'd then have to cut it, which would constitute me buying a lawn mower, which I don't have time to use anyway. So, in retrospect, maybe I didn't envy the neighbors and their lush lawns.

Mary Lou and I entered my house which I'd moved into four months ago. I'd been living in a duplex across town until Carrie Sue's sister, Donna, and her three munchkins moved in next door. I really love kids. Someday, I hope to have my own 2.5 allotted to the average American family, but Donna's little darlings are in a class of their own.

When the owner of my present abode, Mr. Pete Fortney, had to be sent to the Tall Pines Nursing Home down the street, and his son decided to rent out the house, I jumped at the chance to move closer to my work and farther from Donna and her kids, who have been named the most likely to go to jail before the age of fifteen.

I'd showered, washed my hair, and plopped down onto a kitchen chair. Mary Lou had touched up her make-up and added another inch to the height of her hair. She stood ready to turn me into her masterpiece to be presented to the *Cousin from Atlanta, Rupert the Magnificent.*

"Please don't give me big hair, Mary Lou," I begged. One time she'd teased my hair really high for a house-warming party when Carrie Sue got her new, double-wide mobile home. The den had a ceiling fan. Dangling from that little chain thingy used to turn on the fan was a cow with angel wings. Minutes after my unobtrusive entrance, I got that flying cow caught in my big hair.

Evidently, Mary Lou's brand of hair spray is manufactured by the same people who make those fly-catcher strips Grandma used to hang in her kitchen. My hair latched onto the cow and refused to let go. They had to unhook the chain from the fan, and I wore the charming accessory, dangling chain and all, for the rest of the party. If I had a quarter for every flying cow joke I heard that night, Donald Trump and I could be having a financial discussion over dinner right now.

"Are you listening to me?" I asked. "Please don't give me big hair."

"Okay, okay." Mary Lou couldn't understand my objections to anything she had in mind for me. She couldn't operate an electric can opener, microwave, or TV remote. Yet, arm her with a blow-dryer, and I was supposed to believe she was Picasso. I would make my dear, dead uncle, Doubting Thomas, proud.

Don't get me wrong. I love Mary Lou. She's been my best friend since the first grade. But sometimes she's not the crispest cookie in the jar. My family may be responsible for that.

When Mary Lou and I were six, my brothers, Billy and Bobby, talked her into letting them prove they were Hercules by holding her upside down from a branch of a huge oak tree in our yard. Of course, all the boys really wanted to do was look down the legs of her shorts. So there they were; Billy held one leg and Bobby held the other while Mary Lou squeaked with delight at the extraordinary strength of the Byrd boys.

Pop saw what they were doing, came rushing across the yard toward us, yelling, "Put her down. Now!" Billy and Bobby dropped poor Mary Lou onto her head. Although she insisted they didn't do any damage, I'm not so sure.

"Here, take a look." Mary Lou had finished my hair and make up. She handed me a mirror. I slowly peeked into it. Much to my surprise, I looked good. Darn good. My hair had been pulled into a French twist, with only a small amount stacked on top of my head. Tendrils framed my face. A perfect amount of make-up hid flaws, highlighted and contoured my cheek bones, and brought out the brown of my eyes.

"That correspondence course in cosmetology you're taking is paying off, Mary Lou." I hurried to the bathroom mirror to see the full effect under brighter lights.

"I like it." Mary Lou beamed.

"Me, too." I had to admit, my friend had worked a small miracle.

I dressed in a knee-length, black leather skirt, then carefully pulled a sleeveless, white, V-necked sweater over my head. Sitting on the edge of the bed, I slipped one foot into a sensible, comfortable, black loafer. Mary Lou clicked her tongue and shook her head. She handed me a pair of high-heeled, strappy shoes, built for anything but comfort. She had done such a good job on my top half, I decided to let her have her way with the my bottom half too. Surveying the new me in a full-length mirror, I decided I looked pretty good, if I did say so myself.

Mary Lou turned me to face her, then she rolled my skirt at my waist to bring the hem to mid thigh. "Perfect," she said.

I smiled, then when she turned to lead me to the front door, I pulled the skirt back where it belonged. There was a limit to my reform. Sweet Meadow wasn't ready for me in a mini-skirt.

The Dew Drop Inn was jumping. A juke box flashed colored lights from the corner of the dance floor and played "The Devil Went Down to Georgia," Sweet Meadow's National Anthem in over-kill volume. Across the room, a man frantically waved his hand in our direction.

"There he is." Mary Lou latched onto my arm, then dragged me toward his table. I thought about hooking my heels into the wooden floor and refusing to go, but I'd come this far. No turning back now.

Rupert rose to shake my hand. He stood about six inches taller than my five-foot-three. Although he wasn't Patrick Swayze, I wouldn't throw stones at him. I took my seat beside the man, then leaned closer to him to hear what he said.

He'd gone a little heavy on the cologne, one I didn't recognize. Not that I was an expert on men's cologne, but Mary Lou and I have been known to cruise the fragrance counter of Ivey's Department Store. Maybe some of it would wear off during the evening. Level off to a five on my nose Richter scale.

"Would you like to lay on your back?" Rupert asked, smiling widely.

My gaze snapped to Mary Lou, who grinned and nodded in her cousin's direction. I reluctantly looked back at him. "I beg your pardon?" I tried to control the twitch I'd just developed.

"I said," he leaned closer and yelled above the music, "would you like to take up the slack?" He made a circular motion with his hand. "You know, trip the lights fantastic?" He pointed toward the full dance floor. His breath smelled of gin.

"Sure, why not?" Thrilled that I had misunderstood his first request, I followed him to the middle of the other dancers. Wasn't gin a sissy drink?

As he stood, I got my first real, take-it-all-in look at his clothes. His bright red long-sleeved cotton shirt, with several buttons opened, topped white jeans with stovepipe legs pulled over white boots. The small scarf tied around his neck was pink. He reminded me of a tube of tooth paste.

I found Rupert's dancing a little hard to follow, but I just jumped in and held on. At one point, he broke loose and did his rendition of moon walking, which resembled a man walking on hot coals I'd seen at the carnival when I was twelve. I guess that's how they dance in Atlanta. I hoped it didn't catch on in Sweet Meadow.

I finally proclaimed my exhaustion. It wasn't really a lie. He wore me out just watching him. We made our way back to our seats. Mary Lou waited, a little winded from her dance with the long-time love of her life, Rex, the Wonder Dancer. We gave him that name when we were in junior high school, when it was a wonder he could walk, let alone dance.

Rupert ordered another gin and tonic with a twist, then excused himself. Something about seeing a man about a horse.

I quickly turned to Mary Lou, my bestest friend in the whole wide world. "Just exactly what is there about me that makes you think Rupert is perfect for me?" I waited with bated breath for her rationale.

"Yours and Rupert's hips are the same height."

Chapter 2

I couldn't believe my ears. My dear friend, Mary Lou, thinks Rupert and I are a perfect match because our hips are exactly the same height. As if this were the most sensible thing she'd said in years, (come to think of it, it might be) she nodded. I pressed my fingers against my temple and hoped my eyes, which had rolled way back in my head, would not stay that way permanently.

"Even if that had anything to do with anything on God's green earth, he's a good six inches taller than me." My voice screeched several octaves above my normal tone.

"He's only taller from the waist up, but your hips are exactly the same height." Mary Lou put both of her hands on her hips. "It's always been my theory that constitutes a perfect match."

"Is that how you picked your beloved Grant?" I really shouldn't drag her deceased husband into this conversation.

"No, Bertie, and that's why our marriage was on the rocks when the SOB got hit by a dump truck, God rest his soul." She raised her gaze upward.

Now I had a headache the size of Shafer County to match my newly-acquired twitch. "Please. Let's bury this conversation in the back yard. Never to be spoken of again."

"That's what you do with everything you don't want to talk about. Bertie, you need to face your demons and handle them."

I glanced over Mary Lou's shoulder. As if on cue, my newest demon, Rupert, walked toward us drying his hands on his pants. At least, he had washed his hands. Or, at least I think he did.

He scooted his seat next to mine, then put his arm on the back of my chair. "I think we should blow this pop stand and settle in at your place. Mary Lou said you live alone."

I shot her a deadly glance that would have floored a normal person. She just smiled. I decided right then and there that I would personally hang her by her heels from the oak tree at Pop's before the night ended.

Reluctantly, I turned to face Mr. Colgate, as I'd come to think of him. In response to his generous invitation to go back to my house, I tried to be as kind as possible. "As tempting as that sounds, Rupert, I'm afraid I'll have to pass. But thanks anyway."

He gripped the upper part of my thigh, then squeezed. "You don't know what you're missing. I have a seventy-five Johnson outboard motor with an electric starter."

I clawed my nails into his upper thigh and whispered, "I have a .357 Magnum with a silencer."

He moved his hand and arm from touching any part of my body. We both forced a smile at Mary Lou who gave us a moonie-eyed grin like she thought she'd just brought Romeo and Juliet together. Maybe in some twisted way she had, because if this night didn't end soon, I was going to order a shot of hemlock.

For the next hour, Rupert winked at every woman who passed by and sipped his gin and tonics through a straw. Just when I thought my head might explode, Carrie Sue stopped by our table to show me her new wig, a flashy little number with Howdy Doody red spikes. I recognized it as only a slight improvement over the coiffure her sister's kids had given her, but it definitely grabbed Rupert's interest. Soon, they were on the floor, hot-coal dancing.

Forty-five minutes later, they left the Dew Drop Inn. Rupert had someone to go home with, and Carrie Sue appeared to be having the time of her life. She loved showing off her double-wide mobile home. That reminded me, I still had her flying cow in my jewelry box.

"I hope you're not too disappointed about Rupert leaving with that hussy." Mary Lou patted my hand.

Battling wits with her would be a waste of time. We'd be a wit short. "I'll try to get over it. Let's go find something to eat."

Looking at my bar tab, two beers and four gin and tonics, I decided not to say anything to Mary Lou about being stuck for her cousin's drinks. Just to have him gone, it would have been worth it at twice the price.

Mary Lou and I left the Inn, then drove to the new barbeque place over in Shafer. An old McDonald's restaurant had been renovated to house the new establishment. A smoke shed had been attached to the back of the building. The golden-arches were wrapped with tin to represent the hind end of a bovine.

We pulled behind the last of about ten cars lining the drive-thru window lane of the barbeque place called the *Bull's Tail*. From the cooking shed, the tantalizing smell of oak-wood smoke made my stomach growl louder than the music blaring from Mary Lou's car radio.

She looked at me. "Would you rather go inside to order? Might be quicker." She tapped out the rhythm on the steering wheel and nodded her head to the beat.

"Oh, heavens no. With a name like the Bull's Tail, I can't wait to see what we talk into to place our order."

Mary Lou let go with her shrill hyena laugh, sending pain like shards of glass through my throbbing head. When our turn finally came, we placed our order into a speaker phone.

We didn't have to talk into a bull's butt to place our order. My faith in mankind had been restored. However, when we arrived at the pick-up window, my resolve crumbled into a pile. The kid who took our money, then handed us our order, wore a fake bull's nose with a ring in it. At least, I think it was a fake nose.

"Does that hurt?" Mary Lou asked the kid. I looked the other way, not daring to make eye contact.

"No, ma'am." To my surprise, the young man didn't have the least bit of annoyance in his voice.

When we'd driven away from the window, Mary Lou said, "Teenagers today will pierce anything."

Anyone in their right mind would have gotten out of the car right then and there and left Mary Lou to her tapping the steering wheel, nodding her head, and her rationalizing teenagers today. But not me. What fun would that be?

By the time we got back to my house, we were finishing the last bite of our pork sandwiches from the Bull's Tail. While I gathered the trash into one bag, Mary Lou dabbed a napkin daintily to the corner of her mouth, then burped.

"Get any on you?" I asked.

"Oh, you. You always say that."

"You always do that. Goodnight, Mary Lou. Thanks for everything." I waved, then hurried to the house. I needed to get to the bathroom. PDQ.

By the time I reached the front door, I had my shoes in my hand and had unzipped my skirt. I closed the door behind me, then pulled my sweater over my head while my skirt slipped down around my ankles. I kicked it aside and tossed my top on the sofa.

Stripped to my undies, I stumbled through my dark living room until I found the table lamp. It clicked on, flooding the room with pale light.

Reclining in my La-Z-Boy was an old man in his pajamas. Terror thundered through me. I cupped my hand over my mouth to keep from piercing the air with the scream scrambling to escape my throat. Rapidly, self-protection moves, which my brothers had shown me, flashed through my mind. I prepared to fend off my intruder. Suddenly, I realized I'd have to wake him up first. He appeared to be sleeping, or dead, or both.

My breathing slowed to somewhere near normal. I tiptoed toward Sleeping Beauty. His eyes flew open. His scream splintered the quiet. Over and over again, the old man bellowed as if *I* were trying to kill *him*.

Every nerve in my body took on a life of its own. I began to bob and weave in place. Suddenly, I was doing my own rendition of Rupert's hot-coal dance, in my underwear no less.

I didn't know whether to get dressed, call 911, or go to the bathroom, which was where I wanted to go to start with. I grabbed my skirt and top, then scrambled back into them. I snatched my portable phone from the end table and took it with me into the bathroom. All the while the old man continued to scream bloody murder. I slammed and locked the door behind me.

"I need someone over here right away," I yelled at the 911 operator. Okay, so it was just the dispatcher at the local police department.

"What's your emergency?" the placating voice asked through a yawn.

"There's an old man in my living room."

"Who's that screaming in the background?" The woman's calmness plucked my tight nerves like a banjo string.

"It's him." I held the phone in front of my mouth like a microphone, then screamed into it, "It's the old man."

"Are you killing him?" Pluck. Pluck.

"Not yet, but that thought is quickly making its way to the top of my priority list." Maybe sarcasm would work.

"You could go to jail for that." Pluck. Pluck. Pluck.

"Do you have someone on the way yet?"

"Where?"

Boing!

"On the way to my house to get the screaming relic who is stretched out in my La-Z-Boy." Spittle spewed from my mouth.

"I have one of those," the dispatcher said.

"Which one, a La-Z-Boy or a screaming relic?"

I bent at my waist and leaned my head against the cold porcelain sink. All the excitement had caused my pork sandwich to rebel. I hoped I wouldn't lose it.

I kept the receiver to my ear a little longer, listening to Miss Dispatcher talk to someone on a two-way radio. Finally, she came back on the line.

"Are you Roberta Byrd at 203 Marblehead Drive?"

"Yes. Yes, I am."

"Go to your front door. Officer Kelly is there."

I pushed the off button to disconnect from Bonnie Fyfe, then made a mad dash from the bathroom toward the front door. As I sprinted by, I glanced at the intruder who still lay flat on his back in the reclined La-Z-Boy bellowing at the top of his now hoarse voice.

"Knock it off," I yelled on my way by.

Instantly, he stopped. I halted dead in my tracks and smacked myself on the forehead. "I should have done that sooner." I continued to the door, still mumbling to myself. I yanked it open.

A burly, uniformed police officer pointed his big gun at me. "Lace your fingers behind your head and step out of the house."

I followed his instructions to the letter. Danged if my twitch hadn't returned. Once outside, Officer Kelly recognized me as Pop Byrd's daughter. I'd worked a couple of wrecks with the man during the past few years. I hoped he didn't remember me as the tow truck driver who ever so slightly tapped him in the rear one night. And I do mean *his* rear, not his cruiser's. I was new on the job and pretty apt to run into anything that didn't get out of my way.

"Okay, you can put your hands down. What seems to be the problem?" Officer Kelly shoved his gun back into its holster. I couldn't help thinking "My gun's bigger than your gun." I thought it, but I didn't break into song.

"There's a man in my living room. I want him out."

"Miss Byrd, did you just come in from a night on the town?" He sucked air through his teeth.

"Yes."

"Did your date want more than a handshake at the door?"

"He's not my date. I don't know who he is or where he came from. I just want him out of my house. And, this is just a slight request, but could you possibly, if it isn't too much trouble, you understand, maybe get him out of there before sunup?" Puff. I was teetering on hysteria.

For an instant, I wondered if he'd let me borrow his gun. Once I had it in my hand, then I'd figure out whether to shoot him or myself.

"Well, let's go talk to the perp." The officer walked past me into the house.

I followed him across the room, all the while feeling pretty smug because I knew that a "perp" was cop talk for perpetrator. Watching all those reruns of Rockford Files had finally paid off. Once we arrived at the La-Z-Boy and found the said perp, we had to wake him up. It took a few minutes to discover that the old man was Pete Fortney, the owner of the house who now lived at the nursing home down the street. Therefore, he couldn't be arrested for breaking into his own home. Which he didn't do anyway, because he had a key.

Apparently, he'd escaped from this new residence. After making his way home, he pulled a key from someplace, opened my door, then hid the key again. Where it would evidently remain hidden inside the man's mind.

Shortly before the men in white coats, honestly, took Mr. Fortney away, I asked him, "Where did you hide the key?"

The old man stuck his tongue out at me, which, by the way, was cracked and coated with a gray, nasty-looking film. Honestly. "That's for me to know and for you to find out," he mocked.

"Nana nana boo boo." I zinged him with my snappiest come-back, then twitched my way back into OUR house. I closed the door, then collapsed against it.

You're probably thinking to yourself, "Bertie needs to get out more." But I can assure you that after tonight, I may never go out again.

I went to my refrigerator, removed a bottle, unscrewed the cap, and downed a whole Coke. The fizz burned up my nose and down my throat. Still, it didn't erase the vivid memories of the night.

About three weeks following the Friday night from the Twilight Zone, I'd skipped going to the Dew Drop Inn. I'd tried to get Mary Lou to join me for an evening of Nick at Nite with pop-corn and a couple of tons of butter. But she had a hot date with Rex the Wonder Dancer.

I decided I'd be better off staying home anyway. Sometimes a girl needs a little alone time. This night would be mine. Curled in my recliner with a serial killer book, eating a quart of rum raisin ice cream, I'd found my paradise. About every ten pages, I'd take a big gulp from my bottle of Mogen David. Life was good.

Around ten o'clock, someone knocked on my door. I strug-gled, much like a turtle on her back, to push the foot support of the La-Z-Boy down, so I could get up. It hadn't worked right since Pete Fortney had fallen asleep in it. It had worked fine before that fateful night, but not one time since. Because I made him go back to the nursing home down the street, I think Pete put a curse on my recliner.

I finally tussled my way out of the contrary chair, shoved the foot supporter back in place, then gave it a well-aimed kick in the side. By this time, the person outside, evidently an impatient cuss, pounded harder against the heavy oak door.

"I'm coming," I yelled. Forcing my feet into my Marvin the Martian slippers, I hurried to the door, which was now vibrating from the beating it was getting.

I peeked out the window, then opened the door. Mary Lou's face and the rest of her were a disheveled mess.

"What in the world is going on?" I looked beyond her to a car backing out of my driveway. "Is that Rex the Wonder . . . ?"

"Yes, it is." Mary Lou raced to the sofa, threw her purse down so hard it bounced onto the floor. She then threw her body down so hard I expected it to bounce onto the floor too.

"That repulsive . . . doo doo head."

"Simmer down there, Mary Lou. Your language is out of control." Sometimes, mocking her was so easy it took all the sport out of it. "What happened?"

She jumped to her feet and began pacing from the living room to the dining room. Every few seconds, she rotated between a huff and a puff. I swear, if one of the three pigs had been there, she could have blown his house down.

With each step she took, the haystack of hair piled on top of her head, which I'm sure was perfectly fixed when the evening began, bobbed a little further down the side of her face. Runaway mascara blackened her eyes and streaked her cheeks. Bright red lipstick had slipped from her lips and now decorated a wide swipe from one cheek to the other.

At this rate, I wondered if she would ever tell me. "You look like you've been tangling with a mama bear."

"That's pretty much what happened." Mary Lou flopped down again.

I crossed my arms, stood in front of her, tapping my foot.

Finally, she straightened to a half-way sitting position. "Rex and I stopped at the Pack and Sack for some Dentyne. Donna and her tribe were in there buying toilet paper and gummy worms. I had just stepped up to the counter with my chewing gum and cherry Slurpee when all of a sudden, her youngest kid, the one with the limp, snatched my Slurpee." She acted out the snatching part.

"He was almost to the door when I grabbed him by the back of his pants and lifted him off the floor. I'd no sooner latched onto him, then Donna grabbed me by my top knot, swung me and her little helgermite to the floor. Cherry Slurpee flew all in Rex's hair. I caught a peek at him one time as Donna and I rolled around the floor.

"He was dancing around with red juice dripping from his hair, hollering 'What do you want me to do? What should I do? What can I do?'"

She exhaled for the first time since she'd started her story. "You know sometimes, I wonder if Rex's family tree had a blight somewhere along the line."

I burst out laughing. That was probably why Mary Lou was my best friend. I never knew when the light on her front porch would come on. I just knew that when it occasionally did, I wanted to be there.

"Well, did Rex finally break it up?"

"No, Chief Kramer did. The owner of the store decided that if we'd clean up the mess, he wouldn't press charges. Donna's kids cleaned her part. Rex cleaned mine, then I had him drop me off here."

She made a feeble attempt at straightening her hair. "Where's the popcorn?" she asked.

I just stood there, shaking my head and laughing. "You go change your clothes. I'll put some in the microwave." My bedroom slippers and I padded into the kitchen.

"You got an extra football jersey I can wear? Preferably a clean one." Mary Lou pulled hair pins from her bouncing French twist.

"In the basket at the foot of the bed." The same place I keep *all* my clean clothes.

Mary Lou and I watched an old black and white movie. Sometime after one in the morning, she pulled an afghan over her and cuddled deep into the sofa cushions. Marvin the Martian and I retired to my boudoir. Within minutes, I was in bed and sound asleep.

The sun streaked its unrelenting hot light through a crack in my bedroom window. The rays masterfully shone in a narrow strip right across my eyes. I tossed my pillow at the curtain hoping to knock it shut. Since I only have one pillow, and I can't sleep without it, I now had to get out of bed to retrieve it.

While I was up, I might as well go to the bathroom since I would have to get back up in a few minutes anyway. When I finished in there and was almost back to my bed, I heard the tinkle of dishes in the kitchen and smelled the inviting aroma of coffee. I decided to forego my slippers and brave the cold tile to join Mary Lou.

As I rounded the corner leading to the kitchen, I found Mary

Lou and Pete Fortney, in their pajamas, eating breakfast.

Remembering my cursed La-Z-Boy, I bit my tongue against the remarks I really, really, really wanted to say. I flipped through the pages of the phone book, found the number for the Tall Pines Nursing Home. I called them to please come and recapture their runaway. After pouring myself a cup of coffee, I took a seat at the table with the rest of my guests.

"Where's the key, Mr. Fortney?" I narrowed my gaze.

The old man leaned closer, looking deep into my eyes. "Who are you?"

"I'm Bertie Byrd. I rent your house since *you* don't live here *anymore.*"

"Did you say Dirty Bird?" He laughed out loud.

"Oh, that's a good one, Mr. Fortney. I never heard that one before. A real knee-slapper. Where's the key?"

Before he answered my question, the men in the white coats arrived. After they'd walked him to the car waiting out front, and I was sure he was far enough away so he couldn't put a curse on anything, I stepped onto my porch.

"Mr. Fortney?"

He turned to face me. "I don't want to find you at my kitchen table in your pajamas again. Do you hear me, you squirrel bait?"

He smiled and offered a wave, but he never answered me.

The next morning, a beautiful, sunny Sunday, I crawled out of bed, showered, then dressed for church. I was proud of myself. I had time to eat breakfast so my stomach wouldn't growl during the morning worship and still make it there in time for the Garden Club roll call.

I locked my necklace around my neck, then picked up my shoes. On the way to the kitchen, I adjusted the air-conditioner. It seemed a little stuffy this morning. I went into the kitchen.

There sat Pete in his birthday suit. A badly wrinkled, ill-fitted birthday suit, at that.

"You don't have any clothes on, you nitwit."

"You said I couldn't wear my pajamas at the kitchen table any more." He went back to reading MY Sunday paper.

"Oh, good Lord." I threw a towel over his lap, then stormed to the phone. I didn't need to look up the number. I knew it by heart. I chanted over and over, "Thou shalt not cuss. Thou shalt not cuss."

Mary Lou arrived to drive me to church. The people from the nursing home redeemed their prize. I told them they were welcome to take my towel with them since there was absolutely, positively no way I would ever dry my face on it again now that it had swaddled Pete's . . . well, you know. But they left the towel behind.

Mary Lou and I watched the men march Pete to the car, his backside bare, his front side covered with the Sunday morning funnies. I hadn't even read Blondie yet.

Thanks to Pete, we were going to be late for church. We hurried there as fast as Mary Lou's car could go, which is so fast it's scary. When we came to the red light at Liberty and Main, she slowed to a slight roll, glanced both ways, then ran through the intersection. I closed my eyes, sank my fingernails into the dash, and began reminding God of the good things I'd done in my life, just in case He was undecided about whether it was my time to go. Evidently, He had another purpose for me here, because we made it all the way to the parking lot without incident. A true miracle.

As we entered the rear of the church, the organ and the choir were making a joyful noise. Unfortunately, it was so joyful that no one heard us come in. Hence, the Garden Club would not know we were there.

Now, them knowing we were there means as much to Mary Lou as it does to everyone, maybe more. When the music stopped and the minister headed toward the pulpit, Mary Lou fake sneezed the loudest fake sneeze anyone has ever heard. I jumped a good six inches off my seat. When I landed, I gave her a look to end all looks, but she was too busy waving at the Garden Club ladies to notice.

Poor Mr. March, who sat in front of us, straightened his toupee. I'm not sure how it came to be perched at a tilt on his head-my guess would be the force of Mary Lou's sneeze blew it there-but he overcompensated the turn. A little bit of shiny pink scalp peeked at me. The perfectly round spot looked like a big eye hooded by long lashes. A cyclops. When the choir began again, the congregation joined in. As Mr. March moved his mouth to sing, his scalp also moved giving the appearance he was winking at us.

I struggled to keep from bursting out laughing. If I did that, and in light of Mary Lou's horrendous fake sneeze, the whole congregation would swear the two of us had shown up in church still drunk from some kind of wild night of drinking and carousing. They'd probably think I'd spent the evening and into the wee morning hours in a debauched tryst with the devastatingly handsome man who works at the paper mill and whose car I towed last week. A man with dark wavy hair, a smile that could blind any woman. Even his muscles had muscles.

But I digress.

"Let us pray." Reverend Miller closed his eyes and led the congregation in the closing prayer. I was offering my own apology to the Lord for my irreverent thoughts during morning worship. Mary Lou shifted in her seat. I opened one eye and peeked out one millisecond before Mary Lou's index finger touched Mr. March's cyclopic eye. I grabbed her wrist and pulled it back to her lap, then shook my head at her like a mother would a child.

I closed my eyes again. This time I prayed in earnest that lightning would not zap either of us. Or worse yet, that there wouldn't be a pop quiz on Reverend Miller's sermon since I hadn't heard a word of it.

When we were dismissed, Mary Lou and I made a mad dash to her car. Once we'd started toward the Huddle House for lunch, she glanced at me with tears in her eyes.

"Do you think Reverend Miller was talking about me this morning?"

Since I hadn't listened to the sermon, as I've already confessed, I didn't have a clue what she was talking about. "What do you mean?"

"Well, he said that the devil himself sits among us. He looked right at me."

"He wasn't talking about you, Mary Lou. It's just his way of getting his point across that evil can be anywhere, and we have to be on the lookout for it and stay out of its way."

"I don't think that's what he meant at all. I think he meant I am the devil."

I hoped I wouldn't have to perform an exorcism before the day ended. "You couldn't be the devil anymore than I could be the Queen of England."

"Oh, yes, I could. I've had evil thoughts."

"Mary Lou, you don't have a bad bone in your body, let alone anything evil. Kookie, maybe. Evil never." I wanted to reassure her as soon as possible because we were sitting in the parking lot of the Huddle House, and it was rapidly filling up with other church goers with hearty appetites. Apparently, we had to lay this puppy to rest before we could go eat.

"Okay, what evil thoughts have you had?"

"Lots. There was the time I started to put chewing gum in Donna's hair when we were in junior high school. I thought better of it at the last minute, then you said something to make me laugh. I ended up spitting my gum into her hair anyway. It was as if my thoughts made it go there."

I rubbed my throbbing temple.

"Then one time when your brother, Billy, stole my Jello from my tray at lunch, I devised a plan to tie him naked to an ant hill and cover his body with Jello."

"We all wander from reality like that at some time in our lives. The fact remains you didn't go through with it. That's what separates the thinkers and the evil doers. Can we go eat now?" I hoped so.

"But that very day Billy got stung by a bee." She looked on the verge of a full-blown crying jag.

If she started, I feared I might join her. I was totally worn out from just trying to keep up with her thought processes. "What does him getting bit by a bee have to do with anything? It wasn't an ant."

"It was an insect just the same. I wished it on him." She sniffed.

"Well, my dear friend, if you have the power to wish things on a person, there's a man at the paper mill I'd like you to wish on me."

I expected her to laugh at my absurdity. Instead, she calmly removed the keys and started to get out of the car.

"Okay." Her voice took on a long-suffering tone. "I'll see what I can do about that."

I followed her inside. I might have to see a doctor about my twitch.

Chapter 3

After a long but quiet day at work, I pulled my tow truck into my driveway. Monday through Thursday night, I drove it home in case I had to go out on a night call. I didn't have my own car, at least not one that had actually started in the last six months. So, during the week, I used the wrecker for my personal use. If I really needed to go somewhere on weekends, I went with Mary Lou or I borrowed Pop's Cadillac.

Today had been a slow, uneventful day for a change. I had done minor mechanical work on two cars, made a lunch and bank-run for Pop, and did one taxi call to pick up Millie's laundry from the dry cleaners.

The only major thing I'd done all day was lay out a plan of action to find the key that Pete Fortney used to let himself into my home. I'd decided to start at the front porch and look in every conceivable place, working my way clock-wise around the exterior, ground level, and eaves of the house. I'd devote fifteen minutes every evening until I found it. For my own peace of mind, I had to find that key.

Before going into the house, I walked to my curbside mailbox. It's an artsy number left behind by Pete Fortney. The normal metal box was camouflaged by a big rubber bass. I had to stick my hand into his large mouth to retrieve my bills.

"Any mail for me today, Herman?" I asked the fish.

He didn't answer.

I had four pieces. One for a discount on pantyhose at Ivey's Department Store, my *Reader's Digest* (developing my word power is a hobby of mine), my phone bill, and an official looking letter from the Shafer County Zoning Commission.

I opened it immediately. It advised me I was in violation of county zoning laws; parking commercial vehicles in residential areas was prohibited. I would have to cease and desist parking my wrecker at my home.

In my heart, I knew that the zoning people didn't drive by my house and lodge their own complaint. Someone filed it with them, causing the zoning people to take action.

I looked up and down my street trying to decide who would have done such a thing. Surely not Mr. Miller, whom I pulled out of a ditch a month ago, put there because of a suicidal deer. I hadn't even charged him. Surely not Mrs. Weidemeyer. I stop by the grocery store at least once a week for her. Not Mary Lou's cousin, Novalee. I'd brought the air tank to her house at least twice to air up her tires when her rotten, estranged husband had de-aired them during the night, hoping Novalee would be desperate enough to call on him for help. No, there wasn't anyone on my block who would've complained.

But someone had. Now, I had to cease and desist or face a fine. I looked at the phone bill. I could barely pay it. A fine was way out of the question.

First thing the next morning, I told Pop about my notice from the zoning people.

"I dealt with them all the time when I first opened this business. Ask your mom. She'll tell you. They were constantly sending me letters about where I parked customers' cars, the wrecker, my signs. I just told them where to park their letters."

"And they never fined you?" My pulse slowed closer to normal.

"No, siree. I never paid one red cent in fines."

I breathed a sigh of relief. Just then the phone rang. As Pop started to answer it, he called over his shoulder, "I only served seven days of my thirty-day jail sentence."

My heart thudded to my stomach. Dang. I'd have to leave my wrecker at the shop, get my car running and, if I got a night call, I'd have to drive to the shop to retrieve my tow truck.

Pop had finished on the phone and stood looking at me. "Problem?" he asked.

"Yes! The wrecker slash zoning people. Remember?"

"Oh, yeah. I have a solution. You can move back in with Mom and me. Then you'll be right next door to the wrecker. How's that sound?"

I took a few seconds to ponder Pop's precipitous pronouncement. Wow! Improving my word power was paying off. Maybe it wouldn't be so bad. Mom would do my laundry. She'd cook my meals every night. She'd want to know who I was talking to on the phone. Where I was going every time I left the house. She'd be able to analyze why I wasn't married, face to face, instead of over the phone.

When she did my laundry, she'd want to know why I owned black lacy underwear and proceed to keep me abreast of the different infections I could develop by not wearing pure cotton next to my "private parts of my nether region."

"Thanks for the offer, Pop, but I think I'll go talk to the zoning people and see what I can do." I glanced down, then decided to slip out of my coveralls before heading off to fight city hall, so to speak. In the bathroom of the garage, I washed my hands and face, put on a little foundation and lipstick, and took the scrunchie from my hair. I leaned forward and shook my head to give my hair volume. After peeking into the mirror, I combed away the volume. With my blouse tucked into my jeans, I felt I looked presentable.

"I'll be back soon. I better take care of this zoning thing right away."

I drove Dad's Caddy to the courthouse in Shafer. Parking two blocks away, I walked past a park. A homeless man, sitting on a brick wall, offered me a drink from his paper bag. I gave it a hefty consideration, but declined.

Once inside I asked the handsome elderly man, Paul, according to his name badge, at the information desk where I could find George Bigham with the Zoning Commission.

"You can't." The man shook his head rapidly. "He's dead."

I fumbled in my purse and pulled out the letter I'd received. Unfolding it, I showed it to the man. "Mr. Bigham signed this letter I received yesterday."

"So he did. But he's still dead."

"I'm sorry. Was it an accident?"

"I don't think he died on purpose." This clown was serious. He never cracked a smile, just shook his head. As if this were the most profound thing I'd ever heard, I shook my head and clicked my tongue. "Could you tell me where the zoning room is?"

The information man pointed down the hall. "Second door on the right. But you won't find George there."

"Of course not." I hurried away from the little man and wondered if he was only allowed out of the home on Tuesdays. I shook my head and clicked my tongue.

Inside the office, I found several employees, all too busy to notice me. I stepped to the counter separating the public from the zoning people. On the phone a woman, Violet, according to her badge, motioned for me to wait. She'd be right with me.

"Yes, Martha, I know what you mean. Sometimes humans should adopt some of the animal world's practice of eating their young. But, Donna's kids are too old to be eaten now. Listen, honey, I have someone here. Gotta run. Just put ice on your head to keep the swelling down."

Surely the clerk couldn't be talking about Carrie Sue's sister. Donna lived in Sweet Meadow. Violet was in the town of Shafer. Of course, Donna and her kids did have a reputation that could conceivably sweep the whole county.

"What can I do for you, honey?" Violet rose from her chair, then came around her desk to the counter.

"I received this letter saying I can't park my wrecker at my house." She took the paper and studied it.

"This is from George Bigham." Her gaze drifted to me.

"Yes, but I *have* to park at my house. I perform a service that requires I go to accidents in the middle of the night. I have to get there as quickly as possible. I can't waste time going to my garage to get my wrecker, then go to the accident. Sometimes traffic is blocked and I'm needed there immediately."

"He's dead." The clerk shook her head.

I sucked in a sharp breath. "Yes, I know, but surely someone can help me with this matter."

The woman shook her head. "I can help you."

Relieved, I smiled. "Thank you."

"Now, what can I help you with?" she asked.

I wondered if there was a hidden camera somewhere in the office. I wondered because I felt as if I were on an episode of Candid Camera and second, I didn't want it caught on tape when I jumped the counter and beat the woman to death.

"Ma'am, try to stick with me on this. I have to park my wrecker at my house so I can be of service to the community of Sweet Meadow. I can't afford to pay a fine for doing this. Can you help me with that problem?"

"Oh, sure." The woman took the letter, tore it into several pieces and pitched it into a trash can. "I filed it in File Thirteen." She dusted her hands together.

When I left, I was so relieved I didn't even care that it had taken me an hour to solve the problem. I smiled and waved to Paul, the information man. He seemed to get a kick out of my acknowledging him. Why? I haven't a clue, he just emitted a silly giggle. I also said a silent goodbye to George Bigham. God rest his soul.

Thursday I dragged my sorry butt home from work. It had been one of those days when I felt like I'd been shot at and missed. Before I even entered the house, I performed my fifteen-minute key search mission. My third day of prying through shrubbery, probing under rocks, and climbing to places Pete Fortney couldn't reach even if he were in perfect health, but I still couldn't find the key.

I checked my phone messages. Mom wanted to know if I'd heard about the new singles group the church was forming. She wanted me to be a charter member so I could get pick of the litter. That wasn't exactly what she said. It was just my interpretation of the message.

Mary Lou had called. She tends to start her messages in the middle of her thoughts. I always feel I need a secret decoder ring to figure them out. Or, I just wait for her to call back and fill me in on the omitted details. Today's message seemed more cryptic than usual. It piqued my interest.

"I'll be at your house at eight. Keep the bathroom open. I'm bringing a stick." That was Mary Lou's message *du jour*. I found it worth listening to again. Unfortunately, I didn't get any more out of it the second time than I did the first time.

I popped a frozen pepperoni pizza into the oven, then went to take a shower. After I dressed in my best slouchy clothes, I drank half of a bottle of wine and ate most of the pizza. I could almost hear my arteries clogging.

Mary Lou finally arrived. She carried a small brown bag and hugged it to her like it contained something valuable. In my mind, I ran down a list of what it could be. "Did you buy a half pound Hershey bar with almonds? Is that what you're guarding in that bag?"

"No." Mary Lou dumped the contents onto my kitchen table. A home pregnancy test kit plopped out. I slumped into the chair.

"Oh, my God, are you pregnant?" I gasped.

"That's what I'm about to find out." She ripped open the box.

"Does Rex the Wonder Dancer know?"

"Not yet. I wanted to be sure before I said anything to him."

"We may have to change his name. Evidently, dancing isn't all he does." I smiled at Mary Lou.

She gave me a disgusted look and began to read the directions.

"How did this happen?" I asked.

"You need to get out more, Bertie. Then you'd know the answer to that question," Mary Lou said with an even, know-it-all tone.

She was calm and seemingly unruffled by the prospect of being a mother. I, on the other hand, was having trouble sitting in the chair without falling onto the floor. The mere idea of Mary Lou and Rex the Wonder . . . Pantser . . . being parents sent chills the size of ice cubes up my spine. I know Mary Lou has a heart of pure gold and Rex, in his own way, could be as kind as a vintner monk, but they both had a lot of room for emotional growth. Bless their hearts.

While we waited for the peed-on stick to work its miracles, Mary Lou knocked off the rest of the pizza, and I poured myself the rest of the wine.

I told Mary Lou about my undisclosed enemy in the neighborhood who had turned me into the zoning people. She told me she'd like to name her baby "Bill if it's a boy" and "Hillary if it's a girl."

"Good choices," I agreed.

"I think they're strong names. They sound like they could run a country." Mary Lou took a big bite of pizza and chewed thoughtfully.

"You think so, huh?" After downing the last of my wine, I told her about my new friends, Paul and Violet, at the courthouse.

The phone rang. Mary Lou lifted it from the wall, answered it, then, after a few seconds, handed it to me. "It's for you."

"Hello?"

Nothing.

"Hello?"

Again, nothing. I looked at Mary Lou. "There's no one there. Who was it?"

"Some man asked to talk to the rat fink who lives here. I assumed he meant you."

I put the receiver back to my ear and tried again. "Hello? Are you there?"

"Listen, sister, you better move out of the neighborhood and quick while you still have all your fingers and toes." A voice belonging to at least an eighty-year-old man wiggled its way through the phone to my brain.

There was a shuffling noise, then a different voice spoke. "You better listen to us, deary. We mean what we say."

"Jesus, Joseph, and Mary, I'm being threatened by the Rest In Peace gang from the old folks home," I said to Mary Lou. She smiled, then went to the bathroom to check her stick.

"Hey, buster, tell your nurse to come to the phone. I want to talk to her."

The man on the end of the line sucked in a quick, sharp breath, then started to hack. Between coughs he said, "Go get nurse Jane, she wants to talk to her."

In the background, I could hear his accomplice yelling, "Hang up, you dang fool." The line clicked to silence.

"Yesss!!!" Mary Lou screamed from the bathroom.

I sat frozen in my seat, afraid to find out what the yes meant.

She raced from the bathroom, across the kitchen floor, pulled me to my feet and danced me around the room. If she'd made Rex do that, she wouldn't have had to pee on a stick today.

"Okay. Okay. What's the verdict?"

"I'm pregnant." Mary Lou hugged me to her in a way that told me she truly believed this was the greatest thing that had ever happened to her.

Even though, in my heart, I had doubts, I'd never let her know my misgivings about the whole Mary Lou/Rex as parents thing. "That's wonderful. You'll make a wonderful mother." As I danced around my kitchen with my best friend, I actually began to believe my own hype. She *would* be a wonderful mother, as long as she could always remember where she left the kid.

"We're going to have a wedding. You're going to be my maid of honor, Bertie. I'm so excited." Mary Lou and I continued to jump up and down.

Finally, I forced her to stop. "You're gonna bounce that kid right out of there. Don't you think you should talk to Rex, the

Wonder Pantser?"

She cocked her head sideways, then smiled widely. "Actually, Wonder Pantser is a more accurate title for Rex. We both know he never could dance." She rapidly raised her eyebrows several times in succession.

I hugged her again. "Oh, Mary Lou, you are the best friend I've ever had. I treasure you and want only happiness for you."

"Quit it, Bertie, you'll make me cry." She stepped away and sniffed.

"Get out of here. You and Rex have a lot to talk about." I shooed her out the door.

It wasn't until Mary Lou had left that I remembered my phone call from, I was sure, Pete Fortney's cronies. Although they were probably harmless, I decided I'd better let someone at the home know about the call.

"Do you have a Nurse Jane working there?"

"This is Nurse Jane," a lovely young woman answered.

"My name is Roberta Byrd. You have a resident there, Pete Fortney. I live in his house, which is just a few blocks away from you. Do you know Mr. Fortney?"

"Of course, I'm his evening nurse. How may I help you?" She sounded very sweet and kind.

"Well, some of Pete's friends called me tonight and threatened to cut off my fingers and toes. I thought I'd better let someone know."

"Lady, are you nuts?" The lovely woman's tone turned sour. "These poor folks can barely get out of bed alone. Most of them can't even feed themselves. Now, you're accusing them of imitating Mafia members. I suppose you think poor old Pete is their Godfather. I'd be ashamed of myself. Please get a life and don't call here again harassing our residents. If you do, I'll have to report you to the police."

For the second time that night, I sat looking into a dead silent phone.

I went to bed right that minute. Maybe I still had time to wake up from this nightmare day-Paul and Violet, no key, Mary Lou and Rex, aka Mom and Dad, then threats from the "Twilight-Years Zone" were more than any one human should have to endure in one day.

The next two weeks passed quickly. Mary Lou went to the bridal shop and ob/gyn doctor in the same day. The doctor confirmed the stick told no lies. A little Rex would be arriving sometime around Thanksgiving.

At the Sweet Meadow's Bridal Shoppe, Mary Lou found a beautiful white, long, wedding gown which had been discounted seventy-five percent because of a cigarette-burn hole in the train. The owner of the shop assured us she could cover it with a sequin to match the others scattered over the dress. No one would know the difference. I agreed.

So, Mary Lou bought it and was fitted for the alterations, which cost almost as much as the dress. Then we went to the Dairy Queen for a chocolate shake. I also had an order of fries. Mary Lou had a cheeseburger, chili dog, and large onion rings. I hoped she wouldn't have to pay for more dress alterations before the wedding.

I hadn't found the key yet, but Pete hadn't been by for a visit either. I feared he was lulling me into a false sense of security.

On Saturday, I'd planned a bridal shower for Mary Lou at my house. Earlier in the week, I'd bought her and Rex a toaster and a couple of prizes for the cheesy games we were going to play. What shower would be complete without games?

On Friday night, before Pop dropped me off at my house, I picked up a few things from the grocery store. With my hands full of bags, I waved to Pop. After putting the groceries away, I decided to forego my key mission for one night. I did go check Herman, the mail bass.

There, on top of a stack of bills, I found another official letter from the Shafer County Zoning Commission. Things had been going too good.

I tore into it. It was marked second and final notice. Again,

I was told to cease and desist or face a huge fine. George Bigham had signed it. This would certainly put a damper on my weekend. I'd have to put on the gloves and go another round with Violet on Monday morning. This time, I'd get it in writing that it had been filed in File Thirteen.

The next day, shortly before the guests arrived for the bridal shower, I dumped store-bought dip, chips, mints, and nuts into bowls. I laid out an assortment of deli sandwiches. As the center piece I'd bought a mini-wedding cake. Sherbet punch and coffee would give us all what we needed to make our lives grand . . . sugar and caffeine.

Into a brown paper bag, I placed a brand new, pansy covered tea-towel. One of the games we were going to play consisted of my telling them there was a pair of women's underwear in the bag. They would pass the bag from one person to the next like a hot potato. When the music stopped, the person left holding the bag would be led to believe they had to wear the underpants on their head for the rest of the party. Of course, it was really a tea-towel, which they got to keep as a gift. But until the game was over, they wouldn't know that. I said the games were cheesy, but I knew they'd have a fun time doing them. After all, honoring the bride-to-be was important, whether with a tea-towel or underwear.

Mary Lou arrived first, along with her mother, her cousin,

Novalee, and Aunt Shirley. Shortly thereafter, Carrie Sue, her sister Donna, and Millie Keats made their way into my living room. I carefully sat Donna as far away from Mary Lou as possible, lest we forget the Pack and Sack Slurpee altercation.

We'd decided to eat first. As the guests filed around my kitchen table filling their plates with tasty morsels, I noticed one of them needed a shave.

Pete Fortney filled his plate, then took a seat in the corner next to Millie. Within a few minutes, she was wiping frosting from his mouth and they were both giggling like children. I decided not to call the old-folk rustlers. They knew where he was. They'd be along sooner or later.

After we'd eaten, I brought out the paper bag for the hot potato game. Everyone, including Pete, got in a circle. I turned my back to the crowd, then flipped on the stereo. After a minute or so of shuffling behind me, and continuous screeching and uproarious laughter, I stopped the music. When I turned to face the group, Pete sat staring at the bag he held in his bony hands. A silly grin lit his face.

The ladies started egging him on, "Open it, Pete. You have to wear it on your head."

He ripped into the bag, then pulled out the tea-towel. A look of confusion flashed across the old man's face.

"It isn't really underwear, Pete. It's a nice gift," I explained.

"That's a dang fool thing to do to an old man. I was looking forward to wearing women's underwear on my head. Been a long time since I done that."

Time for Pete to go back to the home. "Okay. Come with me." I held out my hand. He took it. Mary Lou gave me her keys, then, hand in hand, Pete and I walked to her car.

You know, I'm developing a fondness for Pete. He gives me diversion from the everyday nuts I come in contact with. Like those Jordan almonds you get at weddings. Sugary sweet at first, but a pure nut on the inside.

As we pulled in front of the home, a nurse saw us. She came out to meet Pete. I called to him, "Where's the key?"

He turned, smiled, then gave me a New Jersey salute.

"You're a nut case, Pete Fortney." I rolled up my window quickly. I didn't really want to hear what Nurse Jane was saying to me.

Back at the shower, Mary Lou opened her gifts: three toasters, two blenders, towels, and a baby layette from Donna, the vindictive. The bride/mother-to-be loved everything and everyone, even Donna.

Early Monday morning, Dad picked me up. I let him out at the garage, then went directly to the Zoning Commission.

As I zoomed by him, Paul waved. I'd worked myself into a dither over my letter. Once inside the zoning office, Violet saw me immediately. "What can I help you with, deary?"

"I received this letter on Friday. You told me I didn't need to worry about this matter and by the way, it's signed by George Bigham."

"He's dead."

"So I've been told, but somehow he keeps sending me letters saying I can't park at my house." My volume was somewhere just below screaming.

Violet took the letter. She shook her head, then handed it back. "You'll need to talk with the people in the permit office. Room 212, second floor."

Good. I could get a permit to keep the wrecker at the house. That sounded simple. I went back to the main lobby. After looking around, I asked Paul, "Where's the elevator?"

He nodded down the corridor. "Around the corner."

I went happily on my way. After pressing the button several times and waiting several minutes, I went back to Paul. "The elevator doesn't seem to be working."

"It isn't. Not since yesterday."

A sharp, stabbing pain shot through the side of my head. I pressed my fingers against it. My whole body twitched. "Then, how can I get to the second floor?"

Paul pointed toward a door located directly behind me. Shaking my head, I yanked the door opened. Before disappearing through it, I gave the man a murderous look.

Room 212 looked exactly like the zoning office. I walked to the counter. An elderly man stepped up to help me. He was older than Paul and Violet put together and almost too short to see over counter.

"Does anyone under the age of seventy work at the courthouse?" I asked.

"How's that?" He cocked his ear toward me to hear better.

"Never mind. I want to get a permit to park my wrecker at my house. I got this letter from the zoning people and they said you could help me."

"This is from George Bigham." The man looked up at me.

"He's dead," I said.

The man, Reuben according to his badge, nodded. "God rest his soul."

I waited patiently while Reuben reflected on the loss of Mr. Bigham. I swear, I think he nodded off.

"Reuben?"

"May I help you?"

"Oh, good Lord. Yes. I need a permit to park my wrecker at my house."

"Well, I can't give you one unless you get written permission from the person who issued the order. That would be George Bigham."

"But everyone knows he's dead. So, who else can help me?"

As if to get out of my reach, Reuben took a step back from the counter.

"I don't know. I've never had this situation before. Whoever does the official notifying is the only one who can give permission to get a permit."

He raised his finger in the air. "Ah hah!" Evidently he had a brilliant idea. "You can go back down to zoning and ask them. Surely, they will know. My hands are tied. I have to have permission from George Bigham."

I snatched the letter signed by the infamous George Bigham from Reuben's hand. I startled him so badly, I thought he might have a heart attack. I didn't care. He appeared to have had a long life. If it was his time to go, then so be it.

I literally ran down the stairs into the lobby. Paul waved and called after me, "No running in the halls."

"Yeah, yeah, yeah." My tone was less than pleasant. I think I may have had drool at the corner of my mouth. I entered the zoning office one more time.

Violet sat filing her nails. She started to approach the counter, looked at the metal file she carried, then looked at me. She took a second to put the file in her top drawer, then locked it with a tiny key which she put into her bra.

"May I help you?"

"I went to room 212 to get a permit. They said I had to get permission from . . ." by now, I was screaming, "George Bigham."

Violet looked a little scared and unsure of what to tell me. From one of the back offices, a younger, meek man stuck his head out. "Did someone call me?"

"No, Junior. This lady has a letter here signed by your daddy. I'm just trying to help her."

The red-faced man came out of his office. He took the letter I held in my shaking hand. "I wrote this letter," he said.

"You? Who are you?" By now, I hung over the counter.

"I'm George Bigham. I used to be George Bigham, Jr. until my daddy passed away."

"God rest his soul," Junior, Violet, and I chimed together.

"So, you sent me this letter?"

He nodded.

"Can you give me permission to get a permit to park my wrecker at my house?"

"Well, I don't know." He raised onto his tiptoes, then lowered himself down. He raised onto his tiptoes, then lowered himself down. If he did it one more time, I would have to beat him severely about the head and shoulders.

"You see, Mr. Fortney said he doesn't want you parking your tow truck at his house. So, when he phoned in the complaint, I had to follow through with it."

"Pete Fortney turned me in?"

"Yes, he called in the original complaint."

"What is the penalty for murdering an old man in the state of Georgia?"

"Well, I . . . I don't know ma'am, I only deal with zoning laws. Murder is out of my realm." Mr. Bigham blanched.

I took several deep breaths and counted to ten. "May I please have written permission to get my permit? I guarantee Mr. Fortney will not pursue this any further."

"Are you really going to kill him?"

I didn't answer. I just glared at George, Jr. He went back to his office. A few minutes later, he returned with my written permission.

I headed for the door, then turned to him. "Do the world a favor. Get yourself a name that is truly your own." I stepped back toward the counter. "Here's a thought. How about George Bigham, Jr., Junior? You could have it slathered on a big ol' name plate. Maybe put it on your desk."

I started to leave again, but turned back. "I'm just thinking off the top of my head here, but, if you're going to be signing letters, maybe you could tell the freakin' zoning people who you are."

I shoved my way through the door. After climbing to the second floor again, I went straight to room 212. I could tell by the look on Reuben's face he had no intention of giving me any further hard time. As a matter of fact, he had my permit ready and waiting.

Downstairs, Paul told me to have a good day. I told him . . . Well, that really isn't important.

I couldn't believe Pete Fortney had caused me all this trouble. Just when I'd starting liking the old cuss. I could feel ulcers forming in my stomach caused by Paul, Violet, and the rest of the zoning people. When I finally got back to the garage, I found Mom and Pop in his office swing dancing to Duke Ellington.

"My parents are so weird," I yelled over the blaring music.

"How'd it go at the courthouse?" Dad topped my yell, never missing a dance step.

"It's a long story. Any jobs come in while I was gone?"

"No, we're all caught up. Go home. I'll call you if I need you." Pop spun Mom around, then dipped her. Filled with dismay, I watched them. I wasn't sure if it was because my parents were acting like children, or if I was jealous because I didn't have anyone to dance with.

Pop jive danced his way across the floor, twisting on his tiptoes, waving his fingers at his side. When he reached the door, he slammed it in my face. From the other side, I heard my Mom giggling.

"Don't make me turn the water hose on you two." Any other time, I would have found them at least slightly amusing. But I was still angry from my George Bigham ordeal.

I drove the wrecker to my house. I could do that now because I had a permit that said so. As soon as I could get into the house, I planned to call Pete's son and tell him what his father had done, the old crow bait.

All the way home, I'd tried to douse my anger by rationalizing that it was all over now. Somehow, I couldn't do that. In my mind, bits of my ordeal kept tumbling like clothes in a dryer. It all spun around . . . Pete, socks, Violet, underwear, Paul, blouse. By the time I arrived at my house, I'd built a powerful desire to hit something.

Herman, the bass, had his big mouth open, like he was laughing at me. I deliberately overshot the driveway and mowed good old Herman to the ground. I got out of the wrecker, then stood staring at the twisted metal box and the ruptured bass lying in the grass. There, sticking from between the metal and the rubber, I found the key.

I FOUND THE KEY!

This might just turn out to be the best day I'd had in a long time. I had the rest of the day off, provided no one needed a tow truck. In a few minutes I'd get to tattle on Pete. And, allow me to reiterate — I FOUND THE KEY!

Chapter 4

Finally, I'd found the key. I set the crushed mailbox upright directly on the ground. I'd really done a number on the mangled mess. So, as I stuck my hand in to get my bills, Herman looked at me with one twisted eye that looked swollen shut. His other eye was stuck to my tow truck bumper. The pole would never stand upright again. Because of my temper, Herman had died a horrendous death. I sort of looked at it as Divine Intervention, the Lord's way of helping end my key mission. I said a silent thank you.

Inside the house, the message light blinked on my answering machine. Mary Lou had called. "Bertie, where are you? Your dad said you went home. I don't ever remember you leaving work this early. Are you sick? If you're there, pick up the phone."

"If I'd been here, Mary Lou, you wouldn't have been talking to a machine in the first place." I cleared the message, then called the insurance company where she'd worked since we graduated from high school. She prided herself on being the office manager in an office that consisted of her and her boss.

"Good morning, United Insurers." Mary Lou sounded rushed.

"Got your message. Are you busy?"

"Boy, am I. Hang on." She clicked me into an elevator. The soft music played for at least a minute.

"Listen, I need some pictures of you and me when we were young."

"Hey, hey, hey. I'm still young, thank you very much," I joked.

"I mean much younger. Hang on."

I stretched the phone cord across the kitchen to the refrigerator. As I stood gazing at the shower leftovers, I hummed to the music and, at one point, broke into a song accompanying it with a soft shoe. If Mary Lou didn't hurry back on line, I'd be too old to *see* the pictures she wanted me to look for.

"Are you there?" Mary Lou returned.

"Yeah, the insurance business must be jumping."

"Naw, I was doing a three-way with the florist and caterer. This wedding stuff is hard work. Anyway, are you sick?"

"No, just need a day off."

"Good. While you're resting would you look for pictures of us? I want to do a collage to set at the reception. Try to find the one where you had your head stuck in the toilet."

Don't ask. You don't want to know.

"Gotta run, the minister's still holding." Click.

"And a good day to you, Mary Lou." She was having the time of her life. That made me happy too. After snagging a hunk of cake from the fridge, I hung up the phone. I licked off all the frosting, threw the cake into the trash, then went back to pour myself a glass of milk.

I called Pete Fortney's son and told him that his father had been trying to force me to move. "I don't want to be a tattle tale," I lied, "but I really like this house, and I'd hate to have to move."

"I'm sorry. I had no idea. I assure you, I'll take care of it. Again, I apologize."

"Well, thank you, Mr. Fortney. By the way, do either you or your father have any emotional connection to that bass mailbox?"

"Not at all, but Dad keeps a key hidden in there. You might want to take it out if you intend to get rid of it."

It never occurred to me to ask my landlord about the key. As I hung up the phone, I gave myself a giant V-8 head smack.

After swallowing the last of the milk, I went into the bedroom, pulled a box from the top of my closet and dumped the pictures onto the bed.

One by one, I sifted through each image of my life. I found several for Mary Lou's collage, including the one of me with my head in the john. I immediately tore it into a million pieces. As I pitched it into the trash, I vowed, "Not in this lifetime."

Having completed my assigned task, I couldn't fight the desire to look at all of the pictures, to tiptoe through the great and not-so-great memories. Many silly poses by old friends made me laugh. A picture of me and Nana Byrd made me cry. A small bundle of pictures wrapped in a black ribbon made me want to barf.

I'd tied them up about six years ago in a ceremony where I'd ridded myself of the anger and hurt Lee's departure had left behind. He'd been put into a witness protection program.

We met a year after I graduated from high school and fell instantly in love. I loved him "with every breath my soul taketh." At least that was what I had written in the poem I'd scribed especially for him. That was back during my awakening period, as I called it. I'd have been better off to have slept through it.

Lee and I had been together for seven years, dating four, living together for three, when things went terribly wrong. He didn't really enter the witness protection program. I just find that easier to say. The truth is, he went to the store for a loaf of bread and never came back. It took me several days to find out he'd run off with Annie, Carrie Sue and Donna's sister. Now, they live in Albany with three kids. From what I've been told, the kids are following in their cousins' (Donna's kids) footsteps. I couldn't wish such terror on anyone better than Lee Dew. No connection to the Dew Drop Inn other than the hours he used to spend there. Lee's name still made me shiver.

That's right. I could have been Bertie Dew. Again, Divine Intervention.

I took advantage of my free time from the garage and caught up on about three years worth of sleep. Around seven o'clock, the ringing phone pulled me from a wonderful, deep coma. Still dazed from my slumber, I reached for the bedside phone. "Hello?"

"Dirty Bird?"

I sat bolt upright. "Pete, is that you, you old reprobate?"

"Yes, my son said I had to call and tell you I was sorry for trying to make you move. He said I caused you a lot of trouble and that you're a nice person and that you're taking good care of my house. I already knew that, 'cause I been keeping an eye on it."

"I've noticed. I found the key, Pete. You can't come in any more."

"That's exactly what Arch said when he called to yell at me today. I won't be bothering you any more. I'm sorry, Dirty Bird."

I swallowed hard to dislodge the lump in my throat. "That's okay, Pete. You were only doing what you thought was best, but I promise I'll take good care of your house. I'll treat it like my own."

"Well, I hope you like it a lot, because Arch said if I run you off he'd rent it to that person, Donna, and her three trolls."

That would scare me too. "I really like it here, Pete. I won't let Donna have it."

"Joyce liked it too. She's been dead twelve years, but I still think of her standing in the kitchen cooking collard greens and ham hocks."

I thought he might cry. "I'm sure you do, Pete. I miss my Nana Byrd, too. I picture her the same way, only in her own kitchen."

"Did she cook naked too?" Pete's tone perked up. I shook my head, like you would a kaleidoscope to scramble visions you NEVER wanted to see. Time to say good night.

"I gotta go, Pete. Thanks for calling."

As I started to hang up, I heard one of his cronies in the background. "Is that her, Pete? Is that Dirty Bird? Want me to go over there and beat her with my rubber catheter hose?"

Pete continued to try to get the receiver back into its cradle. "Oh, shut up, you old *retrotate*."

He finally got the phone hung up, but not before I was laughing myself silly at Pete's misguided attempt to repeat my word power word.

Mary Lou and Rex's wedding plans flowed together nicely. The exchange of vows would take place at the Baptist church Mary Lou and I had attended since we were kids. The whole congregation was invited through the weekly bulletin. Non-congregational members received hand-written invitations which we worked on one evening a few days after she passed the stick test. The reception would be held in the Fellowship Hall at the church.

The whole wedding, from conception (pardon the pun) to execution (again, pardon me) took exactly four weeks. The wedding was four days away, and Mary Lou's condition barely showed at all.

Saturday afternoon I would get to wear my bridesmaid dress-a sleek, yellow, sleeveless number with rounded neck, the hem falling just below my knees. I looked hot in it. Thrilled would not begin to describe my happiness when Mary Lou chose that one as opposed to the orange one with the big ass bow. I use that term not to accentuate its size, but to let you know where it was located. I breathed a heavy sigh of relief and happily accepted the yellow dress as the best choice.

I'd been home about two hours when Pete called. "How are you, Dirty Bird?"

"I'm fine. How are you?"

"Fine, fine, fine. I hear you're going to be in a wedding. Are you the bride?"

"How did you hear that?" Truly interested, I waited for his answer.

"One of the nurses here is going to a wedding. She said you were going to be in it. I just can't remember if you are the bride or the minister."

"No, Pete. I'm not the bride or the minister. I'm the Maid of Honor. I get to wear a pretty yellow dress." I threw that in because I was really, really happy about it.

"Oh, that's nice. I bet you'd make a prettier bride than a minister."

"Thanks. I think." I listened to silence on his end.

After a few seconds, he finally thought of something to say, or woke up, whichever the case. "Okay, I'll hang up now."

"Bye, Pete."

Friday night, several of us took Mary Lou to the Dew Drop Inn for her bachelorette party. Millie Keats had headed it up. Carrie Sue made the bride-to-be a mini-veil to wear throughout the evening. I volunteered to be the designated driver, which was okay with me since I had an aversion to drinking more than my body could hold, then spending the rest of the night on my bathroom floor so I wouldn't have to travel so far to get there anyway. Not that I hadn't done that in my lifetime, but I had funner things to do.

Before we entered the bar, Mary Lou pulled me aside. "Don't let me do anything stupid tonight."

"I'm not sure I'm up to that task, my dear friend. Remember, I'll be without the benefit of booze." Of course, since she was pregnant, she'd be without booze too. But with Mary Lou there wasn't much difference. I didn't think she'd heard me anyway. She'd already run, with her veil flapping in the breeze, to catch up with Carrie Sue and the others.

Later in the evening we'd just ordered another round of Margaritas and vanilla cokes for me and Mary Lou, when a hunk of a man dressed in jeans, a tank top, tool-belt, and hard hat entered the center of the dance floor. Rainbow lights began to dance across the walls and ceiling. The juke box blasted a catchy ditty. The hunky man started to do his job.

He dropped his belt to the floor, then kicked it aside. His body began to move in unbelievable ways. Whoops and whistles came from the crowd. All the women shoved their way to the front, pushing past their husbands, boyfriends, and all the Rupert's in the bar.

By now the stripper had torn off all his clothes except for a shiny, purple thong with almost all of his important parts tucked into a front pouch.

Eighty-year-old Millie was trying to climb onto our table, while Carrie Sue and Donna held her back.

"Who hired him?" I bellowed above the roar.

Mary Lou leaned closer to me, then yelled into my ear, "Millie did."

I looked at the old woman. She'd given up her fight to get on the table. Instead, she was on the dance floor gyrating her hips, shrieking, "Work it, baby, work it."

I rescued the stripper by pulling Millie back to the table. "Sit. Behave yourself," I demanded.

"Spoil sport," she wheezed back at me.

"Go, Mary Lou. Go, Mary Lou." The crowd had now turned their attention to the bride-to-be, which would be the woman with the mini-veil hiding under the table. Several of them dragged her out, then shoved her onto the floor with the hunk. He danced around her a few times. Sweat glistened on his body. Mary Lou flushed a bright scarlet from head to toe.

With Millie settled, I could relax and enjoy the view. The stripper turned toward my section of the room. For the first time, I allowed my gaze to travel from his purple pouch to his face.

"Oh, good Lord," I thundered.

"What's the matter?" Millie asked.

I swallowed hard and shook my head. "Nothing." I wasn't about to tell anyone that the stripper was none other than my handsome fellow who worked at the paper mill. But, I can tell you one thing for sure, if he fell on me with nothing but his purple pouch on, I'd have to believe Mary Lou did possess powers to make wishes come true.

That night, I got everyone home safely who had been entrusted to my care. I had to admit, I had a good time. Jeff, the new wonder dancer in my life, asked for my phone number and promised to call me sometime next week. Somehow, I'd managed to carry on an intelligent conversation with him, in spite of his purple pouch.

I slipped out of my clothes and into my football jersey in record time. Once in bed, I went right to sleep. I'd been dreaming about Jeff only a few minutes when something awakened me. Someone was at the foot of my bed. Fear gripped my entire body.

"I came to tell you good-bye, Dirty Bird," Pete's voice whispered through the darkness.

"For God's sake, you scared me to death."

He stepped closer to the bed. An aura of pale light brought his face into clear view. Pete smiled, his eyes twinkled. "I'll give your Nana your love."

I scrambled to turn on the light. He was gone. Chills chattered my teeth. I tugged the blanket under my chin, then shivered several times in succession.

"How creepy was that?" I asked myself. Although I knew it was a dream, I left the light on and struggled to go back to sleep. Eventually, I did.

The next morning, I gathered all the things I'd need to get ready for the wedding at two o'clock in the afternoon. I locked the front door and made my final trip to Pop's Cadillac which I'd borrowed the night before.

A car pulled into the driveway. I recognized the driver as Arch Fortney, Pete's son. He got out of his car and walked toward me. He wasn't quite six feet tall. With his shoulders slumping his build seemed slighter than I remembered from our first meeting. Sadness shaded his already dark eyes. In my heart, I knew what he was going to say.

"I just left the nursing home. My father died during the night. I wanted to tell you that he really didn't mean you any harm. It was just hard for him to understand that someone else lived in the house he and Mom had shared for so many years."

"I know. We had a few conversations lately." I struggled to hold back my tears.

"He told me on several occasions that he liked you a lot. He wanted me to sell the house to you, if you're interested in buying it."

Just then he choked back a sob. "I'm sorry. I can't deal with that right now. Think about it, and I'll get back to you when things have settled down for me."

He turned without saying goodbye and hurried to his car. As he backed out of the driveway, I saw the tears streaming down his face.

I didn't see a need to tell Arch that his dad had come to say goodbye to me the night before. I'm not sure if I didn't want to hurt his feelings, in case Pete hadn't shown him the same courtesy, or if I was afraid I'd be known as the nutty woman who sees ghosts.

As a matter of fact, I decided not to tell anyone about my final minutes with Pete Fortney. For some reason, I felt a need to keep that information stored in the crevices of my heart.

The wedding went off without a hitch. Mary Lou made the most beautiful bride I'd ever seen. Rex, he cleaned up pretty good too. There couldn't be the slightest doubt of the love those two had for each other, even if the baby she carried did speed up the process a tad. We all knew they'd eventually make the move. According to the smiles on their faces, things couldn't have been better for them.

My tears flowed through the whole ceremony and well into the reception. I tried drowning my sorrow in the punch. Unfortunately, we were in the Fellowship Hall of the church. Therefore, with no alcohol present, the only thing I got from the sweet drink, other than several trips to the bathroom, was the right to cry about everything. I cried because the cake was so pretty. I cried for the happy couple. I cried for Pete. But most of all, I cried for myself.

There would never again be the togetherness Mary Lou and I had shared for over twenty-five years. I would have to take a step back to make room for her husband and her baby. But, even as I accepted the change, and shoved my best friend into her bliss, I ached with emptiness.

Sitting alone at a table near the back of the hall, I looked around the room at all the people I'd known all my life. "Men pickin's are slim in these here parts", Nana Byrd, widowed for thirty years, used to say. God rest her soul.

"They still are, Nana." I said aloud. Surveying the men in the room, I realized we all knew too much about each other in our little town. Yet, venturing from Sweet Meadow had never entered my mind. As our town motto reads, *There's no place as sweet as Sweet Meadow.* I figured it must be true.

A loud, obnoxious laugh caught my attention. Clustered in a corner across from me were the Barrow sisters, Carrie Sue, Donna, and . . . Annie. I hadn't realized she was here. At that very moment, I locked gazes with none other than Lee Dew. Sure took him a long time to get a loaf of bread.

For years, I pretended he really had joined a witness protection program and as part of changing his identity, they'd done plastic surgery on him which went terribly wrong. I used to stand in front of the mirror, making believe he'd come back to beg my forgiveness.

"Take your new face with your two noses and your hunchback and scurry back to Annie," I'd scoff.

Of course, dreams don't always come true. Lee appeared to have aged pretty good. So had Annie. It looked like her plastic surgery had worked well, double D times two.

Maybe someone had slipped some booze into the punch, because I would swear Lee had winked at me. He went to a side door, then nodded for me to follow him. I wished I had a coin to flip to see what I should do, but my sleek, hot dress had no pockets. I took that as an omen, and decided not to follow Lee.

But then again, maybe this would be my only chance to let him know how much I don't miss him and how glad I am he's out of my life.

I rose from the hard chair and had taken only one step when Mary Lou stopped me. She hugged me tightly. "Thank you for being the best friend anyone could ever ask for." She pulled back to look me in the eyes. "You don't need the problems that are waiting for you outside." She nodded toward the door through which Lee had disappeared. "You deserve so much better. Like that." I looked in the direction of her gaze.

Jeff, my new Wonder Dancer/paper mill worker made his way toward me.

"I wished him on you." Mary Lou giggled. "What better way to show Lee how little you need him than with a hunk like that on your arm?"

"How'd you get so smart?"

Mary Lou hugged me one more time. "I had a good teacher." She spun me around to face Jeff.

Through the remainder of Mary Lou and Rex's wedding celebration, I stayed glued to Jeff's side. And what a magnificent side it was. With the combination of Jeff and my shiny, yellow dress, I was, as Pop always said, the cat's meow. Evidently, it showed to everyone. To my amazement, several people congratulated me. It took me a few minutes to realize it was because of Jeff.

What was wrong with these people? Hadn't they ever seen me with a man? I guess most of their memories weren't that long.

Millie slapped me on the back. "See if he has an older brother for me." She then peacocked across the floor with an exaggerated wiggle in her rear. If I attempted that, I'd throw my back out of whack.

Mary Lou's cousin from Atlanta, Rupert the Magnificent, grabbed me by my shoulders, smiled a goofy grin, then hugged me to him in an awkward motion.

"I'm glad to see you've finally found someone else," he whispered in my ear. Every nerve in my body stiffened so hard, I think it popped Rupert's fingers loose from my arms. Quickly, he turned and walked away. His hips couldn't possibly be the same height as mine. His seemed to be resting on his shoulders. The old butt head.

Lee Dew eventually came back into the hall. He gave me a look which asked, "Why didn't you follow me?"

I latched onto Jeff's muscular arm, then gave Lee a look that said, "Nana nana boo boo."

When the time came for the happy couple to leave for their honeymoon in Cleveland, Georgia (Mary Lou wanted to go to the Cabbage Patch Doll Hospital), the guests lined the walkway leading from the Fellowship Hall to the parking lot. Each of us plucked a satin rose stuffed with birdseed from a basket. They'd grown there last week when Mary Lou and I had stayed up until two in the morning building the pretty bouquet.

"You're supposed to throw rice at the bride and groom," Millie announced to anyone who would listen. "Nowhere in wedding folklore does it say throw rice until it becomes ecologically incorrect, then switch to birdseed."

I tried to reassure her it was the thought that counted. Guests were required to send the couple off on their honeymoon by throwing some kind of loose particles at them. Later, in a motel room somewhere, they could perform the animal ritual of picking stuff out of each other's hair as a prelude to making love.

As Mr. and Mrs. Rexall Hiram Jarvis paraded past us, we all threw our best wishes at them in the form of birdseed. Millie threw a large bag of rice.

"Millie!" I stooped to retrieve the missile. A loud rip split the air. Even before I grabbed my backside, I knew my elegant, yellow dress had died a tragic death. Standing up straight, trying to back away from the group, my face flamed.

"It was a joke, Bertie. Jeeze, you are way too stiff. You need to loosen up some." Millie took back her bag of rice.

"She's too loose, now. She's hanging out all over the place." Ethel Winchell added her two-cents worth.

As I backed into the Fellowship Hall, waving at the people who were laughing at me, I held my hand over the tear in the rear of my dress. I wondered, *Where's that big ass bow when I need it?*

From the doorway, I watched Mary Lou and Rex get into his 1970 restored Ford pick-up. I had no doubt they were a perfect couple. Their hips were exactly the same height.

Jeff gave me his blazer to wrap around my waist, to cover my exposed behind. I insisted that Mom drive her Caddy instead of riding with Pop in the wrecker. That freed me to let Jeff take me home.

Chapter 5

As I entered my house and made my way down the hallway, I stopped outside my bedroom door, then peeked inside just in case Pete had decided to hang around. A sadness stabbed my heart. I would miss old Pete, the crazy old goat.

God rest his soul.

I changed into more comfortable clothes (jeans and a T-shirt), then quickly joined Jeff who waited for me in my living room. He'd turned on the television and had already become engrossed in two tag-teams rolling around in a WWF ring.

"I can't believe the top wrestlers are coming to the Armory next Thursday night, and I've been hired to work a birthday party for a sixty-year-old woman." Did he actually have a tear in the corner of his eye?

It appeared my new boyfriend was becoming emotionally distressed because he wouldn't be able to witness an event where grown men parade into a ring in brightly-colored tights. Once there, they proceed to wrestle other men onto a mat because their tights are prettier. And the saddest part is that Jeff would miss this magical event because he had to take all his clothes off and dance in front of a group of heavy-breathing, groping women.

I only have three words to say on the matter. Why me, Lord?

After the wrestling show ended, we turned off the TV, then sat in total silence for a while. Jeff put his arm around me, pulling me closer to his side. I rested my head on his shoulder. Something about him made me know I could get past the Wrestle Mania obsession and the stripper part of his life. I inhaled his faint cologne, then fell into a deep sleep.

When I woke up in my bed, still dressed in my jeans and T-shirt, Jeff was gone. I guess I'd passed out from the wear and tear of all the wedding festivities.

I glanced at the clock. On this day, the Garden Club Ladies would add me to their list of heathens, but I needed my rest. I went to the bathroom, stripped out of my clothes, then snuggled back into bed. Until late in the afternoon, I slept like a new-born baby.

At four o'clock I'm not sure which woke me, the ringing phone or my growling stomach. They performed in two-part harmony.

"Hello?"

"Hey, Sleeping Beauty. When did you finally wake up?" Jeff's kind voice warmed me to my toes.

"When the phone rang."

"Wow. You really were tired."

"Sorry you had to let yourself out. I'm not normally so rude. Did you walk me to my bed?" I asked.

"Nope. I carried you." The thought of my personal Hercules hauling my sleeping butt to bed warmed me even more. I wondered why he hadn't stayed.

"By the way, my name is Jeff . . . House." He enunciated each syllable clearly.

"That's a nice name." I knew by this sharp tone he was trying to tell me something.

"Who is Lee, the Wonder Horse?"

"Oh, good Lord. That horse was put out to pasture many years ago." Yeah, I liked that thought. I might have to move him from the protection program to the pasture.

"I don't think your subconscious would agree with that. How about I come over later and we analyze the source of your psychic energy which appears to be derived from some instinctual need to remember this Lee person?"

I needed my *Reader's Digest*. Now! "Would that entail us having sex?" Tactfulness had never been my strong suit.

"I hope so."

All of a sudden, my heart lodged in my throat. I could think of a dozen reasons why that would be a good thing. But that one nagging thought that I had never been one to jump into bed with someone I really didn't know won the battle raging in my body.

"That's sounds interesting, but . . . "

"But, you think we need more time?"

Perceptive critter, wasn't he? "Would that be so terrible?" No wonder I was thirty-two and still single. I did need psychoanalysis. A hunk of a man wanted to crawl into my bed, and I wanted to think it over. Despite Mary Lou's insistence that having sex was like riding a bicycle-you never forget how-I couldn't help wondering if that was my problem.

"No. I understand." Jeff sounded so kind, I actually believe he did understand. "If it's okay with you, I'll call you later in the week. Maybe we can go out to eat, or to a movie."

"I'd like that." I really would.

I hung up the phone, then sat up in the bed. Could I possibly be afraid of having sex again after so much time? I ran my hand over my shin and calf. Naw, I just didn't want to have to shave my legs right now. That's all.

Also, there was the name problem. Jeff House. Bertie House. I'd have to think that over too.

Okay, so there I was, sitting in Ethel Winchell's Mercedes listening to the radio blasting at full volume. I'd just finished tearing the magnificent machine apart, determined what I needed to repair it, then was told by the parts house it would take two days to get the parts to me. I deserved a break. Pop hollered across the garage, "Chief Kramer said to get on over to 440 at Laney Road. Hurry."

Break over.

I climbed out of Ethel's car and scurried to my tow truck. I call her Bessie. Pop insists it's of the male persuasion, but I know it has to be a woman. She works hard, becomes temperamental once a month, and seldom ever suffers from an over abundance of gas.

I was clipping along humming my theme song, "On the Road Again," when Pop's voice crackled through the dispatch radio.

"Bertie, are you there?"

This question always galls me. He watched me drive away approximately three minutes earlier going hell bent for an accident. The radio is two feet from my face. Where else would I be?

"Bessie is on her way to the accident by herself, Pop. Leave a message and I'll get back to you. Beep!"

"This is serious, Bertie. Chief just called back. He said to hurry. Traffic is blocked both ways. And quit calling that wrecker Bessie. If you have to name it, call it Barney."

I didn't have time to bang my head on the steering wheel. I still had about a mile and a half to go to get to the wreck. Traveling at sixty miles an hour, I'd be there soon.

"Bertie, are you there?" Okay, so I did have time to whack my head one good time.

"Yes, Pop. What is it?" In front of me, a UPS truck slammed on its brakes.

"Tom Mason just called," Pop announced.

I was struggling to get Bessie stopped before she parked herself in the back of the UPS truck.

"Tom said to be careful. Just before you get to the accident, there's something lying in the middle of the road."

The big brown van in front of me swerved to the right. Bessie jumped onto the "something" lying in the middle of the road.

"Jesus, Joseph, and Mary," I screamed. Whatever I'd hit didn't bring Bessie to a complete stop, so I just let her cruise. Surely, whatever I was dragging with me, which was making a heck of a noise, would fall off before I arrived at the scene of the accident about a quarter of a mile ahead.

The halted traffic had already pulled to the side of the road to allow emergency vehicles to pass. As Bessie and I coasted, nose first, right next to Chief Kramer's cruiser, several people frantically jumped into various vehicles and started them up. Like we were at the Atlanta Speedway, they raced away from me.

Deputy Tom Mason yelled for me to get out of the wrecker. Smoke began to fill Bessie. I opened the door, then jumped clear of the flames licking at her undercarriage.

I'd barely abandoned the blazing truck when a fireman sprinted past me with his hose. In a few seconds, he'd drowned Bessie. My knees shook so hard my teeth chattered. Tom asked several times if I was okay. I couldn't find my voice, so I just nodded.

Finally, I found the strength to assess the damage. Sticking from under Bessie's belly were the remnants of a mattress with inner springs. When I ran over it, it ruptured the gas tank and wrapped wire around the drive shaft. By the time I'd coasted a quarter of a mile, mattress stuffings had soaked up the slowly leaking fuel, then sparks ignited the whole mess.

I heard Chief Kramer radio back to his office. He told his dispatcher to call Shafer and get wreckers on their way to us. One for the original accident and one for Bessie.

As they hauled her away, I could hear Pop's crackling voice calling from inside her cab.

"Bertie, are you there?"

The bad news: Seven-year-old Bessie couldn't be repaired. The good news: The insurance check put a big down payment on a brand new wrecker, Melinda or Murray, depending on whether I was driving or Pop.

A few days after the fire, I'd just finished the repairs on Ethel Winchell's Mercedes and had parked it out front for her to pick up any time. Sitting in her front seat, I was singing along to an oldie goldie playing on her radio. Pop is always hollering at me to keep the volume down when I'm working on a car, but what fun is it listening to "Jeremiah Was a Bullfrog" unless it's rocking the rafters.

". . . was a good friend of mine."

"Bertie, go over to The Chow Pal Diner and pick up our lunch," Pop yelled from the doorway.

I turned off Ethel's ignition, then climbed into my new wrecker. As I walked into the diner, several of the happy eaters looked up and grinned at me. I smiled back, but soon I realized they were snickering.

Immediately, I felt the back of my coveralls in case I'd repeated my yellow dress fiasco and hadn't realized it. Finding everything intact and all my parts covered, I averted my gaze to the newest edition of the *Sweet Meadow News Leader*. There on the front page was a picture of me. With eyes the size of saucers, I stared at the mattress flaming under Bessie. The headlines read:

WRECKER DRIVER HAS HOT TIME ON MATTRESS.

It couldn't have been as hot as my face at that moment. Quickly, I paid for my lunch. The diners continued to giggle.

"Cute. Really cute." I smiled and acknowledged their jokes.

As I started backing out the door, I did my Elvis impersonation. "Thank you. Thank you very much."

"Hey, Bertie." I'd almost made my escape when someone from the back of the café called to me. "We think you should get some business cards made. *Have Mattress. Will Travel.*"

Everyone laughed.

"Ha. Ha. Ha. You guys are really funny. When you get done here, why don't you go over to the Tall Pines Nursing Home and take the bolts out of the wheel chairs. Ha. Ha. Ha."

I nonchalantly left the café, walked around the corner to my new wrecker. Once I was out of their sight, I made a face and stuck my tongue out at the solid brick wall on the side of the Chow Pal Diner. They hadn't seen me, but I felt better.

I got back to the garage without killing anyone. Pop and I had just finished our lunches when Ethel arrived to get her car.

She paid her bill and I walked out with her. Belted into her seat, she started the engine. Her blue, wispy hair shot straight up on her head. We both jumped several inches into the air. I dove head first across the steering wheel and Ethel's arms to turn off the blaring radio.

"I'm so sorry. I forgot to turn that back to your station." I felt really bad for the elderly lady who appeared to be terribly shaken.

"And down." She patted her bony hand against her chest. "Turned to my station and down, would have been good."

I pushed her hair back into place and apologized again. As she drove away, she white-knuckled the steering wheel and stared straight ahead. I truly hoped she'd be okay.

When I got home that night, the phone message light beckoned me from across the room. Just as I started to retrieve my calls, the phone rang.

"Is this Roberta Byrd, the celebrity who got her picture on the front page of the *Atlanta Journal-Constitution?*" Jeff, my Wonder Dancer, chuckled into the phone.

"It's the *Sweet Meadow News Leader*, but you were close." What a pleasant way to end a . . . I couldn't call it a strange day, because actually it was a normal day in my universe. Being laughed at by people with mouths full of burgers and fries and apple pie, then scaring poor, old Ethel Winchell out of what wits she has left constitutes an average kind of afternoon for me.

Oh, yeah. Then there was the matter of catching the seat of my coveralls on the oil barrel, but that wasn't important right then. I had a terrific guy on the other end of the phone, wondering if I'd fallen asleep or something.

"No, Bertie. You made the *Journal-Constitution* too. I have a copy right here in my hand."

"You have got to be kidding. Why would people from Atlanta care about something so mundane that happened here in Sweet Meadow?" I just said it was mundane in my universe.

"They called it the Picture of the Week. The caption says *We hope the working women of the red light districts of Atlanta don't start carrying their mattresses with them too.*" Jeff laughed so hard he could barely squeak out his words. "That's funny . . . don't you think?"

I completely missed the humor in the whole matter. I could have been seriously hurt. If it had exploded, others could have been hurt. And, if Jeff didn't quit laughing, he definitely was going to get hurt. I would see to it.

"Yeah, that's hysterical. Is that all you wanted, Jeff? Are you enjoying me being the butt of a joke? Shouldn't you be dancing somewhere with yours hanging out?"

"You know it's funny. Maybe not today, but you'll see the humor in it eventually. Until then, I'll quit laughing." He broke up again.

"Good-bye, Jeff," I growled into the phone.

"Okay. Okay. I'm sorry. Don't hang up. Would you like to go to dinner on Friday?" He cleared his throat several times to stifle his giggle.

"I'll think about it." I tapped my fingernails on the kitchen counter for about fifteen seconds. "Okay. I'll be ready at six-thirty, unless I have to wrangle another mattress out of the road." This time, I laughed too.

After we hung up, I listened to my messages. Three all together. Mary Lou and Rex had returned from their short honeymoon. She'd catch me later.

One was from Pete Fortney's cronies at the Tall Pines Nursing home. They hoped I hadn't taken any offense to their little joke when they'd called while Pete was still alive and teased that they were going to cut off my fingers and toes. They also hoped I hadn't taken a liking to starting fires, especially to mattresses, because the nursing home was filled with them. Someone in the background hollered at the man not to give me any ideas.

I rubbed my temple by my right eye. "Here comes that twitch again."

The third call was from Gabe Nelson from the newsroom at a television station in Atlanta. They wanted to do a remote from my house to the Barry Mateson Show in New York on Friday night.

"Why?" I asked the thin air.

While I was deciding whether or not to return the call, the phone rang. It was Gabe Nelson.

"Mr. Nelson, why would Barry Mateson want me on his show?"

"Do you watch Mr. Mateson? Do you know the kind of people he has on?" Mr. Nelson sounded indignant because I'd questioned the powers-that-be from New York.

I quickly made a mental check of the beautiful, interesting, talented people I'd seen on the late-night show. Maybe it wouldn't be so bad to be associated with the likes of Julia Roberts, Sally Field, and Kathy Lee. I felt my head swell.

"Miss Byrd, you'd be among his memorable guests like the man who collected the biggest ball of tin foil and the midget who drives an eighteen-wheeler."

The air whooshed from my lungs and my head. "Thanks, Mr. Nelson, but no thanks. I have plans for Friday night."

"I'll tell you what, you have a day before I need your answer. Think it over. I'll get back to you." The television reporter hung up on me.

I decided I'd let my answering machine catch all my calls for the next couple of days because I had no intention of talking to Mr. Nelson again.

"And that's that."

When I arrived at the garage on Friday morning, a white van with satellite dishes mounted on top and advertising Channel 11 News sat in our parking lot. I didn't see anyone milling around. Hurrying to get inside to find out what was going on, I ran toward the side door of Pop's office. Fully expecting to find chalk-body outlines on the floor and crime scene tape everywhere, I could barely breathe. I grasped the doorknob, turned it, and tried to enter the office, all in one fell swoop. I slammed head first into the locked door. Dazed, I backed away, then knocked.

"Pop. What's going on? Let me in." I was fumbling through a ring of keys that would put a night-watchman's collection to shame, when the door cracked slightly. Pop peeked out at me.

"Is Mike Wallace with them?" he whispered through the crack.

"Who? What are you talking about?" I pushed on the door. He stepped aside to let me in.

"The Sixty Minute people in the van." Pop pulled down a slat in the blind. "They're after me."

Now, I looked through the small opening. "Why would Sixty Minutes be after you? What did you do?"

"I buried that barrel of used oil out back last year. I knew it was just a matter of time before the Feds found out about it." He pulled the cord and raised the blinds all the way to the top of the picture window facing the parking lot and the empty van. "You'll never take me alive, coppers," Pop yelled at the top of his lungs.

"Stop that." I grabbed him by his arm, then dragged him to his chair. Reaching into his top desk drawer, I took out a prescription bottle. "Here." I handed Pop his pill and a glass of water. "Take your blood pressure medicine."

Through the window, I saw a black car pull up. Three men climbed out. The one with the clipboard was Gabe Nelson from Atlanta. I recognized him from the nightly news.

"You can relax, Pop. They're here for me, not you."

"Why? What'd you do?"

"You remember, I told you they want me to talk to Barry Mateson."

"I think you should hold out for Leno." Pop laid a wet rag across his eyes and leaned back in his chair.

I decided to face them and get it over with. As I walked across the lot, Mr. Nelson saw me and came to meet me. "I told you I couldn't do this. I have plans for tonight."

He shook my hand like he was priming a water pump. My whole body quaked. "That's why we're going to tape it now. It'll run during tonight's show." He motioned to one of the other men. "Over here, Jake."

Jake charged our way with a camcorder. The other man, with a toothpick in his mouth, held a microphone.

Gabe Nelson led the way to the corner of the lot where they could get a full view of the garage and my new wrecker. I stole a glance at myself in Melinda's side-view mirror. Since I'd just arrived at work, my hair and face hadn't yet done battle with axle grease. I looked okay, but to talk to Barry Mateson, King of Late Night, I wasn't so sure.

"Miss Byrd, we're ready," Gabe called.

"Guess I am too." Doubt wiggled and niggled and tickled inside me, kind of like the spider the old woman swallowed in the nursery rhyme. "Where's Mr. Mateson?"

"Oh, well, you see, I'll ask the questions, you'll answer them. Tonight, they'll have Barry ask the same questions, then play your responses. Okay? Ready?"

Dang. Just my luck. I'd be interviewed, which I didn't want to be, by someone I wouldn't even see or hear. "I guess so."

"Okay, what is your name?" Jake's tone bordered on boredom.

"Roberta Byrd, but you can call me Bertie."

"That your new wrecker?"

"That's right. Pretty, isn't it?"

"Yeah. So, you hit a mattress."

"A mattress with inner springs."

"So, you ran over it or what?" Did Gabe just yawn?

This is my debut. Where's my motivation?

"Bessie, that's what I called my old wrecker, she was like a friend, jumped on the mattress. She and I rode it a little ways until . . . well, all of a sudden, it broke into flames. Then I jumped out and ran for my life."

"That'll take care of it, Miss Byrd. Thanks. Jake," Gabe called to the man with the camera, "span across the front of the building, get the name of the business."

Just like that, Nelson hauled his body back to his car, and the other two men jumped into the van. They disappeared like the last of a tornado tail, leaving a wake behind it.

That night, Jeff and I went to dinner. We hurried back to my house, then snuggled on the sofa ready to watch the Barry Mateson Show. When I realized my segment was coming on, I became giddy with excitement.

"We want you to meet this little lady right here." Mr. Mateson held up the newspaper picture of me and flaming Bessie. The camera had just the right angle. Maybe I didn't look too bad. Barry told the story of my near tragedy.

"We have the female tow truck driver on satellite from Sweet Meadow, Georgia. What's your name?"

"Roberta Byrd, but you can call me Bertie."

"Did you say Dirty Bird?" Barry asked. The audience chuckled.

"That's right, pretty isn't it?" I replied. *That's not what Gabe asked me*, I mouthed, but the words didn't come out.

"Oh, yeah, catchy name. In your recent accident, you lost a piece of equipment you use to make your living with. What was it?" Barry appeared to be trying to hold back a grin.

"A mattress with an inner spring." I heard my words, but I just couldn't believe it. The audience roared with laughter.

"Well, what happened?" Barry Mateson was smiling widely.

"Bessie, that's . . . my friend, jumped on the mattress, then rode it until it broke into flames. I ran for my life."

By this time, even Barry Mateson was lost in hysterical laughter. I groaned and slumped away from Jeff, laying on my side, and curled in a fetal position. A lesser woman would have been reduced to slobbering and imitating Mom's hyper poodle, Fifi, who couldn't walk without peeing. But I lack the gene that would have allowed me to do that.

Instead, I began to laugh so hard that tears soaked my face, and I had to go to the bathroom. I'm not sure how that differed from slobbering and Fifi's habit, but, trust me, it did.

When I got back from the bathroom, Jeff had a plastic bag full of ice. He led me to the sofa, then put the bag on my head. Every once in a while, I'd burst into laughter. Jeff would just pat my back and hum a sweet lullaby. Finally, I fell asleep.

Chapter 6

I awoke in my bed, in my clothes, and Jeff was gone. This was getting to be a habit. I got up and peeked out my window. No news vans. I breathed a sigh of relief.

Strolling down the hallway, I glanced into the spare bedroom. Every time I looked in there, I felt a stab of guilt. I'd been in the house for five months, and that room still held stacks of unpacked boxes.

I started thinking that, since I hadn't needed anything in there in five months, maybe I didn't need it at all. Maybe I'd just haul it all to the dump. That was another gene I lacked, the throw-away gene. I'd kept everything I'd ever owned. Throwing it away was never an option for me.

I pulled the door shut. Maybe if I didn't see it, I wouldn't feel so guilty.

In my living room, on my sofa, laid a lump covered from head to toe with an afghan. One long, definitely male leg stuck from beneath the cover.

Ah, how sweet," I whispered. Jeff hadn't wanted me to be alone, but he'd hadn't taken advantage of my impaired thinking last night. He'd slept on the lumpy couch.

That really touched me. My heart swelled with love? No, my heart swelled with strong fondness. Our only two dates had ended with nothing more than me falling asleep and him putting me to bed in my clothes. We hadn't even kissed, but I had a strong desire to kiss him now.

I knelt in front of the sofa, ran my hand along his exposed leg, under the cover, and as I planted a kiss on the blanket where his face would be, my hand reached his backside. I expected to feel the firm, cute butt I'd seen dancing around Mary Lou at her bachelorette party. But instead I found a flabby broad one, barely covered by old boxer shorts with a hole in them. I uncovered Rip Van Winkle's head.

Oh, my God. I'd kissed Prince Charming and turned him into my brother! Screaming, I jumped to my feet, trying to brush the cooties from my hands and shivering to my toes.

"Brrrrrr. Bobby, what are you doing here?"

My brother, whom I hadn't seen since Christmas, bolted upright and clutched his fist to his chest.

"Jeeze, Bertie. My ticker ain't what it used to be. You could've killed me."

"Well, you didn't do a heck of a lot for me either." Again, I shivered violently and rubbed my hands on my jeans in an attempt to get rid of the Bobby residue.

The phone rang. I pointed at my brother. "Don't go away, I have lots of questions."

"Hello?"

"Good morning. I hope I didn't wake you. I assume you've found your brother by now." Jeff sounded a little too chipper for my frame of mind.

"Did you let him in?"

"Yeah. He said he was your brother."

"How could you have been sure? Didn't you notice he bears a striking resemblance to Hannibal Lechter? I could have woke up dead this morning," I yelled at the person I'd had such sweet thoughts about only minutes earlier.

"I'm sorry," he said. "He seemed to be telling the truth. I thought you'd be glad to see your brother. Aren't you having a good day?"

"Oh, peachy. In the last few days, I've had a near-death experience, been ridiculed on national TV, and I just felt up my brother. I may break into a chorus of 'Who Could Ask For Anything More.' "

"Wait a minute." Jeff stopped right in the middle of his horse laugh. "This feeling up your brother thing, was that intended for me?"

How much mortification does it take to cause a person to spontaneously combust? Stick with me, and you might learn the answer. "Well, it certainly wasn't intended for my brother."

"That's the way things go for me," Jeff said. "I finally get lucky, and I'm not even in the room."

Well, at least that told me he wouldn't have run screaming from me. "That's my life in a nutshell too." I glanced from the kitchen to the living room where Bobby sat watching cartoons. "For me, luck is a four-letter word. I've got to go. I haven't had a chance to find out why my brother's here." I wasn't sure I wanted to know.

"Okay, I'll take a rain check on that other thing." Not until Jeff laughed out loud did I get his meaning.

"I've suffered a traumatic experience. I may have to seek therapy before I engage in any such activities ever again."

"Ever again?" Jeff sounded disheartened.

"Only time will tell. Bye." I hung up the receiver, then went to join Bobby on the sofa. As the Roadrunner flew off the cliff with his leg tangled in a rope attached to a crate from Acme, I watched my older brother giggle. On a forty-year-old man, it wasn't a pretty sight.

"Hey, Bobby, where's Estelle?"

His giggle stopped. He looked at me. "She threw me out."

I thought he might give a few more details on that bombshell, but the silence hung as heavy over our heads as a wrecking ball at a construction site.

"Why?" I asked.

"Because of that ugly matter with her sister." He chewed on his bottom lip and shrugged.

I felt like the wrecking ball had fallen on my head. "Oh, no. You had an affair with Estelle's sister?" I found it hard to breathe.

"Bertie." Bobby jumped to his feet, then hurdled the coffee table. Quickly, he reached back to retrieve the afghan from the sofa. Wrapping it around his shoulders, he looked like an Indian Chief. At least it covered the hole in the back of his underwear.

"Jeeze, what's wrong with you?" The veins in his neck pulsated, turning his face almost purple.

"You said you were an ugly matter on Estelle's sister." I was matching his indignation ounce for ounce.

"No, I didn't. Estelle wanted her sister to move in with us, but she's a troublemaker. When I put my foot down, my loving wife of twenty years put my clothes out in the yard."

"Let me get this straight. Cute little Mona wanted to live with you guys, but you didn't want her. So, my wonderfully thoughtful sister-in-law sent you to live with your sister. What justice is there in that for me?"

"Estelle'll get over it in a few days. She figures you'll drive me so nuts that I'll be thrilled to come home to her and her sister."

I've never understood how I can just be sitting around the house minding my own business, and bamm! I get blind-sided by people who profess to love me. I guess Bobby just doesn't realize what a low blow his wife's words, spewed in the heat of an argument, delivered to my heart. At least my own flesh and blood hadn't originated the statement.

"Well, I told Estelle she was in for a shock. I can endure you a lot longer than she can. I told her not to look for me back anytime soon."

Wow. Bobby sucker punched me twice with that one. First, because he concurred with his wife that I could conceivably drive him nuts (it really would be a short ride), and it sounded like he intended to be in town awhile, probably at my house. Translated that means; there goes my neighborhood.

"Okay, so, you got into town late last night and didn't want to wake Mom and Pop. I can understand that. How about I help you gather your things?" I picked up his jeans from the floor. "Then I'll ride over to their house with you. You know, help you unpack. There!" I refused to breathe.

"I don't want them to know I'm in town."

I still refused to breathe. A massive lack of oxygen might help my situation.

"How do you expect to be in Sweet Meadow and Mom and Pop not know? It wouldn't surprise me if they already know and are on their way over here right now." I continued to gather his scattered belongings, forcing a smile all the while.

Bobby raced to the front window and peeked out. I wouldn't have been surprised if he'd yelled "You'll never take me alive" like Pop had a few days earlier. He didn't, though. He just slinked back to the sofa. Then, so he wouldn't have to listen to me anymore, he turned up the television to rock-my-teeth volume.

I thought about going to the phone and calling Mom and telling her that Bobby was at my house, and he'd driven all the way here with a hole in his underwear.

Before the sun was high in the sky, Mom appeared on my doorstep reprimanding me for hiding my brother and wanting to know why Bobby had deserted his family, which is what Estelle had said when she'd called my parents' home that morning. I bowed at the waist, made a grand gesture signaling for her to enter my own personal WWF ring. I went outside, slammed the door behind me, and left Mom and Robert Ulysses Byrd (R.U.B.) to figure out who had the prettiest tights. I wanted no part of the rumble that would be taking place in my living room. I'd rather stroll through my brown grass and decide, if I bought the place, where I'd put my petunia commode.

By Sunday morning some of the dust had settled. Estelle and Bobby had decided they needed some time apart. He would take a two-week vacation and visit with his family while Estelle helped her sister get her life together and find a place to live. Then, everyone would live happily ever after. I had trouble with the whole matter because, in the interim, I had custody of Bobby.

Although eight years older than me, he seemed to be twenty years younger. I love my brother, but I'm always on guard where he's concerned. He's never seen the harm in doing things like replacing after-bath dusting powder with itching powder he'd bought at the magic shop on a trip to Stone Mountain. Or, handing someone a metal container filled with substances which explode when opened, leaving the opener devoid of eye lashes and brows. For several weeks following the incident, I had trouble looking surprised.

Sunday morning, Bobby and I rode to church together. Before

services started, I needed to make a stop in the restroom. Alone in the three-stall bathroom, I'd taken my place, leaned on the toilet paper holder, closed my eyes and . . . rested. Thoroughly enjoying the only peace and quiet I'd had in days, I started singing, "I am on the Glory Road." I'd just hit the chorus when...

"Bertie, you have a beautiful voice."

Jerking from my leaning position, I opened my eyes to find that the stall door had ever so quietly swung open and before me stood Glorie Thorpe.

"Honey, you need to join our choir." She smiled widely.

"Excuse me." I closed the door in her face, gently, of course, then slumped into my head-bowed-in-humiliation position which seemed to be happening with great regularity lately. There I'd been singing Glory in front of Glorie in all my glory.

She hooked her fingers over the door, raised on tiptoes, and peeked down at me. No use objecting. What could she see that she hadn't already? "We need a voice like yours. Please say you'll come join us."

"If I agree, will you go away?"

"Oh." She giggled and moved away from the stall. "See you Wednesday night for practice."

I waited until she'd finished what she'd originally come there for and left, before I ventured from my hiding place. At the end of the hallway near the nursery room, Bobby stood talking to a nice looking woman. I strolled their way. He stopped in mid-conversation and introduced her to me.

"This is Karen Battles. Excuse me, it's Karen Kelly, now. We graduated the same year."

I'd seen her at church a few times, but really didn't know her. "It's nice to meet you," I told the lady, who had a dazzling smile. After a few seconds of idle conversation, I excused myself. Bobby and Karen picked up their conversation in whispered tones.

Once we were seated in the church, I looked for Karen. She sat a few pews away beside a burly guy. After a couple of minutes racking my brain, I realized the man was Officer Kelly who had rescued me the first night my dear, departed Pete Fortney appeared at my house.

The Kellys made a lovely couple. Karen turned in her seat and flashed a big smile at Bobby. It's dazzling brightness set off warning bells the size of Big Ben inside my head.

I sat munching on a doughnut and drinking coffee in Pop's office. Mom had just left to go to my house to pick up Bobby's laundry. I begged her not to get mine. I'd take care of it myself. Thank you very much.

The phone rang. Pop answered it. "For heaven's sake. Well, sure. She'll be right there." Pop twisted his mouth into a thoughtful grin. "Okay, I'll tell her."

I wondered if the party on the other end of the line would ever let Pop go. Finally, he grunted, then hung up.

"You're needed on Highway 440 out by the old fruit stand." Pop went back to his doughnut.

I rose, checking my pocket for my keys. "What's going on out there?"

"It seems a plane made an emergency landing in the middle of the road."

"I can't tow an airplane," I protested.

"Well, you could if you had to. But a couple of rubber-neckers locked bumpers. Be sure you have a crowbar on Murray." Pop disappeared through the side door.

"Melinda," I called after him.

Sure enough, there in the middle of the highway squatted a single-engine plane, white with blue stripes. Also, there were two cars with their rubber bumpers locked together.

The officer in charge commenced to tell me how to separate them. "Back your wrecker up here." He pointed to the rear of the second car, whose front bumper was jammed under the rear of the first car. "Hook onto it here." Again he pointed. "Then pull them apart."

I stood staring at the well-meaning man who evidently didn't understand that if I pulled the second car, the first car would come with it. I flashed him my best thank-you-very-much-but smile. I walked to the point of impact, sat on the hood of the second car, placed my foot on the rear of the first car, then began to push with my legs and bounce with my . . . well, you know. Finally, the two vehicles broke free. The crowd watching me work applauded. I curtsied. The cars pulled out of the way.

Just then, the plane started its engine. "Bertie," Tom Mason hollered at me. "Pull that chalk block out of there." He pointed toward the landing gear. I hurried to the belly of the aircraft, then started to remove the yellow plastic wedge jammed under its tire.

The plane lunged, jumping the block, landing on my hand. My scream was lost in the roar of the engine. I sank to the ground and tried for about ten seconds not to cry, but it was a hopeless case. Lying there in the middle of the road, watching the Piper Cub take off, I had to face the very scary fact that I'd just been run over by an airplane.

Entering the front door of my house, I really didn't feel any pain in my recently-broken hand, because I'd been fed some really good pain pills. It didn't even matter that my brother lay sprawled all over my sofa, surrounded by soft drink cans and my package of Chips Ahoy. That's how good the pills were.

Bobby jumped to his feet, then rushed toward me. "Bert, what the heck happened?" He kicked his tennis shoes out of my way.

With Mom's help, I made it to the recliner. "I got ran over by a plane."

"If you don't want to tell me, just say so." He turned to our mother. "Mom?'

She shrugged. "Bertie got ran over by a plane."

"That's amazing. I've never known anyone who had that happen to them. Have you?" Excitement supercharged my big brother. He danced around like he might have to go to the bathroom. "Let's call Ripley's. I'll bet they'd like to know about you."

He sucked in his stomach, pushed out his chest, and cleared his throat. "Believe it or not." He forced his voice into a bass tone.

As if shot from a cannon, I jumped to my feet, grabbed Bobby by the front of his shirt then, with my unbroken hand, twisted the material and a few chest hairs. "Don't even think about it."

"Ber . . ." he winced.

"No, I see it in your eyes, you're thinking about it." I wound my grasp tighter. "Don't." I'm not sure if the drugs had given me extra strength, or if Bobby's sedentary lifestyle had made him a wimp. I definitely had his full attention, but to reinforce how much I would dislike being visited by a Ripley representative, I raised on tiptoes and looked my brother directly in his eyes. "If you do anything so stupid as call Ripley's, I'll take my .357 Magnum and turn you into a eunuch. Then you can be put into the museum with me. Believe it or not."

"Okay. Okay." He pried my hand free, then quickly moved out of my reach.

"You two, behave." Mom stood with her hands on her hips.

Jeeze, maybe my new friends, the pain pills, were turning on me. I felt like I was eight years old and back at my parents' house. I shuddered, then collapsed into the chair.

"Can I get you anything, sweetheart?" Mom fluffed a pillow, then stuffed it beside me so I'd have a nice, soft place to rest my hand.

"I'm fine. Thanks, Mom." She kissed my forehead. Turning to Bobby, she gave him a peck on the cheek. "Take care of your baby sister, Bobby. She needs rest, so don't give her a hard time."

He rubbed his chest. They walked toward the door. "It's a good thing you're here," she said to Bobby. He raised his eyebrow, inquisitively. "With Bertie laid up, your father'll need your help. I'll see you at the garage in the morning."

"Sure, Mom, I'd be glad to."

How wonderful that Bobby so readily agreed to help out during his vacation. He really surprised me. I regretted threatening him and pulling his chest hairs.

Mom looked at me. "I'll come over early tomorrow and stay with you until Bobby gets back tomorrow afternoon."

I waved, then closed my eyes. If this day would just end soon, when tomorrow came I'd face my new demons with a smile. Well, maybe.

As soon as Mom pulled out of the driveway, Bobby appeared to have grown pointed ears and fangs. Right before my eyes, he turned evil. I didn't care. That's how good the pills were.

"Thanks a lot, Ro-Ber-Ta." He glared at me, then flopped onto the sofa. "Now, I have to drive the wrecker tomorrow. I hate driving the wrecker. That's why I left home, so I wouldn't have to drive the wrecker."

I grinned at Robert Ulysses. "That's funny, I left home so I could live alone."

"What's your point?"

"Never mind." Evidently, sedentary lifestyles also cause brain density.

I dozed for a little while. Bobby woke me around seven. "Would you like some of my pizza?"

He can be so kind sometimes. He'd taken the pizza from *my* freezer, which *I'd* bought and put there, baked it in *my* oven, then woke me from a sound, drug induced sleep to see if I wanted what was left of *his* pizza-burnt crust with all the cheese and pepperoni picked from it. I ate two pieces, then made my first attempt at going to the bathroom since I'd gotten run over by an . . . well, you know. It was a struggle, but I managed just fine.

Back in the living room, I noticed a canvas bag by the front door. "What's that?" I asked Bobby, who was washing dishes.

"Oh, yeah. Your mailman brought you that today. Said it wouldn't fit in that sad mailbox of yours." Bobby lifted the bag, which appeared to be heavy, onto the sofa next to me. "He sure is a whiny fellow. He said, 'Please tell her to get a new one so I don't have to climb out of my truck to make her deliveries.' " Bobby imitated the man's sniffling voice, or Bobby's shorts were too tight, I'm not sure which.

Looking inside the bag, I found a bunch of letters. What in the world could they be? I pulled out a handful. They appeared to be from all over the United States. The addresses covered every possible anagram or configuration possible of my name. Miss Byrd, Dirty Byrd, Birdy Byrd, and my personal favorite, Bird Lady from Sweet Meadow.

Bobby watched me struggle to open two of the envelopes. "Well?"

My stunned gaze slowly drifted to him. "They're fan letters. All these people saw me on the Mateson show."

"What do they say?"

"These two said they thought I was brave to have jumped from a flaming vehicle." At the time, it appeared necessary to save my butt.

"This is so cool. Let's read them all. Maybe some of them sent money." Bobby went to the kitchen, got a steak knife and started opening the envelopes, making it easier for me to pull out the letters. We read for several hours. Bobby counted them. Seventy-three total.

Most of them were very kind with their remarks and compliments. A couple went a whole different direction.

"Listen to this one," Bobby said. "'How dare you destroy a perfectly good wrecker because you failed to have your vehicle under control? That could have just as easily been a dog or a deer standing in the road. You would have mowed it down, possibly caught it on fire, you Fire Bug, with no regard for the fact that they could have puppies or little deer at home waiting for them. I should report you to the animal rights activist, then you'd be sorry.' " My brother doubled over with laughter.

"That sounds a little scary. Where's that one from? Is it signed?" I wondered who could be over the top enough to have actually rationalized that in their tormented brain.

Still chuckling, Bobby looked first at the envelope, then the letter. "No return address, but it's post marked from Sweet Meadow. It's signed, *Jack*. Oh, listen to this. 'Here's a tip for you-If you know what's good for you, you'll keep your eyes on the road ahead of you and concentrate on everything going on around you.'" Bobby's smile faded. "That's a strange one, huh?"

I'd inherited Nana Byrd's intuition. Something told me to hold onto that letter. I took it from Bobby, glanced at the childlike pencil scratchings and laid it in a pile by itself. Something about the letter creeped me out. Bobby got me a grocery bag, and I shoved all the mail into it. All but two: Jack's threatening letter and a marriage proposal from a man who professed to be old and rich.

Bobby looked at me questioningly, then put the canvas bag by the door to be returned to my whiny mailman.

"Who knows," I giggled. "This proposal might be worth checking out." I went to bed.

Chapter 7

The next morning Bobby rattled, banged, and slammed his way out of the house. He wanted to be sure that if he had to work in my place, I at least didn't get any extra sleep. His mission was a success.

When Mom arrived I'd been up about an hour and had just finished eating a bowl of cereal, one handed. She marched in and demanded to know about the letter I'd gotten from the rude person who had threatened me. Robert Ulysses strikes again.

"That was quick. Did Bobby wait until he got in the door to tell you that, or did he just holler it across the parking lot so he wouldn't waste time?"

"He's just concerned, that's all." As usual, Mom defended him.

"I'm not worried about it, so you shouldn't be either. Did Bobby tell you I got a marriage proposal from a rich old man?"

"As a matter of fact he did. He told me to try to get it away from you so you don't do anything you'd regret later."

"The only thing I regret is having Bobby here. His ability to keep a secret has always been zippo. I see that hasn't changed."

"He's just looking out for your best interests. Can I get you something?"

"No, thanks. I feel a lot better today. You really don't need to stay with me. I'm just going to rest." I needed my alone time.

"I could do your laundry." She started toward my bedroom.

A vision of lacy undies stuffed in my hamper assaulted me. "No. That's okay, really. I appreciate it. Really. Why don't you go back and help Pop? He'll have his hands full with Bobby there." I hoped my pleading didn't sound as whiny to Mom as it did to me.

Someone knocked on the door, interrupting Mom's lists of reasons why she should be hanging around my house driving me crazy. She answered it. I saw a man standing on the porch just outside the door.

"Is the lady who lives here at home right now?" Although I had not officially met him, I recognized the man from the house next door. He and his wife kept a nice yard. I hoped he hadn't come to complain about my lack of zest for yard work. Maybe I'd just tell him that I planned to plant cacti and turn it into a desert oasis. Yeah, that's the ticket.

I walked up behind my mother.

The man saw me. "Oh, hi. I'm sorry to bother you, but I heard about your unfortunate accident."

Mom took a stand between me and the man. "Did you write her a threatening letter?" she asked.

The man took a step backward, flushed scarlet, then stammered, "Well, no, of course not."

I stepped around Mom, literally pushing her aside. "I'm sorry. Is there something I can do for you?"

"Actually, I was hoping we could do something for you. I figured you'd be home today and my wife is home every day. Would you like her to come over and sit with you a while? She could fix your lunch or get you things," he nodded at my cast, "since you're a little under the weather."

I couldn't answer fast enough. "I think that would be very nice. My mother was just leaving, weren't you, Mom?"

"I guess so, if you're sure." Mom picked up her purse.

"I'm positive."

"I'll go tell my wife. She's been wanting to come calling, but she's very shy." He hurried away.

Mom stared at me like I'd grown two heads. "Are you crazy? You don't know these people."

"It'll be fine. I'll feel better knowing you're helping Pop since I'm not there. You can answer the phone and help with the customers. Okay?"

Reluctantly, she left. My underwear was safe. Within a few minutes, timid and pretty Barbie Jamison arrived, followed by her husband, Rick. He left for his work at an accounting office in Turner. Barbie sat on the edge of the sofa. She appeared to be braced for the shot to start the race. I hoped thunder didn't clap, or she'd be out the door in a flash.

We sat for a few minutes not saying anything. "Awkward silence closed in on us.

"Would you like something to drink?" I asked.

She shook her head.

"Would you like to watch television?"

She nodded.

"What do you like to watch?"

She shrugged.

Where's my mommy when I need her? I may have been hasty in my choice of babysitters.

Accepting the fact that Barbie was painfully shy, I'd just take advantage of the peace and quiet. Sitting back in my recliner, I flipped through the channels, finally settling on The Price Is Right. The four people were in Contestants Row studying a big refrigerator. The first one bid a thousand dollars.

"That's ridiculous." Meek Barbie shape-shifted right before my eyes. "Everyone knows you can't get a 26.8 cubic foot, energy-efficient, side-by-side refrigerator-freezer combination for less than eighteen-hundred dollars."

She slammed her body back against the sofa cushion, propped her feet on the coffee table. Crossing her arms, she appeared to be settling in. Suddenly, she dropped her feet to the floor, then leaned forward, resting her elbows on her thighs.

"Stupid witch," she yelled at the television.

I sat quietly wondering if I had to defend myself against the woman, just exactly how much pain would I endure for whacking her over the head with my cast. Mr. Barker announced that the price of the refrigerator was one thousand, eight hundred, and thirteen dollars.

"There," Barbie shouted at me. "Didn't I tell you? I know my prices."

"You certainly do. You were right there with that one."

"I'm right there with all of 'em. You'll see."

I'd seen all I really wanted to. Thank you very much. But evidently not enough.

"That's what's wrong with the world today." She turned in her seat, then propped her feet on the sofa.

I nodded my head in agreement, although I wasn't sure what I was agreeing to, but it seemed like a safe way to go.

Barbie continued, "People are so stupid. They don't know their rears from their ears."

"Would that be all people, or just the ones on The Price is Right?" I asked, practicing my karate moves in my head.

"Why, all of them, of course." As if disgusted with me and the world, she shook her head.

"Of course," I agreed.

"Yesterday, in the express line at the grocery store, the witless person in front of me had twelve items in her cart. She had the nerve to try to make me think that a six pack of coke was one item, instead of the six that they really are. Did you ever hear of anything so stupid?"

"No, can't say that I have." Boy, that was a true statement. Never had I heard anything like that.

Silence befell my living room. Dark, menacing silence. Even though it was time for a pain pill, I chose to brave the dull throbbing in my hand. I feared going to sleep in the same house with Bats-in-her-Belfry Barbie might be the mistake of my life. So, there we sat for several hours with my hand aching, watching several soap operas.

Since I'm normally at work during soap opera time, I didn't have a clue how the man hiding behind a bush outside a mansion spying on the pretty blond lady intended to get out of there without being discovered. Barbie, however, thought she could help.

"Go around to the back yard, Davis. Go. Go."

Davis evidently heard Barbie, because just then he started running, then slammed right into another man who pummeled him within a inch of his life, or at least until he bit the food coloring capsule in his mouth and fake blood ran over his lips. Boy, I tell you that was the worst fabricated fight I'd ever seen. Barbie became very upset about the whole matter.

"He shouldn't have done that to such a sweet man." With that profound statement, Barbie began to sob. Her waterworks were still going strong when Rick arrived to retrieve his wife. When he volunteered to bring her over again the next day, I quickly declined.

"That would be lovely, but I'm going to work tomorrow. I can answer the phones and things like that at the garage, so that's where I'll be. But, I can't tell you how much I appreciate Barbie keeping me company today. Please, feel free to come over and visit anytime."

I closed and bolted the door behind me. "Or never again in this lifetime." I whispered a heartfelt goodbye to Rick and Barbie Number one, Barbie Number two, and Barbie Number three. I literally ran to the kitchen and took a pain pill.

When Bobby came home from work, he brought me a plate Mom had sent, liver smothered with onions, mashed potatoes, and okra and tomatoes. I ate the center of the mashed potatoes, being careful not to accidentally get any that had actually touched liver or okra. Mom called a little while later to make sure I'd eaten all of the nutritious meal she'd sent. She had taught me to be honest. "Yes, ma'am. I ate every bite, and it was really good. Thank you."

She had also taught me to be kind.

I needed to see if I had any mail. Before going outside, I peeked out the window hoping I wouldn't find Barbie trimming her hedges. I didn't see her anywhere. A huge oak tree grows just on her side of the property line. I felt it had eyes. Glancing that way, I didn't see anyone. Maybe my pain pill had made me a tad paranoid.

In Herman the mailbox, I found about twenty fan letters. Giggling with heady excitement, I declared, "I'm a celebrity."

Carrie Sue and Donna's cousin, Novalee, lives a few houses down the street. In her front yard I heard childish laughter. Using a piece of my mail I shaded my eyes from the setting sun and watched a group of kids having a good time. Donna's kids, Pam, Randy, and Jude (I think that's short for Judas) were taking turns throwing Novalee's son, little Ralphie, to the ground in a body slam that would make any wrestler proud. The small child, about five-years old, would break free, then come right back for more.

I inhaled a few deep breaths of fresh air and tried to rid myself of traumatic flashbacks of Billy and Bobby throwing their sweet baby sister around in the same manner. I, too, would get up and go right back. What was I thinking?

Since I'd enjoyed as much of my trip down memory lane as I could stand, I started back toward the house. Rankled by the nagging feeling someone was watching me from behind the massive oak, I decided to check it out. I walked to the tree, then all around it. I didn't see anyone. I glanced over Rick and Barbie's well-manicured lawn at the windows facing their front yard. Still, I didn't see anyone anywhere.

"Hello." A voice boomed from above me.

"Jesus, Joseph, and Mary." Had I not been weighted down by the mail and my cast, my feet would have left the ground. I looked above me. There, perched on a limb hidden by the fullness of the beautiful green leaves sat petite, blond Barbie holding a cat.

"What are you doing up there?" I snapped at the obviously deranged woman.

"Damien got caught up here." She stroked the huge black and

white cat. "I came up to get him."

"Damien, huh?" I had a strong desire to form a finger cross and back away from the tree, but I still had the hands-full-of-mail-and-cast problem. So, I just scurried across my yard.

"Gotta go," I called to the giant goonie bird.

"Come back and visit soon," she said.

Not in this lifetime.

Once inside my house, I breathed a little easier. Bobby sat at the kitchen table, giggling into the telephone. Evidently, he and Estelle were working out their problems. That made me happy. At the end of two weeks my two nephews, although almost fully grown, would get their daddy back and I would get my house back.

I got my steak knife and opened my fan mail. It was mostly a repeat of the day before, including one from Jack. As I sat reading that one, Bobby finished his call and came to join me.

"Listen to this," I said. " 'I've called the animal rights activists AND the Wrecker Association to report your willful disregard for animals and wreckers.' "

Bobby took the letter from me. "Maybe we should call the police about this. This guy is too weird to ignore. Don't you think?"

"I don't know. What else did he say?"

He looked back at the letter. "'Here's a tip-never leave your blow-dryer on the edge of a free-standing bathroom sink. It could be knocked into the water while you're brushing your teeth and fry you to a crispy critter. Jack.'"

With one eyebrow raised and his other eye closed, Bobby deepened his voice, "You're surrounded by stripped-geared rum runners."

I laughed out loud. "I thought I was the only one who had noticed."

Worn out, I decided to go to bed. First, I stopped by the bathroom.

"Bobby," I yelled.

Instantly he appeared at my side. "What is it?" His heart seemed to be lodged in his throat. Mine, too.

I pointed to the free-standing porcelain sink. There on the edge lay my blow-dryer. That's where I usually kept it, but how could Jack know that? I looked to the uncurtained, high window over the bathtub. "Could someone have looked in the window and seen that?"

Bobby shrugged. "I don't know. I'll go out and look around. It would be a good guess that, since this is an old house, there wouldn't be counters in the bathroom. And, even though you don't look like you use one," he ruffled my hair, "most women have a blow-dryer lying around the bathroom." He planted a kiss on my forehead. "Don't worry about it."

Bobby went outside. I used the bathroom, but I kept an eye on the darkness outside the window. If I got another letter, I would have to call the police. Yeah, three strikes and *Jack in the Mailbox* would be out.

Bobby came back into the house to report he'd seen nothing out of the ordinary outside the bathroom. I'd decided that the adrenalin shooting through my veins needed a shot of milk to calm down. Going to bed now appeared out of the question. I turned on the television and glanced at the clock. Nine.

"I'm going for a ride in the tow truck," Bobby announced.

My gaze snapped in his direction. "Developing a fondness for Melinda, are you?"

"His name is Murray." Bobby went toward the door. "Want me to bring you anything?"

I shook my head. As he left, I couldn't help wondering where he could be going at this time of night. He'd been out the door a total of one minute when he burst back in.

"Call the police," he shouted.

I sprang into action. "Is Jack out there?" My heart pounded so loudly I could barely hear his answer. I grabbed the phone.

"Who? Oh, no. There were three kids playing around the wrecker. That's an expensive piece of equipment. No place for kids."

I'd punched in 9-1. I hung up the receiver, then picked it up again and entered Novalee's number. She answered on the second ring. "Good evening, this is Bertie."

"How are you? I hear you've had quite a time lately," Donna's cousin purred.

"Pretty typical in my world. Is Donna still at your house?"

"Yes, do you want to talk to her?"

Since I'd rather wrestle an alligator, I quickly said no. "Would you mind telling her that Pam, Randy and Jude were just down here messing around with my tow truck. I'm afraid they might get hurt."

"Are you sure you don't want to tell her yourself?" Novalee's voice carried a smirk.

"No, you tell her. Thanks." I hung up before she could give me any more grief. I opened the front door, looked around, but the kids were already back at Novalee's sitting on her front porch with the light shining directly on them. They wanted to be sure anyone could see they were behaving like angels. I saw them, but I didn't believe it for a minute.

I stood in the doorway watching Bobby drive away. I still didn't know where to. A minute or so later, Donna and her kids drove by at a high rate of speed. She blasted her horn. I guess she might have been a bit put out that I'd tattled on her junior Satans.

I turned in the doorway, bent at the waist, and started to moon her, when an uncontrollable shudder flew through me. What if Jack was out there, in the dark, watching me? I ran inside, slamming the door behind me. Until it faded in the distance, Donna's horn continued to blare. I went to bed as soon as she had tooted her way off my street, then tossed and turned until the sandman finally showed up to dust my eyes with sleep.

I'm not sure what time Bobby came home.

The next morning, when I heard him fumbling around in the kitchen, I crawled out of bed and got ready to go to work. I joined Bobby for some of the strongest coffee I'd ever put in my mouth. I told him so.

"Coffee should have a heavy taste. As Nana Byrd used to say, it should put hair on your chest."

I peeked down the front of my blouse. "This could do that, and grow grass."

He smiled. I think he was glad I'd be with him in the tow truck. Until yesterday, I don't believe Bobby had even looked inside one since the day he left home twenty years ago. My new hat should read *Baby Sister/Technical Advisor.*

As we walked toward the tow truck, I saw Barbie snipping her hedges with a big pair of clippers. I wondered how wise Rick could be to allow her to play with sharp objects. Wanting to be sure she knew I was headed to work, I waved wildly. She shyly rippled her fingers in my direction, then ran into the house. "Holy flying cows," I managed to say through the chilled shivers that were dancing their way through my body. "That is one strange lady."

Bobby laughed.

When we were almost to the garage, Pop dispatched us to pick up out-of-fuel-again Ethel Winchell.

"We've got a can on the back, we'll go fill it up." Bobby did a U-turn in the middle of the road to go back a few blocks to get the gas.

"We can't do that. Ethel has a diesel. You can't just fill it up like gas-using cars. You'll have to remove the fuel filter, then prime it. Let's go pick her up and take her back to the garage. She and I have this maneuver down to a science."

Bobby made another U-turn right in front of a garbage truck. We made it okay, thanks to God, but I couldn't believe the language. When the dust settled, I vowed to never talk like that again.

While Bobby hooked up Ethel's Mercedes, I scooted to the middle of the seat, then helped her climb into the wrecker. We were cruising at about forty-five miles an hour.

"Look, Bertie, that car looks just like mine." Ethel pointed out the passenger window to a driverless vehicle passing us on the right. Quickly, I turned to look out the rear window. Her car was no longer attached to the back of the wrecker. All around us wheels were squealing, horns were blaring. Someone was screaming. I think it was me.

Just then, Ethel Winchell's 1982 silver Mercedes, a fine piece of machinery, plowed into a phone booth. Bobby swerved off the road to an abrupt halt.

"I'm glad Superman wasn't in there," he said. I think he might have been in shock.

We all got out and joined the others who had stopped along the highway. When my shaking brother squatted to check the straps which had held the now-destroyed Mercedes, he found that the bolts had somehow come loose, releasing the vehicle and sending it free-wheeling on its way.

The embarrassed redness that glowed across Bobby's face turned to a bright fuchsia. "Those kids did this." He jumped to his feet, then kicked the wrecker sling several times.

I quickly looked around us. "What kids?"

"The ones from last night. What were their names? Ram and Pandy. And the little one, Juke."

"You mean Donna's kids?" I looked closer at the sling. "They're too little to remove heavy bolts like the ones that held all that together."

"That's right where they were messing around last night, those little . . ."

"Show's over, folks." I started moving people out of the way. Ethel was rubbing the side of her car with soothing strokes. While I tried to console her, Bobby called Pop to tell him my brother, the insurance salesman, had killed a car and phone booth in one swipe.

Our father brought the parts we needed to put the wrecker back together so we could tow Ethel's car for a different reason now.

Mom called the rental car place. When we arrived with poor, dejected Ethel, a brand new, red, sporty car waited for her. The little blue-haired lady positioned herself behind the wheel and for the first time smiled like a Cheshire cat. As she pulled out of our parking lot she squealed tires, laid rubber, then fish-tailed onto the road.

"I'd better make sure the sling is together really good. We may need it again real soon," Bobby said.

Chapter 8

Late in the afternoon Jeff called the garage looking for me. He'd been working a lot of overtime at the mill and had danced outside of Atlanta the night before. Someone had just told him about my run-in with the airplane.

"It's not as bad as it sounds. It's a simple break. With everything that's been going on, I really haven't had much time to dwell on it." I kicked back in Pop's chair in his air-conditioned office. Through the picture window, looking out into the parking lot, I watched Bobby using hand signals to demonstrate exactly how Ethel's car had mowed down a defenseless phone booth. He'd told the story to the policeman at the scene, then to Pop when he arrived with the parts to reassemble the sling, to Mom when we got back, now to the insurance appraiser who had just shown up. Each time he told it, the Mercedes picked up speed, and Donna's kids became more evil. We couldn't prove they had anything to do with it, so the little termites from hell would go free.

"I wish I could come by to see you tonight, but we've got problems at the mill, so I have to work late again. That is, unless there is something you really need me to do for you." Jeff's deep, kind voice caused my heart to thunder like the hooves of a runaway horse. I had to pull in the reins on that stud. Every time I felt that much enthusiasm for a man, I got thrown from the saddle in less than eight seconds.

"Actually, I have choir practice tonight. I appreciate your offer, but I understand you have to work."

"Maybe we can get together over the weekend. I'll call you." We hung up.

Shortly before the end of the day, a florist van pulled to a stop in front of the garage. A petite teenage girl slid from the front seat of the vehicle, then went around to the back, out of my sight. She came back into view staggering under the weight of a horseshoe-shaped wreath covered with red roses. By the time she dragged the massive thing through the door, Bobby and Pop were trailing close behind her.

"Here, let me help with that." Bobby lightened the girl's cumbersome load, then set the flower arrangement on its tripod legs.

"This is for Roberta Byrd," the delivery person said.

My mouth dropped open. I couldn't imagine why someone would send me such a monstrosity.

"That would be Ro-Ber-Ta." Bobby pointed to me. "What'd you do, Bert, win the Kentucky Derby?"

I shot Bobby a lethal glare, but everyone knows looks can't kill. If they could, he'd have been dead years ago. As the delivery girl made her departure, I found the card. *Here's wishing you only good luck from this day forward. Jeff.*

I clutched the note to my chest and felt the beating of my heart. Taking a deep breath, I cautioned myself that things were moving too fast, and I was allowing my emotions to boot rational thinking out of the way. Putting my nose close to the beautiful red roses, I inhaled their sweet essence. I couldn't help myself. Maybe my luck *was* changing.

"I'm ready to go home, Bertie." Bobby handed Pop the truck keys. "You sure you don't mind me using the Caddy tonight?"

"It's fine. It won't kill me to do wrecker calls one week night. See you two in the morning." Pop looked tired. I gave him a quick peck on his cheek. "Good night, sweetheart," he said.

"Night, Pop." I watched him disappear into the garage to turn out the lights.

At home, I wrapped my arm in a plastic garbage bag, then show-ered in record time. With only one working hand, I fixed my hair the best I could. I'd have to go to the beauty shop and get Bonnie Boo to fix it for me, or maybe Mary Lou. Maybe.

Bobby drove me to church. Immediately following the Wednesday evening service I attended my first choir meeting. Director Homer King told me where to stand then, so our heights would form a "church steeple," he moved me again. I'd have to re-member not to let Mary Lou give me high hair, or I'd throw Homer's pyramid out of kilter.

He told us what page we'd be starting on. While we were flip-ping noisily through the hymnal, Glorie Thorpe tried to sneak into her place.

"Maybe I need to go over the choir rules for the benefit of new and old members alike." He glared at Glorie, who blushed a glorious pink. Homer's nostrils flared. "Wednesday prayer meeting ends at seven-thirty. Choir practice begins at seven thirty-five on the dot. All members will be dressed in their robes and lined in the hallway in their appropriate places, according to their height, at ten fifty-five on Sunday morning. Any questions?"

"No, Homer," most of us chimed. Glorie raised her hand. With his baton, the director pointed at her.

"I'm sorry I was late. I had to meet with Reverend Miller to set the time for the Helping Hand Committee to visit the nursing home in the morning."

As if in prayer, Homer closed his eyes. After releasing an audible sigh and mumbling something about his cross to bear, he opened them again, then pointed to Bea at the organ. Instantly, she began to play. The choir began to sing.

I noticed that about every tenth key, Bea would hit a sour note. To keep from being distracted, I zoned away to my tropical isle. Only this time, instead of being slathered with suntan oil by Antonio, a native cabana boy, I pictured myself dressed in a white choir robe, complete with angel wings and halo, facing the ocean and singing praise to the heavens.

I'm not sure how long I'd been in that euphoric state before I realized no one was singing but me. They were all staring at me. Like an unwinding Victrola, I eased to a stop right in the middle of my Amen.

"Well, well, well. What have we here?" Homer looked about to burst.

"I'm sorry. I guess I wasn't paying attention."

"You don't have anything to be sorry about. Does she, ladies and gentlemen?"

Nos of all pitches sang through the choir loft.

"Bertie, you are truly a rose among the thorns." Homer scrambled through his briefcase. "Here. Try this." He handed a paper to me. "Solo."

"Solo?" Jesus, Joseph, and Mary. I couldn't sing by myself in front of the church. In the shower was one thing, but the whole congregation was more than I could handle. Was this my punishment for the foul words I used earlier in the day when Bobby turned in front of the garbage truck? I'd apologized over and over again. What more could I do?

"Sing," Homer demanded. Bea played. I sang.

When I made my way to the parking lot, with my music sheet in tow, I found my brother in a close conversation with his old schoolmate, Karen. Were they both crazy? Her husband, big strapping, gun-toting policeman Officer Kelly, apparently hadn't made it to the prayer meeting. When Bobby saw me, he waved. Before they stepped away from each other, the last few words of their conversation made their way to my ears. "Nine-thirty."

Yeow. That wasn't good. I feared for my brother's safety. If Officer Kelly didn't kill him, Estelle would. I might help her.

Once inside the car, I waited all of thirty seconds for Bobby to explain himself. He didn't. So, I picked up the slack. "Are you nuts?

Don't you realize her husband carries a big old gun?"

"Oh, Bertie. Don't worry your pretty little head about little ol' me. I'm a big boy. I can take care of myself."

"You're not a big boy, you're an idiot boy."

When we arrived at my house, I stormed inside. Bobby followed close behind. The phone rang and we both dove for it. He won. He took the portable out the front door. Shortly, I heard him giggling like a child.

Maybe I was being unfair about him and Karen. After all, when I found them they were only talking, not intertwined in a lip-locking embrace. Now, he was laughing and cooing on the phone with his wife of twenty years. Jeeze, I needed a pain pill.

The front door opened. Bobby came inside. "You have a call, Sister Dearest."

I snarled at him, then took the phone. "Hello?"

"Hey, Bertie. How's your hand?" Mary Lou sounded her usual chipper self.

"My hand is healing just fine. I guess marriage must agree with you. You sound happy."

My bestest friend in the whole wide world began to bawl into the phone.

"Mary Lou? Honey? What is it?" I felt so helpless.

"I don't know. One minute, I'm happy as a lark, the next I feel like oiling the wheels on a grocery cart and running away from home." She spoke through quick, short sobs.

"Oh, now, I'm sure it's just hormones." I'd heard that somewhere, but what did I know? At the rate things were going for me, unless you could get pregnant using a public toilet, I'd never know anything about those kind of hormones.

"I'm sure you're right. It's just so strange. I went from being single and loving it to being a wife and mother-to-be in a few short weeks. I guess my mind hasn't caught up with my brain. Surely, it will, don't you think?" Mary Lou sniffled.

Okay, she wasn't feeling well, so I decided to give her a break. However, several really good zingers almost choked me to death. "You're probably just tired. Why don't you take a warm shower and go on to bed?"

"That's what Rex keeps telling me. I'm sure I'll feel better in the morning. Oh, how did things go at choir practice?" She sounded a little better.

"Yucky. I have to sing a solo on Sunday morning."

"Oh, my God. You don't think you'll pee down your leg or something, do you?" She was really peppy now.

"Well, until now, that thought hadn't even entered my head. Jeeze, Mary Lou, I better go before I start bawling too."

"Okay." She sniffled again.

"I'll tell you what, Mary Lou. If I can manage to drive with my broken hand, I'll come by and see you at work tomorrow."

"I'd like that. Good night." She hung up.

"I've got an errand to run." Bobby jingled a tune with the car keys.

"Let me guess, it's almost nine-thirty." I stole a glance at the clock.

Bobby frowned at me. "So?"

The next morning, Bobby and I had very little to say to each other. We rode to work in total silence. Maybe after I'd been fortified with the doughnuts and coffee Pop had waiting for us, I'd broach the subject of Bobby's infidelity. As if he read my mind, my brother sneered at me over his sticky bun.

"I'm gonna tell on you," I sniveled. I hate it when I do that.

"If you do, you better not open any metal containers for the rest of your life." He issued several evil grunts which may have been loosely interpreted as a laugh. I rubbed my eyebrows, thankful they'd grown back.

Bobby went into the garage to do a tune-up on a Jeep. I sprinted around Pop's desk to my huge flower display which Jeff had sent me yesterday. I stroked it like I used to rub my white rabbit's foot for good luck. I checked the floral foam to see if it needed water. Just then, the same florist van which had delivered the horseshoe-shaped wreath the day before pulled to a stop right in front of the picture window.

Instead of the tragically thin teenager who had delivered the flowers, an older, heavier woman climbed out of the van. From my vantage point, I could see that the handsome lady had satiny smooth skin, short, white minx hair, and a cute little dimple in her chin. I took a sniff of the roses and waited for her to get her hair just the way she wanted it, then straighten her pink smock.

When she came into the office and I got an up-close look at Pidge, according to the name embroidered in purple on her pocket, I saw that her velvety skin had been stretched to the max. She'd obviously gone under the knife several times. Her translucent make-up, impeccably applied, allowed her porcelain skin to show off the flawless marksmanship of a plastic surgeon. The closest thing we had to one of them in Sweet Meadow was John the Taxidermist.

"I'm looking for Roberta Byrd." Pidge, who looked to be about sixty going on twenty, looked around the office. Before I could admit to being the person she was looking for, the woman stepped up to my good luck bouquet, picked it up, and started out the door.

"Hey. Hey. Hey. What do you think you're doing?" I raced to her.

"I'm taking this back to my shop." Her face sagged.

So did my mouth. "It's mine."

"Not unless you want to pay me the four-hundred and fifty dollars owed on them."

"My boyfriend sent them to me." I hoped I wasn't going to cry.

"Well, there's been a mistake. I have yours in the van."

My bottom lip quivered. I watched the old hag go outside, then return with a dinky vase with one red rose and a plastic horseshoe tied around it with a ribbon. "I don't understand," I told her.

"Your boyfriend can't pay for the spray, so I have to take it back and try to salvage some of the flowers."

I stared at the shrew's dimpled chin. I'll bet that was really her belly button. She looked me over from head to toe, shivered then left. I looked down at my jeans and T-shirt. "Your point is well taken, my dear Pidge," I said to the empty room.

That's really a low blow. My toast to better times, my good luck crest, my Kentucky Derby wreath, whatever name you wanted to give it, had just been repossessed. That wasn't a good sign.

During the day, I refused to go with Bobby on any calls. I hung around the office, answered the phones, and paid a few bills. Around three o'clock the phone rang.

"Byrd and Sons."

"Bertie? Hi, dear, this is Mrs. Weidemeyer. Would you

please bring me a loaf of bread and a gallon of milk on your way home today?"

Helen Weidemeyer lived next door to Novalee. She didn't drive, so at least once a week I picked up a couple of things for her at the grocery store.

"My brother is coming for dinner tonight. I'd like for you to meet him. I think you two would make a perfect match."

"How high are his hips?" I asked.

"I'm not sure. Would you like me to measure him when he gets here?" the woman asked.

"No, ma'am. I'm just kidding around." I tried to imagine a male version of Mrs. Weidemeyer. All I could come up with was Charlie Brown on a bad hair day. "Well, maybe I'll get a chance to meet him this afternoon. I'll be glad to pick up those things for you. Do you use skim milk?"

"Lord, no. Don't bring me any of that blue water. I go for heavy duty, super duper stuff. Straight from the cow, if they have it." She snickered into the phone, then hung up. I wished I was so easily amused today.

I'd hoped to go by the insurance company and visit with Mary Lou for a few minutes, but the day had slipped by me. Actually, my discouraging experience with Pidge had left me wallowing in self-pity. I couldn't raise my spirits with a forklift. I certainly couldn't have raised Mary Lou's.

Bobby stood hot to trot, probably a bad choice of words, right at five o'clock. We were taking the tow truck home. Pop said he felt too tuckered out to get up in the middle of the night again.

When I told Bobby I had to stop at the store, he showed a little speck of irritation. Jerking to a stop in front of the store, he told me to hurry. He had things to do.

I slid from the wrecker. "I'll bet." I glanced at the markings on the pavement. "You're in a tow-a-way zone."

"If they call a wrecker to tow me away, I'll already be here." He reached across the seat and pulled my door shut. I scurried into the store.

At home, Bobby skidded into the driveway, then hurried inside the house. I struggled with my broken hand to carry the milk and bread to Mrs. Weidemeyer's.

"Hi, Bertie." Helen took her groceries, then handed me the money. All the while, she blocked the doorway. Usually she insisted I come in for coffee. Today, she rudely hurried me on my way. The fact that I didn't have time to go in for a visit was irrelevant. Her actions compelled me to knock again.

She peeked through a crack just under the latched security chain. "Yeah, Bertie."

"I thought you wanted me to meet your brother. Is he here yet?"

"Yes, but he's sick. He has diphtheria." She closed the door so fast the force knocked me back a step.

I would not be deterred. I knocked again. This time Helen hollered from the other side of the door.

"What is it, dear?" She'd thrown down the gauntlet.

I rose to the challenge. "Diphtheria? Isn't that pretty serious?" I stepped closer to the door. "Can I get him some juice?"

The door opened. Helen looked very uncomfortable. "I'm sorry, dear, but my brother doesn't want to meet you. When I suggested it, he got very angry with me. He had to take a pill."

"That's okay, Mrs. Weidemeyer. No problem." I didn't want to meet the old doo-doo head anyway. A movement from a window in Helen's house caught my attention. Someone peeked out at me. I said a quick goodbye, then left.

"That was too strange." I started walking back toward my house.

"Oh, Bertie," Novalee called to me from her porch. "I'm having a Tupperware party on Monday. Will you come?"

"Will Donna be there?" I hollered across the yard.

"She will, but Pam and Randy and Jude won't." She smiled.

"Okay, I'll come." I could take Donna for a minimal amount of time, but Ram and Pandy, and Juke, as Bobby called them, were another story.

By the time I got back to my house, Bobby had already showered. I heard him in the bathroom gargling and blow-drying his hair at the same time.

I made a bologna sandwich and a cup of hot tea. Shortly, Bobby came into the kitchen, grabbed an apple and planted a kiss on my forehead. "Don't be mad at me, Sis. I'll be back early."

Robert Ulysses left.

During his dinner break, Jeff called. "I'm sorry about the mix up with the flowers. I told them I wanted a rose with a horseshoe. They sent a horseshoe with roses. I apologize."

"That's okay. No problem at all." I didn't tell him that before his call, I'd planned to make a voodoo doll that wore a pink smock and had a navel in her chin. Or, that I couldn't have experienced more disappointment if I'd found out he was married. Ha. Ha. Ha. How absurd.

"Are you married?" I asked.

Dead silence.

Why did I ask that ridiculous question? Where were my pills?

"My wife was in an auto accident." Jeff's voice quivered.

"I'm sorry," I managed to eke out.

The sadness in his voice said it all. I decided to let him talk about it when and if he wanted to. I'd not mention it again.

I heard the whistle sound through the phone, signaling the end of Jeff's dinner break.

"I've got to get back to work. Can I see you on Saturday night? Maybe I can bring in some Chinese, and we'll watch a movie at your house."

"Sure." I'd really like that. We hung up.

I scrounged around and found Vienna Sausages and popcorn for dinner. My bologna sandwich hadn't done the trick. A couple of antacids later, I went outside to check the mailbox. Barbie and Rick were edging and sweeping their walkway.

"Yoo hoo." Barbie whooped.

I thought about ignoring her, then had a vision of being whacked to death with a weed-eater. So, I braved a smile, but kept on trucking toward the mailbox. A moving target is hard to hit.

I bent down to the dead fish and pulled out my letters. The fan mail was still trickling in. When I turned, I came nose to chest (her nose, my chest) with my nutty neighbor. I took a couple of steps backward, then looked down at Petite Barbie.

"You had company today." The woman smiled.

"Really. Who?"

"I don't know. Some man in a white car. He looked in your window."

Alarm rattled my eye teeth. Could it have been Jack? "What did he look like, Barbie?"

"I can't say for sure. It's hard to see really well through the slats in my attic air vent."

My gaze snapped to the octagon-shaped louvers in the eaves of her house. I glanced back at my own. I had some too but, Lord knows I'd never crawl up there with the spiders and whatever else is up there. Evidently, Bats-in-the-Belfry Barbie hung out in hers.

Shivers crawled up my spine, into my hair, down my front, and out my toes. To Barbie, I must have looked like I was having a spell.

"Something wrong?" she asked.

"Nooo. What cannnn you tell meeee about the maaaan?" I continued to shiver.

"He walked funny."

"How so? Did he have a limp?"

"No. At first, he walked just fine, then he walked like this." Barbie spread her arms out to her side, then did the best pantomime of a person sneaking along a wall I'd every seen. The next time I played Charades, I wanted her on my team.

"He walked like that across the yard?" I was flabbergasted.

"Of course not."

"Then where?"

"Along the side of your house. When he got to the living room window, he did this number." Slowly, she inched up on her tiptoes like a secret agent or Peeping Tom would do.

"He sneaked along the side of my house, then peeked into my window?"

"Yes." Barbie began to clap.

I put the clues together and won the game. I jumped up and down. Barbie joined me in my enthusiasm. It took a few seconds to realize this wasn't a game, and that I'd just been told someone had been snooping around my house. My heart told me it was my stalker, Jack.

I stopped jumping. Barbie didn't. She jumped, hopped, and skipped all the way home. I ran into my house. Quickly, I looked through the ten or so letters I'd just received. Thankfully, none of them were from Jack.

I had to find something to take my mind off my pounding, terrified heart. Bobby should be here protecting his baby sister. What else were big brothers for?

Thinking of the slug, anger filled me again, this time for what I was pretty sure he and Karen Kelly were doing. When Officer Kelly had answered my 911 call the first time Pete Fortney had let himself into OUR house, it was late at night. Therefore, I could only assume Officer Carl Kelly handled the evening shift. How convenient for Karen to have a tryst with her boyfriend, AKA my married brother, while her husband defended the community against crime.

Irked to the max, I called Mary Lou. "Come and get me. We're going to find Robert Ulysses and drag him back here by the hair of his head."

"Now, Bertie, that's not your job. Call Estelle and let her do it."

"No, if I can talk some sense into him, she'll never have to know about Bobby's indiscretion. Hurry over here." I started to hang up. "Oh, by the way, dress in black."

"I just bleached my hair. I have to put color on it."

"Just cover it with a scarf. We need to be able to fade into the darkness. We may have to sneak around at first to make sure he's at Karen Kelly's house."

"Hang on a second, Bert. I need to ask Rex."

Before I could object, she was already yelling to her husband, "Can I go hide in the bushes with Bertie?"

"Sure, honey. I'll finish watching this sci-fi movie. Just don't be too late. You know how cranky you get when you don't get enough sleep." Good old Rex. Nothing about Mary Lou surprised him.

"I'll be right there."

After we hung up, I changed into a dark T-shirt, then forced my way-too-long auburn hair under my Braves baseball cap. Before Mary Lou could even stop in the driveway, I shot out the door to meet her. I climbed inside her car. "The Kelly's live on Marriott Drive. I don't know if that's where Bobby and she are meeting, but we have to start somewhere."

We found the street with no trouble but, in the dark, the house numbers were hard to read.

"Rex has a flashlight under the seat." Mary Lou pointed to the floor near my feet.

I reached there and found a heavy metal object which could have been a flashlight, in outer space. "Is this it?"

"Yeah, the switch is right here." Mary Lou pointed to a huge button on top. I aimed it toward the house we thought might be the Kelly's, then pressed it on. A light, bright enough to be seen on Venus, bathed the entire home and surrounding yard. I felt like hollering "You're surrounded. Come out with your hands empty." After the shock wore off, I turned it out. "Did you see a number?"

Mary Lou pulled the car to the curb a few houses away. "Yeah. That's it. Now what?"

A street light lit the inside of the car. For the first time, I noticed that Mary Lou's hair shone a neon yellow. "What happened?" I took a piece of it and looked closer.

"I told you I'd just bleached it. I'm going blond. I haven't put the color back."

"But, you glow in the dark. Where's your scarf?"

"I don't have one. I brought this." Mary Lou raised a black, macrame purse into the beam of the street light. I recognized it as the one she'd made when we were in Girl Scouts many years ago. It had two big handles. She pulled it over her head. The plastic hoops looked like earrings. I just stared at her.

"Are we going?" Annoyance filled Mary Lou's voice.

"Okay. Let's see if we can peek in a window." Barbie had shown me exactly how to do that just this afternoon. I was prepared.

"I hope we don't have to witness them doing anything we wouldn't want to witness them doing." Mary Lou had a good point. I'd make her look first.

We got out of the car. When Mary Lou came around the front, I couldn't believe my eyes. She had on a black and gold Hawaiian shirt, a pair of Rex's dark boxer shorts, and a pair of high-top black tennis shoes with gold socks folded to a huge bandage over the laces. Of course, she had the purse pulled over her head with the hoops hanging onto her shoulders.

"Would dark jeans, T-shirt, and a baseball cap have been too much to ask?" I shook my head in amazement.

"Well, excuse me, Miss Fashion Police. I don't know how to dress for spying."

"Good point." Who knows, she may have been perfect. I could have been the one making the *faux pas*.

We made our way back up the street toward the Kelly's house. A cat scampered from under a mailbox, scaring Agent Double 0-0 and Agent Double 0-0 and a third, half to death. We inched by an empty phone booth with its light shining brightly on us. Hurrying away from it, hoping not to have been seen, I tripped. Fearing I might fall on my already-broken hand, I struggled to right myself.

"Quit kidding around, Bertie."

I rolled my eyes at her, but her purse hat had slid over her eyes, and we were in the dark, and she didn't pay any attention to me anyway.

A light shined from one of the front rooms. I led the way along the hedge surrounding the yard then, bending at the waist, I hurried to the corner of the house. Once there, I edged my way through the two-foot or so clearance between the wall and a line of tall azalea bushes. Jeeze, I hoped no snakes lurked in the shrubs. When I got to the window, I ducked under it. While I took my position on one side, Mary Lou fell into place on the other.

Light from the uncurtained window shone on a square patch of shrubbery. I motioned for her to take a peek. Slowly, she eased up. She ducked down, then eased up again. She ducked, then looked about three more times. "What's going on?" I whispered.

"They're boogying."

"Oh, my God." I squeezed my eyes closed against visions that invoked.

Mary Lou reached out to touch my shoulder. "They're dancing, Bertie. You know, like your parents do. Jitterbugging."

"They're dancing?" I looked through the window. Sure enough they were cutting a rug. On the sofa, watching them, was Carl Kelly.

"What in the name of all that's holy is going on?" Maybe I'd said that just a tad louder than I should have. Officer Kelly glanced at the window.

"Let's get out of here," I told Mary Lou. "Run."

We took off across the yard. Being pregnant had not slowed her down any. She sprinted way ahead of me.

"Don't let them see you, Mary Lou. Hide." Just as the words left my mouth, a hand grabbed the back of my T-shirt, jerking me to a sudden halt. Officer Kelly stepped in front of me. For the second time in a few months, I stared down the barrel of his gun. As I looked past his shoulder, I saw Mary Lou standing inside the phone booth with the door shut and the light shining down onto her purse hat. She had her hands clamped over her eyes. I assumed this was Mary Lou's version of hiding. She must be doing a good job of it. After all, she wasn't the one looking death in the face.

As I alternated my gaze from the gun to the phone booth, I had one more revelation. I don't know why I had been concerned about Mary Lou's attire; at least the gold in her Hawaiian shirt and the gold in her socks matched. I, on the other hand, was going to jail dressed like Johnny Cash.

Chapter 9

Bertie, what do you think you're doing?" Bobby raced across Karen and Carl Kelly's lawn toward me. With my hands high in the air, my knees shaking, and my stomach rolling, I couldn't take my eyes off the hunk of blue steel pointing at me.

"Please, don't shoot me. I've never even been married."

"For the sake of the men of Georgia," Officer Carl Kelly said, putting his gun back in its holster, "I think I'll lobby for a law against you *ever* getting married. You're a hazard."

"Hey. Hey. Hey." I started to object, but why? My life's roller coaster had always clacked just a tad off its track. Oh, sure, most of the time it could climb the hills, and even weeeeeee down the other side, but every once in a while it jumped the track, then bounced to the ground with a thud. This was a big thud.

"You really thought that Karen and I were having an affair, didn't you?" Bobby, Carl Kelly, and his wife stood staring at me.

"This is all your fault, Robert Ulysses. You had a good old time letting me think that you were . . . well, you know." I could feel my face flushing like hot embers. My audience laughed their butts off.

"Yeah, well, if you think I'm funny, look behind you." I pointed down the street.

They turned to the phone booth where Mary Lou was still *hiding.* I wondered how long she would have stayed in there.

"Who's that?" Carl asked.

"That's the other half of Bertie's brain. Put together you still only have a half of one." Bobby didn't even try to hide his laughter.

"Hey." I hit my brother with my good hand. Pain vibrated up my arm. He walked across the yard toward the phone booth. When Bobby opened the door, Mary Lou screamed. He grabbed her, forcing her hands and her purse hat away from her eyes so she could see that it was him. When her fear had subsided, she hit him too.

Karen and Carl graciously invited us, Nut Case and her sidekick, into their home. There we were given a glass of iced tea and a full explanation.

"Estelle has always wanted me to learn to dance like Pop. So, last week, when I ran into Karen at church, I remembered how well she used to dance at school functions. She agreed to teach me."

"He's a natural. He just needed a little practice. Watch." With that, they jumped to their feet. Carl turned on the stereo, and Karen and Bobby began bopping to a tune straight out of the fifties. She was right; my brother could move with the grace of Thomas Byrd, AKA Pop. Estelle would be so proud.

As thrilled as I was to have been wrong in believing Robert Ulysses capable of infidelity, the evening's events had given me a headache the size of Barbie's oak tree. I had to go home.

The next day, Friday, I treated Bobby a little better than I had for a few days. Truly sorry for mistrusting him, I even rode with him on his wrecker calls and supervised his work to keep him out of trouble.

Shortly after lunch, Carrie Sue came by.

"Would you like to go to the Dew Drop Inn with me tonight?" She'd just had her hair fixed. It had finally decided to grow back after Donna's kids had scalped her. Bonnie Boo had done the best job she could with what she had to work with. I personally thought Carrie Sue's dark, wiry do looked like a Brillo pad.

"I'm still recuperating." I waved my cast and feigned considerable agony.

"I'll go." Bobby came into the main office out of the bathroom.

"Great. You want me to pick you up?" Carrie Sue jumped at the chance to go out with my brother.

"I'll meet you there. Can you do the Electric Slide?" Bobby did a fancy step across the floor.

Who did he think he was? Fred Astaire? I bayonetted him with my stare.

"Now, Ro-Ber-Ta. Didn't we just go through this? I've got to get in as much practice as possible before I go home next weekend."

He was right. I needed to have more faith in him. "All right," I conceded. His date left.

Mary Lou called.

"Did you tell Rex about our big adventure?" I chuckled into the phone.

"Yeah. He said to tell you he'd appreciate it if you didn't get me killed while I'm carrying his child."

"He knows I wouldn't bring any harm to the mother of my god-child," I said.

Without missing a beat, she said, "Speaking of the baby, my underwear's getting tight."

Leave it to Mary Lou to work the words baby and tight underwear into a sentence. "Really? Is there a lot of that going around?"

I asked.

As usual, she ignored me. "Donna's gone to work at that new lingerie shop in Turner. She gave me a coupon for ten percent off. Let's go shopping there tomorrow so I can get some looser drawers."

I needed new undies too. "Sure. Let's go around lunch time. By the way, what's the name of the place?"

"Panties R Us. Bye." She hung up.

That evening, after Bobby had left for his date with Carrie Sue, I watched the rolling guide on television and hoped I'd find something good to watch. I didn't. I stuffed my feet into my Marvin the Martian slippers, then traipsed into the kitchen. I made a pot of coffee. While it brewed, I sat at the kitchen table and propped my feet on a chair. Softly practicing the song I'd be singing in church on Sunday morning, I made Marvin sway to the rhythm.

I looked around the kitchen. Everything could use a good cleaning. The floor needed scrubbing. For a little while, my broken hand would put a damper on things like weekly cleaning. Since I truly believed that housework makes you old before your time, most of it didn't matter to me. But, for some strange reason, I can't stand a dirty kitchen floor. I had the whole evening ahead of me. I decided to tackle that job one-handed. Just then, Jeff called.

"Hi, cutie." Just the sound of his voice warmed me to my bones.

"Are you working again tonight?" Marvin really danced now.

"Yes. But, I won't have to work at the mill tomorrow night. I have to dance at seven, then I'll be at your house, with food, by eight-thirty. Is that okay?"

"Sounds great."

"I've missed you, Bertie," Jeff whispered.

Evidently, he was in a break-room and didn't want his co-workers to hear him talking to his girlfriend. How sweet.

"Tomorrow night, I'm yours, totally and completely. I'll do anything you want." His innuendo jump-started my sexual engine and pushed my desire into overdrive. Just thinking about it, my breath threatened to stop. What would I do when I stood, or laid, whatever the case might be, face to face with Jeff, my Wonder Dancer?

"Tell me really slowly what you'd like me to do for you." Jeff sounded like he might be hyperventilating. My nerve was dying a slow, painful death. In my sexiest voice, I whispered, "Scrub . . . my . . . kitchen . . . floor."

Jeff burst out laughing. "I think you're afraid of sex."

"No, I'm not."

"Are too."

"Am not." Through the phone, I heard a door open and a woman's muffled voice.

"They need me back on the floor. We'll finish this discussion tomorrow." Jeff hung up.

As I poured myself a cup of coffee, a shadow flashed across the kitchen window. I jumped and rushed to it to close the curtain. Just then, a knock sounded at the door. I hurried to peek out the window. There on the porch I found Arch Fortney, Pete's son. I opened the door. Beside the man stood a cute little girl with blond pigtails.

"I hope it isn't too late. My daughter and I were in the neighborhood, and I need to talk to you about whether you're interested in buying Dad's house." He appeared uncomfortable.

"I like your slippers," the girl said.

"Thank you. We can discuss the house now." I stepped aside to let them in.

"This is my daughter, Petey," he said.

I narrowed my gaze at Arch.

"Penelope Tam. P.T." He shrugged. "Dad named her."

That explained it all. I missed Pete, the old goat. I bent to talk to his sort-of namesake. "My name is Bertie. How old are you, Petey?"

She had the prettiest green eyes I'd ever seen. With a bright smile, she looked me straight in my face, which wasn't a big task because I had leaned down to her level.

"I'm ten and a half and my hearing is really good, so you don't have to lean close to talk."

I backed away. "Sorry about that."

"That's quite all right. All grown-ups do that."

Arch pulled Petey next to him. "That's enough. We get the point." She accepted the reprimand with grace.

"Please, have a seat. May I get you something?"

"Do I smell coffee?" Arch smiled.

"Yes. As a matter of fact, I was just going to have a cup myself." I started to bend, then quickly straightened. "How about you, Petey?"

She sniffed the air. "Do I smell hot chocolate with marshmallows?"

I chuckled. "Yes, you do. Come with me. You can help me make it."

Petey followed me into the kitchen. "You don't have a maid?"

"I'm afraid not. We'll have to wait on ourselves. Isn't that terrible?"

"Disgusting." The child took the milk from the refrigerator.

I got a pot from the cabinet. "I guess you have a maid."

Petey giggled. "No. That's why I know how disgusting it is not to have one." We both laughed out loud.

"What does your dad like in his coffee?"

"Just a little cream, then I cool it off like this." Petey blew into the cup. "He says that makes it sweet." I looked down into her angelic face. Her apple cheeks glowed. She had Pete's eyes. A strange feeling filled my heart.

She carried her cup to the living room. I carried mine and Arch's. Petey and I found her dad sleeping in Pete's recliner. Arch's previously tense jaws relaxed, softening his features. I hadn't noticed how handsome he was. I felt a little guilty watching him sleep. The girl and I looked at each other.

"He's been working real hard lately," she said.

"Let's not wake him."

Petey nodded. We went back to the kitchen, drank our hot drinks, and played Hangman and Tic-Tac-Toe. When Bobby came home just before midnight, that's how he found us. Petey and I at the kitchen table, the floor still dirty, and Arch sleeping in his dad's chair.

Arch apologized profusely for falling asleep and for leaving his daughter to my care. Little did he know it should have been classified the other way around. Petey kept watch over me. Twice, I sneaked an *X* into a Tic-Tac-Toe space. Both times, she caught me.

Her knowledge and wit far exceeded any child of ten I've ever meet. Oh, sure, Donna's ten-year-old had a lot on the ball, but I'm not talking about criminal masterminds. I'm talking about a fifth grader who can beat the heck out of a thirty-two-year-old in a game of Hangman. Of course, the oldest of the two women had a broken hand. Surely, that should count for something.

Arch promised to get back in touch with me soon about my buying his dad's house, then he and Petey left. Bobby danced his way into the spare room to get his pillow and blanket, then skipped and bounced back to the couch.

"I take it you had a good time." I made sure the doors were all locked.

"I sure did, Sis. I can't wait to see Estelle's face when I take her dancing next Saturday night. She won't believe how I can move." He jived his way across the floor, spun me around and dipped me. I laughed in spite of myself.

The next morning after breakfast Bobby cleaned the kitchen, scrubbed the floor and vacuumed the whole house. I did the laundry. Mary Lou picked me up just before lunch. We zipped through a drive-thru, then ate our burger and fries on the way to Turner. We didn't want to waste any time getting to Panties R Us. With a big sale going on, all the merchandise would be picked over. Lord knows, I don't like any one messing with my underwear, unless . . . well, you know.

As we entered the lingerie shop, Donna waved to us from behind the register. She finished her transaction and hurried in our direction.

"How may I help you?" Donna exaggerated her saleswoman

approach. She and Mary Lou gathered in a giggle huddle. I passed on that adventure and moved to a display of see-through nighties. Fluff from a marabou trim stuck to my lip. I tried blowing it off. No luck. I looked around for a mirror. Peering into one, I was happily picking a processed turkey feather from my mouth when I saw Donna's sister Annie and her husband, my ex-boyfriend, Lee Dew, enter the shop.

Next to Sasquatch, Lee Dew was the last man I wanted to run into. I ducked behind a sale rack and hoped he wouldn't see me. Moving to a table in the far corner, I pretended to be a normal, everyday shopper. I glanced around. Donna headed my way. Dang.

"Aren't these great, Bertie?" She picked up a pair of red polyester panties.

"I'll take them." Foolhardily, I pressed a bill in her hand, along with the undies, hoping she'd go to the register, ring them up, put them in a bag, then bring them back to me. If only I lived in that perfect world.

Donna made it as far as the register, at the same time as Annie and Lee.

"Those are pretty," Annie said, admiring my underwear.

"They're Bertie's." Not only did Donna mention this fact, but she used my unmentionables to point in my direction.

Mortified, I waved to them, hoping my face wasn't as red as it felt. Deciding the jig was up, I joined them to get my change and package. Donna finally quit waving them around like a banner and almost had them in the bag. "You never struck me as the kind who wore crotch-less underwear," she said.

I don't, my mind screamed, but my throat wouldn't squeak out the words.

"She doesn't." Lee managed to find *his* words just fine.

I hit him squarely on the shoulder with my good fist. Donna hit him on the other side. He winced. I gloated, took my change, then grabbed Mary Lou, who, with enthusiasm, was digging through a bloomers bin. I dragged her out of the shop and to the car.

"I didn't get to buy anything," she said.

"We'll come back when Annie and Lee leave."

Mary Lou patted my hand. "Okay. Let's go get a milkshake."

"You just ate."

"No, I didn't. I fed the baby. Now, it's my turn." Mary Lou started the car.

With my eye twitching in doubletime, I thought she might have a good idea. "I guess I can have something light." My stomach continued to quiver like a bowl of Jello. Just like we did when we were teenagers, we plopped our bottoms onto the soda fountain stools and ordered.

We were sucking down double Dutch chocolate malts, and listening to an old song on the juke box. "Why don't we ever come here any more?" Mary Lou asked.

"Because we grew out of the teeny bopper scene and staggered into the Dew Drop Inn. Life hasn't been the same since." Through a straw, I slurped the last of the ice cream.

Mary Lou chose to raise her glass and drink the last of hers. She smiled at me with a brown mustache like she used to do when we were sixteen. "You're silly." I handed her a napkin.

She reached to take it, then let go a blood-curdling scream. I slid off the stool.

"What's wrong?" She was rubbing her wedding ring in a frantic state. Her mustache was fading.

"I've lost my diamond. It's gone." She began to cry. "My wonderful diamond is gone."

"When's the last time you remember actually seeing it in its setting?"

"When we were at Panties R Us. It's bigger than Donna's so I waved it under her nose a couple of times to make sure she saw it." Mary Lou dropped her head into her arms which were folded on the counter. Earnest sobs shook her body.

I gathered our purses, paid the tab and helped my dear friend to her car. "Let's go back there and look for it. It's big enough we should be able to find it." At the lingerie shop, Donna, Annie, Lee, and I helped Mary Lou look.

Donna used her clerk authority to organize us. "Annie, you check over there by the bras. Bertie, you check the crotch-less panty table. Mary Lou, you check the panty bin." Excitement lit Donna's face. "By the way, I was promoted to Panty Bin Manager just this morning. These are all mine." She waved a demonstrative hand over several displays of (what else?) panties. We offered our weak congrats, then scrambled to our assigned hunting grounds.

"Oh, Lee." Donna pointed to the front of the store. "You check the floor from the entrance back."

"I want the crotch-less panties." Lee beamed.

Donna sharply jabbed her finger into his chest. "Go," she said. He scooted on his way. We all looked in every possible place, but we didn't find Mary Lou's diamond. The poor girl was distraught. To compensate for her loss, Donna sold her five pairs of cotton briefs and two bras, and allowed Mary Lou to take advantage of the employee's forty percent discount.

"It's a good thing you lost it today instead of yesterday." Donna seemed really happy about that fact.

"Why?" Mary Lou asked.

"Yesterday I was just a sales associate. You'd have gotten those bloomers at only a thirty percent discount."

Mary Lou couldn't find the will to smile. We just left. We were almost home when I saw something sparkling under the brake pedal. Leaning down, I picked up her diamond. I could see the relief relax her tense jaw line.

"Let's go to the jewelry store," I suggested.

"Yeah, they can reset it, and Rex will never know." She turned right at the next corner. "Do you think I should go back and pay the difference between the regular and the employee discount?"

We looked at each other. Together we sang, "Not."

Mary Lou and I arrived at the jewelry store.

"How much would it cost to have my Hopeful Diamond remounted?" She handed her ring and stone to the man behind the counter.

The jeweler furrowed his brow. "Hopeful Diamond?"

"Sure, I'm hopeful that if I fertilize it enough with dish water, it'll grow to a full carat."

The man belly-laughed. "I'll do it for free. It's well worth it just for the chuckle."

While he worked on Mary Lou's ring, she and I walked a few doors down the street to a book store. She searched the shelves for mother-to-be books; I perused the romance section. If I couldn't partake, I could at least read about it. I chided myself for thinking in such negative ways. After all, I did have a date with a hunky guy later that night.

Jeff would be at my house, with Chinese food, right after he undressed for other women. Okay, so my self-directed pep talk needed work. I moseyed around the corner of a shelf and came nose to nose with a man whose face looked familiar. When I backed up a few steps so my vision could focus, I realized he was George Bigham, Jr. from the zoning office. "Hello," I said.

"Excuse me." He walked around me. I guess I didn't leave as big of an impression on him as he'd left on me. Around the next shelf, my neighbor, Helen Weidemeyer flipped through a magazine. We exchanged typical niceties.

After a few minutes, she said, "I'm here with my brother. He's ready to go." She nodded to someone behind me.

I turned, hoping to get a glimpse of her illusive sibling, but saw no one. A humorous idea wiggled its way into my thoughts. Wouldn't it be funny if George was Helen's brother? A much younger brother, of course, since he couldn't be more than forty, and she had to be ninety in the shade. I stepped into the aisle where I had a clear view of the exit. Sure enough, Helen and George left together. At least that explained why he'd refused to meet me when I'd dropped off her groceries. He'd seen me in angry action and probably feared for his safety. At the very least, he didn't want to risk me going off on another tangent about his name. Personally, I didn't feel I'd lost any great shakes either.

When Mary Lou dropped me at my driveway, she waved with her left hand which flashed her repaired ring. I checked with Herman to see if I had any mail. On top of my three fan letters, two advertisements, and two bills, I found a hand-written note from my mailman. He put me on notice that he would not deliver any more mail until I had a regulation mailbox. He'd left me specifications about what would be considered regular. A dead fish on the ground wasn't it.

Inside my house, I kicked off my tennis shoes and slipped into my fluffy Marvin the Martian slippers. I still had time before Jeff came, so I sat down to read my fan mail. One was from Jack. It read: *You delight in killing for your own pleasure, don't you?*

A shiver shook me.

What kind of critter had to lose its life for the green slippers you stuff your feet into?

I glanced at Marvin. *How long will you go on before people get wise to you and stop you?*

I hadn't a clue what kind of bee this lunatic had in his bonnet, but his statements were so stupid, it all had to be a joke. My shoulders relaxed. Of course it was a joke. This letter featured the author's tip of the day.

Here's a tip for you: Always keep your doors locked. Someone might go in and change the expiration dates on your milk prod-

ucts. Then you'd be sorry. Jack.

Now, I had a big decision to make. How stupid would I look for reporting these letters to the police? Clearly, they were too silly to be taken seriously. I read it one more time, then broke into heartfelt laughter. It had to be one of my friends with a warped sense of humor. That list could take a while to weed through.

I called Mary Lou and told her about my newest letter.

"Surely, it's a joke, don't you think?" I'd hoped she'd start laughing and tell me which one of my friends had sent the funny letter. But she didn't.

"Jeeze, Bertie, you're the only person I know who could be stalked by Jack the Tipper."

My twitch was back. "Thanks, Mary Lou. By the way, did you tell Rex about losing your diamond?"

"Yeah, all he wanted to know was if I'd gotten a pair of those crotch-less panties like you did."

"Oh, no. Don't tell anyone about those things, for crying out loud." Filled with embarrassment, I sank my head onto the kitchen table.

"Let's just hope Jack the Tipper doesn't find out about them." Mary Lou, always thinking ahead.

I heard a commotion on her end of the line. "Hang on. Okay," she called to someone. "I've got to go. Rex has his ear caught in the vacuum cleaner. Again."

"Wait." I wasn't sure I wanted to know, but "How did he do that?"

"He thinks he can hear dust mites talking, so he . . ."

"Sorry. More info than I needed. Bye." I hung up as soon as I could find the strength. My life and the people in it were tearing down my resistance. I may have to check myself into the cashew farm any day now.

I practiced my solo a couple of times. Except for one part near the end, I found it pretty easy. I'd just concentrate really hard, and I'd make it through the whole song just fine. I hoped this was only an initiation into the choir, not something they'd expect me to do every Sunday. I ran through it one more time, focusing on the one scary note, then went to shower and dress for my date. If a man brought food to your house and watched a movie with you, was it still considered a date? Maybe an almost date.

Jeff and I had just finished eating moo shu pork and crab rangoon when Bobby came home. I glanced at the clock. This was the earliest he'd been in since he'd learned to dance. Of course it would be tonight. Bobby took up his sentinel post on the sofa and picked through our left-overs.

"Do you like wrestling, Jeff?"

Oh, no. Not the W word. So much for a cozy, possibly intimate evening with the finest looking man I'd been on an almost date with in a long time. Maybe ever. I tried to watch the goings-on inside the ring, but my mind couldn't stay with it enough to keep from going numb. I moved to the recliner and tried reading for a while. Eventually, when wrestling went off and a war movie came on, and Jeff and Bobby appeared to be doing the male bonding thing, I slid quietly into the comfort of my bed, snuggled against the pillow and, until I fell asleep, thought of what might have been.

When Bobby woke me for church the next morning, I was in the middle of a dream about being on my tropical isle with Antonio, my cabana boy. I hated to leave the sun and sand, but I had a job to do. Today, for the first time in my life, I would sing in front of a church full of people.

The choir lined up in the church hallway according to height. Since my solo would be first, Homer King told me to enter last. We had practiced my song twice on Wednesday, and I had sung through it several times during the three days since. But, suddenly it didn't seem enough.

I thought I could hear my knees clacking like someone playing the spoons. I know that most Southern women don't perspire, they merely form a demure sheen on their skin. I must be part

Northerner because I was sweating like a stuck hog. As I dabbed at my upper lip, I made eye contact with Homer. With a swirl of dust behind him, he hurried in my direction.

"Are you going to be all right? You look a little green around the gills." He patted me on the back between my trembling shoulders. "I can't have you fainting and disrupting the choir's performance." His hand slid down my robe to my waist.

"I'll be fine." Lord, please let that be true.

"Good." The choir members began to file through the door to the loft. "Now, get out there and show the congregation the wonderful talent the Lord has given you." The old buzzard patted me on my behind. I spun to face him. He pointed his baton toward the others, directing me to follow them. I marched back to face him.

"You ever do that again, and they'll be pulling that stick out of your . . ." Instantly, I remembered I was in church. ". . . ear. You old goat."

I marched into the choir loft with a purpose and more confidence than I'd ever thought I possessed. I sang from the bottom of my heart, sending my voice to the rafters and beyond. Still fueled by the anger I'd experienced when Homer had fondled my backside, I belted out that one scary note with so much volume and grace, I almost felt I should thank the old goat for his motivation. In my heart, I knew I'd done good. The smiles, nods, and misty eyes throughout the entire congregation told me I was right.

When the choir had finished the rest of the songs and we had taken our seats to listen to Reverend Miller's sermon, I scanned the faces of the people crammed into the pews and found Mom, Pop, Bobby, Mary Lou, Rex, and George Bigham.

Good Lord. I'd never seen him at our church before. Evidently he was visiting with his sister, Helen. I picked her out a couple of pews away with the Sweet Meadow Garden Club. I could feel George staring at me, but when I glanced his way he averted his gaze.

Maybe I'd been too hard on him that day at the zoning office, but a little of my mom's Irish temper had flared. Okay, a lot of my mom's Irish temper had flared. Perhaps my singing had shown him my softer side, and perhaps I should apologize for my actions that day.

When the service ended, a mob gathered around me. "That was wonderful," most of them told me. Close friends and family hugged me. After a few minutes I went to the choir office to hang up my robe. The other members had already left. I stepped into the dark room, flipped on the light, and turned to find Homer standing just inside the door.

"Jesus, Joseph, and Mary. You scared me to death. What are you doing here in the dark?" I walked across the room and hung my robe on the empty wall hook. When I turned, Homer was blocking my path to the door.

"You did a good job out there." He stepped closer. I could tell by the look in his eyes it was going to turn ugly.

"Get out of my way, Homer King." I raised my broken hand and braced for the pain I was sure would come when I bashed him up the side of his head. He didn't seem to care. He edged closer.

"Miss Byrd, may I speak to you a minute?" Homer and I both froze like statues. He turned, and I glanced over his shoulder. George Bigham stood in the doorway. I hurried around Homer and gave a silent thanks that I'd been rescued.

"Of course, Mr. Bigham." I latched onto his arm and practically dragged him down the hallway. Once outside, I turned to him. "What did you want to talk to me about?"

"Nothing. I just happened to be passing by and thought you could use some help."

"You were right. Thank you, and I'm truly sorry for hollering at you that day. I was overwrought."

"Sure." That was the sum total of his reply. We parted ways. Well, at least I'd apologized.

Deep in conversation with Carl and Karen Kelly, Bobby sat in the wrecker waiting for me. When I walked toward them, he stuck his head out the driver's window. "Good job, Sis."

"It certainly was a moving song. You have a wonderful voice."

Karen gave me a quick hug.

"Thanks." I shifted my gaze to Carl. "I need some advice. I've been getting letters from a real nut case. One minute, I think it might be from someone I know who's playing a colossal joke on me. The next, I'm just plain scared."

"Yeah, they're really strange," Bobby said. "The scariest part is that they say specific things about the inside of her house."

I told Carl the meat and bones of the letters. He agreed. "That's really strange. It does sound like someone who knows you."

"Or, a Peeping Tom. My neighbor saw a man in a white car outside my house. He looked in my window."

"I think it might be worth checking into. I'll see what I can do." Carl and Karen waved, then started to walk to their car. A white vehicle crept by us. Inside, Homer King stared straight ahead.

Chapter 10

On Monday afternoon, I went to the hardware store to buy a mailbox. I opted for a normal black one with a pole and concrete block attached. After work, Bobby dug a hole and planted my up-to-specification, regulation letter receptacle. I gathered up Herman and headed to the trash. Bobby dragged the pieces of the shattered post and stacked them alongside the mailbox. Just in case the mailman had changed his mind, I took one last look inside. I found a letter from Jack. My heart slammed to my throat. That meant he'd hand delivered it.

I looked at the envelope, then saw something very strange. If it were hand delivered, why did it have a postmark from the Sweet

Meadow post office? My hand shook. Bobby and I went into the house. He opened the letter.

Just because you can sing doesn't mean you'll be admitted to heaven. You will have a lot to make up for. Here's a tip for you; Whambo in the fifth race. Jack

"What the heck does that mean?" I didn't know whether to laugh or cry.

"I think it means there's a wacko in our midst. I'm calling Carl." Bobby picked up the phone. I hurried to get dressed for Novalee's Tupperware party. Suddenly, I had an idea. I hurried back to the kitchen. With the receiver to his ear, Bobby listened intently. I tapped him on the shoulder and startled him.

"Hang on, Carl." He looked up at me. I took the phone from my brother.

"Do you happen to know where Homer King works?" I asked.

"He works for the post office. Why?"

After I'd almost swallowed my tongue, I told him about my encounter the night before with Handy Homer in the hallway, then later in the choir office. I also told him that my mailman had refused to deliver to me, so my last letter had to be hand delivered, yet it had an official postmark.

After a few seconds, he told me to go about my business as usual, and he'd do a full scale investigation. I'd hear from him soon. Back to my business as usual? He really didn't know what he was saying.

While I walked to Novalee's house, Bobby watched from the end of my driveway. I would call him when the Tupperware party ended and Bobby would meet me.

At the party, I watched the lady demonstrate how to burp her bowls. We ate some really good stuff, all served in Tupperware. By the time I was ready to leave, I'd ordered a bowl big enough to take a bath in and a child's toy, should I ever get married and have one. A child, not a toy.

When I called home, Bobby didn't answer. I walked onto Novalee's front porch. Evidently, my brother had been called out because the wrecker was gone. I decided to brave walking home alone.

The street light in front of Novalee's house shone just to the edge of Helen Weidemeyer's yard. The next light stood on the other side of Rick and Barbie's house. My home hid in the black hole in the middle. Just as I neared the trash pile at my driveway, I caught sight of a man's silhouette crouching under Barbie's tree. He faced my house, with his back to the road.

It must be Jack.

If I ran to call the police he'd get away, and I was tired of worrying about the whole being stalked issue. If I just walked up to him, he might kill me. Or worse.

I had to subdue him myself.

My eyes had adjusted to the darkness. At my feet were the remnants of the mailbox post. Quietly, I picked up a huge chunk of wood which fit my unbroken hand perfectly. It had good leverage.

I edged along the road, cutting my way through the void between the lights like a stealth bomber. Directly aligned with the big oak I squatted, then duck-walked my way to the figure still hunched beside the tree. I crept behind him, raised the log, and whacked him.

"Damn." The man lunged forward. I prepared to hit him again. As he rolled onto his back, the light from Barbie's yard illuminated his pale face. I dropped to my knees beside him. Pressing my fingers to his throat, I hoped I hadn't killed Officer Carl Kelly.

"Speak to me," I begged.

"You don't really want that. Not right this minute." Carl sounded okay. I certainly hoped he would be.

"Are you okay?"

"If I say yes, are you going to finish the job?"

"Carl, please. I thought you were Jack."

"I've heard stories about you. I should have realized you could fend off a mere lunatic. Here's a tip for Jack: Run. Run for your life."

"Okay. Okay. You should have told me you'd be out here."

"It's not your fault. I failed surveillance 101 at the police academy. It's not my strong suit." He struggled to a sitting position.

Just then, Bobby pulled into the yard. While Carl and I sat under the neighbors' tree, Bobby walked directly toward us.

"What are you two doing out here? And don't tell me dancing."

"Carl had my house under surveillance. I thought he was Jack, so I sneaked up on him and hit him with a stick."

"Stick, my foot." Carl stood. "It felt like a railroad tie."

I took his arm. "Let me help you into the house."

He pulled away. "No, thanks. I think I'll be fine." We stood there a few more minutes making sure he was okay. I took the flashlight from his belt and shined it into his hair looking for signs of blood. I saw nothing but a deep red streak across his scalp. It would be black and blue by morning.

"Maybe we should take you to the hospital and have it checked out," I said.

"I've had a lot worse. I'm fine."

"I think she's right." Bobby stepped closer to take Carl's arm.

Carl pulled away. "I tell you, I'm fine."

"Will you guys go away? I have to go to the bathroom," a voice boomed from above us.

Carl and Bobby jumped. I didn't even flinch. I knew who lurked there. I shined the flashlight into the branches. There she was. She and Damien, the cat. Same branch. Same position.

"Barbie, what are you doing up there?" I asked.

"I don't have to answer that." Annoyance spiked her voice. "This is my tree."

"Can I help you down?" Bobby raised his hands. She slid from the bough into his arms. Just then her husband Rick walked up.

"Just exactly what's going on here?" His tone seemed a mite put out.

Bobby almost threw Barbie to the ground. "I was just helping her out of her tree."

Oh, my dear brother. She was out of her tree long before you met her.

"Come on, it's time to go in." Rick put his arm around his wife and led her away.

The three of us retreated to my house. "Boy, that's a bag of mixed nuts." Bobby chuckled his way into the living room.

"This whole street's full of them." Carl glanced at me and gently rubbed his head. "How do you think she got up there?"

I poured us all a glass of Coke. "It wouldn't surprise me if she had sprouted wings and flew up there."

The next morning, at the garage, things moved at a snail's pace.

The only call we had came from Millie. She needed a prescription picked up at the pharmacy. Bobby delivered it. Pop did one minor repair on a motorcycle. I dusted the office, then decided to drive across town to visit with Mary Lou. When I arrived, she seemed a little more rattled than usual.

"What's going on?" I propped my elbows on the counter above her desk.

She looked up at me. "This has been a peculiar day."

Uh oh. I hated it when she started a conversation like that. Peculiar to Mary Lou was like icebergs to Alaska-quiet, beautiful, ever-present, but when one of those suckers broke loose, there could be hell to pay.

Her boss' door opened. Gary Landon hurried out lugging a pull-along suitcase. "Got that file, Mary Lou?" He looked at me. "Oh, hi, Bertie. What a day."

She handed him a huge folder. He tucked it under his arm, then hurried out the door, dragging his suitcase like a tail behind him. I hooked my thumb in his direction. "Where's he off to?"

"He has to testify in court on a claim we handled a few months ago. He should be gone for the rest of the day. Yippee." With a box cutter, she sliced the tape off a package sitting on her desk. "Supplies from the home office," she told me. Mary Lou stood and began pulling forms and booklets from the box.

"I had the weirdest conversation with the delivery man this morning." She loaded some of the stuff into her desk drawers. "He wanted to know if my boobs had gotten bigger now that I'm pregnant. Do you think that's a strange question from a person I only see about every six weeks when he makes a delivery from the home office?"

"Yeah. What did you say to him?"

"I said yes. But then he said he thought I must be proud of the fact since I was wearing a banner to advertise it. What do you think he meant by that?"

"I don't know. But did you hurt him when you slugged him?"

"Naw. He caught me by surprise and with my added weight, I'm not sure I could have taken him."

"I got a railroad tie you can borrow," I joked.

"Huh?"

Before I could tell Mary Lou about my latest adventure with Carl Kelly, she rose from her seat and crossed the room to a filing cabinet. Dangling from the waistband of her stretch pants hung a bra. One end was caught by the hooks in the knit material, while the other end tapped right above her calf. The bra looked like Old Glory. It flashed red, white, and blue. I didn't know whether to laugh or salute it.

"Mary Lou, you have a bra hanging off your butt." I don't believe I've ever had to make that statement before in my life.

Instead of reaching back there to capture it, she tried to look at it over her shoulder. Soon, she twirled in a circle chasing her tail like a puppy.

"Stop." I went around the counter. "You're going to make yourself dizzy and fall down." I removed her banner.

"Good Lord." Mary Lou pulled out the front of her blouse, peeked inside, then breathed an audible sigh of relief. She waved the bra in the air. "I must have sat on this one when I put my shoes on." She stuffed it into her purse.

I left my dear friend in the middle of the tizzy she'd worked herself into. I waited until I was out of her office, then started chuckling. Laughter and tears are said to cleanse the soul. I should have the cleanest in the South.

I had tittered my way across the parking lot toward Pop's car. Almost there, my bra strap broke. I raised my gaze toward heaven. "Your point is well taken." I climbed into the car and drove to my house to change.

In my driveway, I found a white car.

Jack.

I parked across the entrance to my driveway, blocking the car. Seeing no one in the yard, I went to the back of the house. There, on his hands and knees, weeding around a scraggly rose bush was

Arch Fortney.

"What are you doing?" I asked.

He looked up and smiled. "Just tending to a couple of Dad's favorite flowers." He rose and dusted his hands together. "They're looking a little sad."

"Did you come by last week and look in my window?" Could Arch be the man Barbie had seen?

"No. I've only been here the night I fell asleep." A sadness clouded his brown eyes. "The truth is, I got to missing Dad and felt like coming home for a few minutes. I hope you don't mind."

"Of course not." The words worked their way around a lump in my throat. "It is your house."

"Yeah, we need to work out the details for you to buy it. How about tomorrow night?"

"Church." I shrugged.

"Petey has asked a couple of times if she can come over and play with you again."

I smiled. "How sweet. How about Thursday night? Around seven?"

"Okay. Would it be okay if I finish up here before I leave?" Arch asked.

"Sure, I've just got to . . . get something from inside, then I'll be gone. Bye." Inside, I changed quickly. Peeking through a small opening in my bedroom curtain I watched Arch work. From his profile I could see a strong resemblance to Pete. Arch's heart appeared to be like his father's too. Sentimental. I liked that in a man.

I went back to work. Dad sat talking to a young man who seemed nervous. I pretended to be busy at the other end of the office.

"You've done recovery, roll-overs?" Pop asked. Was he interviewing the fellow for a job as a wrecker driver? My father hadn't mentioned taking on another employee, but now that I thought about it, that could be a good idea. I still had my hand in a cast, Pop had been extremely tired lately, and Bobby would be going home to Estelle first thing Saturday morning. I already had my alarm clock set so I could wake him up.

"Yes, sir. I can do anything with a wrecker. I worked for Craig's in Atlanta for six years."

"Why did you leave there?" Pop rested his arms on his desk.

The man appeared uncomfortable. "Mr. Craig and I had a difference of opinion."

Pop and I both leaned closer. "About what?" He asked.

"About marrying his daughter, Broomhilda."

"You mean he fired you because you wanted to marry his daughter?"

"No, sir. Because I didn't marry her. She's a real witch."

Pop and I both laughed. I had a sneaky feeling he hadn't told us the complete truth. "Her name isn't really Broomhilda, is it?"

A grin smirked its way across his lips. "No ma'am. It's Judy."

We all laughed. "Lincoln Johnson, this is my daughter, Bertie. She's really the boss around here. But, you can see she's had a little accident. Her brother is helping out until Friday, then he'll be leaving."

He stood and we shook hands. "Linc," he said.

"You'll work eight to five weekdays, then be on call every other night and every other weekend. I'd like you to ride with me and Bobby for a couple of days to see how you do. Can you start tomorrow?" Dad asked.

"Yes, sir. Thank you." Linc smiled widely.

Our new employee said his goodbyes and promised to be at work by eight the next morning. I felt relieved that Pop had made the decision. I didn't like how tired he'd been looking and, with Bobby leaving, I wasn't sure how I'd manage with my hand still in a cast. Linc could be the answer.

Wednesday night I dreaded going to church, and especially to choir practice. I wasn't looking forward to facing Homer King after his slip from reality last Sunday morning. He must have thought himself a magician, with his sleight-of-hand trick. That, coupled with my suspicion that he might be stalking me under the guise of Jack the Tipper, made me very uncomfortable. Officer Kelly had promised to check out Handy Homer, but I hadn't heard anything yet. I would try to control myself, but one false move on his part, and he'd be singing soprano for the rest of his life. I braced for the confrontation, then made my way inside the church. Glorie Thorpe waved to me from across the aisle and hurried in my direction.

"Hi, Bertie. Did you hear? We won't be having choir practice tonight. Homer's under the weather."

"Good." That slipped out. "I mean good gracious, that's a shame."

Glorie smiled, then took her chipper self off to her next task. Relief flowed so heavily through me that I had to go to the bathroom. I checked my watch. I had plenty of time.

Someone occupied one of the stalls. I entered the next one. As I settled onto the seat, the neighboring lady said, "Hello."

Friendly person. I don't usually carry on a conversation while using a public bathroom but, after all, it was a fellow parishioner. "Hi."

"Everything come out okay?" the woman asked.

Feeling a tad uncomfortable at such a forward question, I stumbled for what I should say. "So far."

"Did you tell him to shove it?"

"Well, no. He's not here tonight." Good Lord. Who was that over there who knew about my conflict with the choir director?

"When that happened to me, I got my foot stuck in there."

This had to be one of the strangest conversations I'd ever had. "I'm sorry. I don't recognize your voice. Who are you?"

"Hang on," the woman said. She rapped sharply on the wall dividing our stalls. "Excuse me, but I'm on my cell phone over here. Do you mind?"

Jeeze. "Sorry." I swore I'd never go back into that place ever again.

For the second time in two weeks, I slunk out of the church bathroom. Mary Lou had saved a seat for me. I slid into it and looked around for a woman with a cell phone. Of course, I didn't see one.

Mary Lou leaned close to me. "Would you and Jeff like to come to my house for dinner Saturday?"

"I'll have to check with him, but yeah, that would be great." I don't remember Mary Lou ever cooking anything other than peanut butter and dill pickle sandwiches. But never let it be said I couldn't roll with what life dealt me, or what Mary Lou served me.

Linc Johnson showed up for his second day on the job. He

hadn't fibbed about his wrecker skills. He'd handled a couple of calls with Bobby.

"He's good," my brother reported to Pop and me. "He gets out, hooks up, and gets back in the truck while I'm still standing there scratching my head trying to figure out the best way to handle the situation."

"Good. So you'll be packing up tomorrow night. Right?" I waited with bated breath.

He gave me a rough, brotherly hug. "Yes, Sis. I'll be out of your hair early Saturday morning."

"Well, I know you're anxious to get home to Estelle and show her the fancy dance steps you've learned." I scurried from the garage into Pop's office.

Bobby called behind me, "But not as excited as you are to have me gone."

I pretended not to hear him. He knew I loved him, but he needed to go home.

"Byrd and Sons." I answered the loudly ringing phone.

"Hi, Bertie. I have a doctor's appointment at ten." Millie Keats sounded a little puny. Arguing that I didn't run a taxi service proved fruitless with most of the citizens of Sweet Meadow but, with Millie it could be dangerous. "Okay, someone will pick you up about ten till."

"Send that new hottie I saw putting gas in your tow truck yesterday at the filling station down the street." Millie had perked up.

I glanced out the window. Long, lanky Linc loped across the parking area. His lengthy, unruly brown hair boinged from under his cap. His brogans, buckskin colored, appeared to weigh more than he did. He looked like an exclamation mark in motion. Hottie? I didn't see it. "I'll try to send him, Millie."

When Linc returned from his Millie mission, he looked a little rattled.

"Would I be jeopardizing my job if I refused to pick that woman up from the doctor's office?" He removed his hat and scratched his dark curls.

"No, but you have to tell me why." I was already laughing, and I hadn't heard the first detail.

"It's kind of embarrassing." He blushed.

"Yeah, those are the details I want." I couldn't help myself.

"She asked me my name and when I told her Linc, she said she'll call me John."

"That was her husband's name. He's been dead about ten years."

"That's what she said. She refused to call me anything but John. When she got into the truck, she said she was afraid of falling out, so she slid next to me."

I gave him a sympathetic nod. All the while, I chewed on my bottom lip.

"You don't understand," he appeared flustered. "She . . . sat . . . next . . . to . . . me." Linc pressed his body against the wall, imitating Millie against him.

Wide-eyed, I watched him. His shoulders slumped. "She ran her hand up my thigh." His face reddened.

Chewing on my bottom lip no longer worked. I cracked up. "I'm sorry." I tried to stop, but it wasn't happening. I guess Linc decided if you can't beat'em, join'em. He, too, started laughing. We shrieked for two or three minutes. Suddenly, he went stone-faced.

"You won't make me go back, will ya?"

When the time came, I sent Bobby. When he returned, not seeming any worse for wear, I told him about Linc's experience with Millie.

"Oh, really," my brother snapped. "What's he got that I don't?"

I narrowed my gaze at him, then tapped the side of my head hoping to loosen the vision his indignation caused. Forty-four hours and twenty-three minutes before his departure, but who's counting?

Chapter 11

J ust before Bobby and I headed home from work, Helen Weidemeyer called. She needed a tomato for dinner. I picked one up at the produce stand just down the street from the garage. By the time I'd delivered it, then walked back to my house, Arch and his daughter, Petey, were pulling into my driveway. The girl, carrying a pizza box, bounded out of the car.

"Hi, Bertie. Dad and I hope you like sausage and lots of cheese." Her smile beamed from ear to ear.

"Who doesn't?" I put my arm around her shoulder and walked to the door. Arch caught up with us. "You didn't have to bring dinner." I unlocked the door.

"We wanted to." His brown eyes sparkled. His soft tone jerked a knot in my heart. Maybe it was pre-pizza indigestion.

I led the way to the kitchen. While I put ice in glasses and got the Cokes from the fridge, Petey and Arch took plates from the cupboard. By the time Bobby finished his shower, we were well into the pizza. He said his hi's and goodbye's, snagged a piece for himself, and headed to the Dew Drop Inn for a final night of dancing. Cha-Cha-Cha.

"How's Helen doing?" Arch asked.

Petey chewed daintily, then took a drink. It took a second for me to remember he'd seen me coming back from Helen's house. "I take it she lived there when you were growing up here."

He nodded.

"She seems to be doing fine. Just needed a tomato for her salad. So, I brought it to her."

"Have you ever met her brother, Junior?" A smiled played at the corners of his mouth.

The only thing that played at my lips was a smirk. "Yes, unfortunately, Junior's the one your father called when he turned me in to the zoning people."

"Oh, yeah, that's right. I'm sure Junior took a lot of pride in harassing you. He's always been a twerp."

"I had to make a couple of trips to the courthouse to straighten it all out. Evidently, Junior didn't leave much of an impression on his co-workers because they didn't know him. Of course, by the time we got to the bottom of all of it I was on the verge of murder. I've since come to regret my overreaction to the matter, but I can't take it back." I took a big bite and chomped thoughtfully.

Swallowing, I continued, "You should have seen his face when I told him he needed to get his own personal name. You would have thought I'd thrown cold water on him."

"Oh, Lord. I can imagine. When we were kids, he always said some day he was going to change his name so he'd stand out in a crowd. We parted ways because of his name."

Interesting. I raised my eyebrows and looked at him, waiting for an explanation.

"When we were about sixteen, I told him that being a junior was like being a wart on his dad's butt. Meek little George Bigham, Jr. beat the stew berries out of me." The smile he'd been flashing faded. "He has a wicked side. That was the last time I talked to him until I called him and told him that I'd grown several inches taller than him and now outweighed him by about twenty pounds and for him not to bother you about the wrecker anymore, even if Dad did call again."

I saw sadness inch its way across Arch's face. Placing my hand on his arm, I hoped he'd realize I, too, missed Pete, the old nitwit.

God rest his soul. Petey eyed me skeptically. As if I'd been burned, I jerked my hand away.

"Do you like my daddy?" Petey asked.

"I don't really know him very well." *Well, that was awkward.*

"What do you want to know about him?" The girl bounced in her chair like she had a spring attached.

My gaze snapped to Arch. He was enjoying my discomfort, and his smile had returned. Two could play this game.

"How old is he?" I sneered at him.

"I'm not sure. I know he's old, but he has his own teeth." I wanted to pinch her apple cheeks. She was too adorable for words.

"Can I check them out?" I looked at the handsome man across the table from me. He exaggerated his grin, exposing his pearly whites. "If I count the rings around them, will I be able to tell how old you are?"

"I'm a man, not a tree." Arch mocked indignation. "I'm thirty-four. How old are you?"

"Thirty-two."

"You said that so quick, you must be proud of it." He took another bite of pizza.

"With the way my luck runs, I'm just glad I've survived to this age." Arch and I laughed.

"Was that funny?" Petey's green eyes shone brightly.

Her father nodded. She laughed with us. I couldn't remember the last time I felt so comfortable in the presence of a man. Maybe the fact that we had his father in common, and maybe since we were going to discuss the business of my buying his house, put our relationship in a plastic bag. We could both see through it.

I realized Arch and Petey were staring at me. I jumped into action, closing the top of the empty pizza box.

"Well, how much do you want for the house?" I gathered the remnants of our dinner and threw them into the trash can.

"I've been giving that a lot of thought. I'd feel guilty unloading this place on a single woman with all the repairs it needs. So, I've decided to fix it up, then have it appraised by the bank. They'll loan you more if I spiff it up some."

"I don't expect you to do that. Just sell it to me, then I'll take care of the repairs myself."

"My heart won't let me do that. If I wouldn't be in your way, I'd like to work on some of the things over the next few weekends."

I didn't know what to say. Would that jack the price of the sale up? Was that the motivation behind it? Or, do they really make men with that much compassion for other people? Not! "I really don't want you to do that."

"I insist." He glanced at Petey. "We insist."

The sweet girl nodded. "We insist."

"It's your house. I can't stop you from working on it. Or, force you to sell it to me. So, have your way with my precious home." I bowed my acceptance.

"Good. I'll start on some of the repairs on Saturday." Arch motioned to his daughter. "Time to go, Sweety Petey." The girl twisted her lips into a pout and shrugged. Hurrying, with her pigtails bouncing, past her dad, she waited at the front door in the living room.

"She's a great kid," I said.

"It could have been a tough job raising her alone, but I think she's taken pity on her poor old dad and made it as easy as possible."

"How old was she when her mom passed away?" I'd gathered from a conversation I'd had with Pete Fortney that Arch's wife had died several years ago. I hoped it had been long enough that my question didn't strike sensitive nerves.

"Petey was three months old. Her mother was on her way to work and had just dropped Petey at day care."

That would have been over ten years ago. A slight cloud of regret veiled his expression.

"Nola, that's my wife, was late. She ran a stop sign on 440. A four-by-four hit her. She died two days later."

"Was that at Clemmons Road?" As I remembered a young woman, pale and badly injured being loaded into an ambulance, I swallowed hard. She'd called for her baby.

"Yeah." Arch realized I might remember the accident. "She drove a Honda Civic."

"That's too many cars ago for me to remember the exact ones, but the truck was red and the car was dark green."

"Tahitian green." He cocked a crooked smile. "So, you picked up the wrecked vehicles?"

"One of the first ones I ever worked." His relaxed nature told me it was okay to talk freely. "I saw them put her into the ambulance. I prayed for her daily, and I called the hospital a couple of times to find out about her. I even talked to her husband. I guess that would have been you." Nervously, I smiled.

"I'm afraid I don't remember that. Too many things going on and so many calls." He shrugged.

"Dad. I'm waiting here. It's getting late and *one* of us needs our sleep." Petey stood in the kitchen doorway.

"Yes, I do." With his arm on his daughter's shoulder, Arch walked to the door.

"I'll be here early Saturday morning."

"Okay." Yuck. Other than sleeping, I hated doing anything *early* Saturday morning.

After they left, Nola's face haunted me. Normally, when I arrived on the scene of an accident, if someone was hurt, they had already been transported to the hospital. She'd been one of the few I'd actually seen seriously hurt, and she'd left an impression on me. Now, to know her husband and the baby I heard her call for in her last hours of life, shrouded me with sadness. Strange, how life twisted . . .

The ringing phone pulled my mind from its morbid corner, a place I normally steered clear of. "It's your dime," I said into the receiver.

"How are ya?" Jeff asked.

"I was just thinking about you." He couldn't prove I wasn't.

"Did it involve massage oil and a mink glove?"

That image would leave a mark. "No, but I'll file that under *Possible*. Mary Lou has invited us to dinner Saturday. Can you make it?"

After a second or two of silence, I assumed he was checking his calendar to see if anyone, other than me, wanted to see him naked. "I can make it, but it'll have to be an early evening. I have to drive to Atlanta afterward."

There was so much I didn't know about Jeff, like why he would have to drive to Atlanta late on a Saturday night. I also didn't know if I had a right to ask. Of course, right or not, I'd ask anyway.

"What's in Atlanta?"

"My mother. I promised I'd go to church with her on Sunday.

She's being presented with an award for Mother of the Year. So we'll all be there. My brother the lawyer. My sister the teacher. My other sister the mother of six. And me, the paper mill worker. I don't think she's ever mentioned to her church organization that I'm also a male stripper."

"If they knew, they'd probably take away her plaque." I chuckled. "Okay, pick me up at six. You might want to eat a little before we go to dinner at Mary Lou's. She said something about making a new recipe from the Roadkill cookbook she got as a wedding gift."

"That is a joke, isn't it?" Did Jeff's voice tremble?

"Uh, yeah. Sure." *If that's what you want me to say.*

The next morning, Friday, Bobby's last day at work and at my house, started out normal-strange, strange, strange.

Donna called requesting a tow truck. Her daughter, Pam, had locked herself inside her mom's car and refused to open the door.

"What do you think we can do about that?" I asked.

"I want you to tow the car to her daddy's job. He'll get her out of there."

"You are kidding?" I looked around the office. "Am I on Candid Camera?"

"No. I'm serious, you twit. Get someone over here. I'm getting ready to call AAA to see if they'll cover the charges."

Twit. She called me a twit. "We'll be right there, doo doo head." Guess I told her.

Linc and Bobby went together. When they returned, both looked like they'd been tangling with a wildcat.

"What the heck happened to you two?" Pop snorted.

"Donna rode with us in the wrecker. When we pulled into the parking lot, her husband came out, took his key, opened the door, and took the girl out." While he talked, Bobby tried to straighten his clothes. Linc just continued to shake his head in dismay. "When Udell saw Donna slide out of the wrecker, he went wild. He said that she could have gotten Pammie out of the car, but that evidently Donna wanted to ride around town sandwiched between two studs."

My gaze snapped to the disheveled, anything but studly, men still trying to get themselves together.

"Has Udell had his eyes checked lately?"

Bobby shot me a killer look. He held his dangling shirt pocket in place with one hand, giving the appearance he was about to recite the Pledge of Allegiance.

"His eyes appear to be fine. He popped Donna soundly up side her head. Then, lanky here," he hooked a thumb at Linc, "decided he'd protect her."

I looked at the our new wrecker driver. "I assume you discovered the hard way that Donna didn't need protecting."

"Yes, ma'am, I did."

"But not until I had to get into the action." Bobby combed his hair back into place.

Just then, Tom Mason called.

"Bertie, we need a wrecker out at the bridge that goes over the creek. Right at Black's Fish Camp. A car went over the bridge onto the boat ramp parking lot below and the boat it was hauling is lodged on top of the railing. It doesn't look none too steady, so hurry."

Bobby and Linc headed to the old fish camp. I called Mary Lou and told her Jeff and I would be at her house about six-fifteen Saturday evening. I tried to find out what we would be dining on. She insisted it was a surprise.

The drivers had been gone about an hour. Pulling a boat off a railing might be a challenge to Bobby, but I had a lot of faith in Linc's recovery ability. Surely, they would be along soon.

At that moment, Tom Mason pulled to a stop in front of the office and climbed out of his cruiser. Our wrecker parked beside him. Linc got out, but I didn't see Bobby. When they came inside, I hurried around the counter to meet them.

"The other driver you have," Tom said, "isn't he your brother?"

"Yes, do we look alike?"

"No, but there are other family resemblances." He smirked.

"I'm really sorry, Miss Bertie. It just slipped." Linc's blanched skin sported sweat drops.

Panic grabbed me by the throat. "What slipped? Where's Bobby?" Good Lord. What had happened to my brother? Linc's face paled even lighter. I thought he might faint.

"He's going to be okay, but he'd walked down under the bridge to decide the best way to roll the wrecked car over," Tom began.

"I was hooking the chains to the boat on top of the bridge. Somehow, it slipped and fell down." Linc slumped to a nearby seat.

"Fell? Fell where?" Terror paralyzed me.

"It fell on Bobby. I'm so sorry."

"Is he dead?" I screamed.

"No, he heard it coming and dove for cover. It fell on his legs. We're pretty sure he broke both his ankles."

"Oh, my God. He won't be able to dance."

Tom stared at me with his mouth open. "Well, there's that too, but my first thought would have been that he won't be able to walk. But whatever tweaks your cheeks."

With that, Tom left me to console Linc who now blubbered into his hands. I rubbed his back. It seemed like such a minor thing, but evidently it opened a door for him. He threw his arms around my waist and buried his head against my stomach and sobbed openly.

I felt like joining him. Tom had said that Bobby would be okay. I wasn't sure I'd be. Did this mean my brother wouldn't be going home? He'd stay here to recuperate? Please, no. Say it isn't so.

What kind of demon had possessed my heart? My brother lay in the emergency room with two broken ankles, and all I could think about was that he wouldn't be leaving my home to dance with his wife.

Dang, on top of that, whether it was a wrecker, plane, or boat, I could also see the family resemblance.

On Saturday morning, Estelle arrived around eight o'clock to take possession of my brother. You know, the one with two broken ankles. With my hand still in a cast, I helped load Bobby into the car and his wheelchair into the trunk. My sister-in-law glared at me, then climbed into the driver's seat and drove away. Surely, she didn't blame me for the pathetic state in which I'd returned her husband. When the boat fell on him, I wasn't even on the scene. Until Bobby could drive again, I got to keep his car. Maybe Estelle was unhappy because I got the best end of the deal.

Jeff picked me up at six for our dinner at Mary Lou's. Standing next to the handsome hunk, I knocked on the door. Rex greeted us. He ushered us into their living room. A crash sounded from the kitchen.

"Oh, my God. What's happening?" I rushed toward the sound. "Jeff, old buddy, if I were you, I wouldn't go in there." Rex flopped onto the sofa. My date joined his host.

"Cowards," I called over my shoulder.

In front of the fridge, Mary Lou, on her knees, chased baby pickles which had scattered from a broken jar. "Well, there goes the dinner."

"Pickles? Was that the main course?" Oh, me of little faith.

"No, but once things start going wrong, it's usually downhill all the way for me." She rose and threw her gatherings into the trash. I mopped up the rest of the juice.

The smoke detector blasted through the room. While I clasped both hands over my ears, Mary Lou jerked open the oven door. Smoke billowed out. I rushed to the window over the sink, opened it, and barely made it out of her way before she dumped a flaming piece of beef into a pan of sudsy dish water. The fire, along with our dinner, had been doused.

"Told you." Unruffled, Mary Lou rinsed the soap from the roast, put it in another pan, and placed it back into the oven. "I'll just reheat it a little. Can you set the table with only one hand?"

"Sure. It doesn't hurt that much; just awkward sometimes." I reached to open the dishwasher. Sticking out the side of it was an electrical cord. Slowly, I eased the door open, then followed the cord to a crock pot nestled inside. "Mary Lou, honey. You didn't wash this in here, did you?"

She looked surprised at my question. "Sure. Rex said I shouldn't get the plug wet. The directions didn't say how to wash it." She tapped her finger to her temple. "But I figured it out." She smiled so widely, I didn't have the heart to tell her. I just hoped she wouldn't get electrocuted the next time she plugged it in. The first chance I got, I'd alert Rex.

Once dinner made it to the table, everything else went really well. The roast was perfect. Maybe giving it a bath had tenderized it. The conversation covered a wide variety-Rex and Mary Lou's baby, Bobby's accident, my accident. I noticed we talked about everything but Jeff. Any question we asked about him bounced in a different direction.

"How'd you escape the bonds of matrimony?" Rex took a drink of iced tea.

"My wife was in a car accident." The sadness in his eyes made the rest of us uncomfortable.

"How 'bout them Braves?" Rex yanked the subject in a different direction.

"Do you live here in Sweet Meadow?" Mary Lou handed Jeff a big piece of chocolate cake straight from the Piggly Wiggly bakery.

"Yeah. I don't get to see many of the Braves' games. I've been working a lot of overtime or I have a party to dance at almost every night."

Okay. Jeff was a widower who worked at the mill, stripped for money, lived in Sweet Meadow somewhere, had beautiful blue eyes and great looking buns. That's all I needed to know.

Mary Lou went to the kitchen to get Rex some more tea. I leaned close and whispered to him, "Your crock pot has water in it."

He stole a quick glance over his shoulder. "She's just a little bloated from being pregnant, but she'll be all right."

My eye twitched for a second. I rubbed it and tried to keep my voice to a whisper. "Please stick with me on this, Rex. I said crock pot, not crack pot. Mary Lou ran it through the dishwasher. You might want to check it out before she uses it again."

"Oh, okay. Actually, I think I'll get rid of it. She made moo glue gai pan in it yesterday."

"You mean moo goo gai pan." I corrected him.

"No, I ate it, remember. It was moo *glue*."

We were laughing when Mary Lou returned.

"I heard that." She set the tea down, then sucker punched Rex in his arm. "Now tell Bertie how much you ate."

A smile played shyly across his lips. "Two plates. I also had two plates of sticky rice. I think my insides are stuck together."

Mary Lou smacked him again, then joined in our laughter.

Jeff walked me to my front door. The moonlight shone all around our front yard. I had an eerie feeling someone was watching us.

"Would you like to come in?"

"I think I'd better get on the road to Atlanta. Your friends are nice people."

"Thanks. I think so too."

Jeff moved closer to me. I concentrated on aligning my lips with his. Should my nose go to the right or the left? Should I put my arms around his neck or his waist? I should have chewed a mint. I strained to see the look in his eyes, but they were shadowed. Finally, I could feel his breath on my mouth. I met his with eagerness and waited for the fireworks.

They didn't come. The magic I'd imagined would happen with our first kiss never materialized like a white rabbit from a top hat. Dang. He had all the right things going for him. All his parts appeared perfect. But, he kissed like a guppy. And, I would know. When I was five, Bobby convinced me that if I kissed our guppy, Bart, he would turn into candy. I did. He didn't. But Jeff vividly brought back the memory.

As I ran my unbroken hand over his broad, well-built chest, I decided I could learn to live without fireworks.

"When are you coming back from Atlanta?"

Jeff ran his hands down the length of my back, then pulled me against him. "I'm taking the day off Monday and staying there with my mom. Then I'm dancing at the Women's Club in Marietta. One of the ladies is retiring after ten years as the president. They want to do something special for her."

"Like what? Give her a heart attack?"

Jeff chuckled and gave me a peck on the cheek. I heard a rustling in Barbie's tree. Surely, it was the wind. She didn't usually hang out there this late in the evening. Probably a bird.

"I'll call when I get back to town. Good night."

From the doorstep, I watched Jeff back out of the driveway. As I turned to go inside, two shining eyes glowered at me from Barbie's tree. I couldn't believe she was up there at this time of night spying on me while I was guppy kissing.

I made my way to the side of the house, turned on the water at the garden hose, then walked like I might be going to tend to my dead grass. When I came within squirting distance of her branch, I pulled the nozzle and sprayed water into the tree.

A vicious, hissing critter sprang from the leaves and landed near my feet. I screamed and ran toward the house. With each step, my feet sprang out in front of me like a drum major leading a band. At one point, I glanced over my shoulder to see if the creature was in hot pursuit. His eyes glowed from where he'd landed under the tree.

When I reached the front door, I braved a harder look. An opossum slowly moved from my yard toward the road. With each step, he appeared to wince with pain. *Is nothing safe around me?*

First, I turned off my weapon of choice, the water hose, then fumbled my way into the house. I hoped the poor opossum would be okay.

Chapter 12

Monday morning I drove Bobby's car to the garage. Linc was already there waxing Melinda's bright red hood.

"Pop in the office?" I paused by the wrecker.

"Haven't seen him yet."

I glanced toward my parents' home right next door. My dad carefully made his way from the front porch. When had his peppy step turned to a slow pace? When had it become obviously painful for him to bend to pick up the morning paper? When had he gotten old? It appeared to have happened overnight.

"Morning, Pop. You're late. Are you feeling okay?" I unlocked the office door and waited for him to catch up with me.

"Of course I'm okay. Can't a fellow be a few minutes late without everyone fretting over him? Jeeze, first your mother, now you." Pop scooted past me.

I guess we all have an off day now and then. Without a moment's hesitation, my father flipped through the work orders lying on his desk. He pulled one from the stack.

"Call the parts house and get me what I need for this Buick." He thrust the paperwork into my hand. "Oh, Bobby called last night. He made it home okay. Estelle is fussin' over him like a mother hen. He loves it." Pop laughed all the way into the garage. I watched him from the door. Before long, he had parts flying from under the hood of a Buick. Everything as usual, including his whistling louder than the air compressor clamoring in the corner.

I shrugged and went back into the office to call the parts house. While I waited for them to answer, I locked the receiver to my ear with my shoulder. Using a plastic ruler, I tried to relieve the itch inside my cast. Hopefully, it would come off next week.

Finally, the parts house answered.

"Hey, Joe. I have an order for you." I hoped Joe Richardson, owner and operator of Joe's House of Parts, and a New York transplant, would just take my order and skip his usual habit of tossing horse puckets.

"Yo, Bertie. How ya doin'?"

"Fine. I need . . ."

"I know what you need, doll, and I'm just the man to give it to you."

"Where's Constance? I'll give her my order." Asking for his wife usually put Joe in his place.

"Gone to her sister's. That leaves me free as a bird. Have dinner with me and you can pick the place. The sky's the limit. Denny's? Waffle House?"

"Joe. Take my order or I'll switch to Monroe's Auto Parts. They'll give me a better discount anyway."

"Oh, Bertie, where's your sense of adventure? I can take you places you could only dream of."

Denny's? Waffle House? Be still, my heart. "Do you want this order or not, Mr. Lewd and Lascivious?"

"I went to school with them," Joe announced.

"Who?" I rubbed my temple to ease the nerve twitching a happy rhythm in my eye.

"Sharon Lewd. Anne Lascivious." He hee-hawed his annoying donkey laugh.

When I didn't say anything, he finally relented. "Okay. Okay. What'd you need?"

I rattled off my order and hung up the phone. Shortly, it rang again. There'd been a wreck at the intersection of Franklin Road and

21st Avenue. I dispatched Linc, then began paying company bills.

Minutes after he left, Linc radioed back to the office. "I used the last ticket in my book last night."

"You don't have time to come back. You go on, I'll bring you a new one." I grabbed a fresh invoice book from the supply cabinet, told Pop I was leaving, jumped in my loaner car, and headed to Franklin and 21st. As I pulled onto the shoulder of the road, an ambulance sped away. Linc had already backed up to one of the vehicles and was hooking it up. When he saw me, he came over to my car and took the ticket book. I started rolling the window back up.

"Hey, Bertie." Tom Mason waved frantically and ran my way.

I rolled the glass back down. "Yes, sir?"

"Here." He thrust a plastic baggie filled with ice toward me. "Get this to the emergency room at the hospital, ASAP."

"I'm not UPS, but I'll do it." I took the cold package and laid it on the seat next to me. "Did the hospital run out of ice?" I smiled at him.

"The man who just left in the ambulance lost a finger in the accident. We didn't find it until they'd left." He slapped the roof of my car and backed away. "Hurry; they need it right away."

I glanced at the ice bag next to me. Good Lord. I had a finger as a passenger. Shivers climbed from my toes and shot out the top of my head. Surely, my hair was standing on end. I was afraid to steal even the slightest peek at the bag with the finger. What if it beck-oned to me? Instead, I sped away from the accident scene, trying to make the car go faster than the seat next to me where a body part lay. I didn't even know who the finger belonged to. Every thirty sec-onds, my whole body shuddered violently.

I skidded to a stop at the emergency room door. Looking around, I hoped to find someone who would retrieve the parcel next to me. When I didn't see anyone who could help me, I knew I'd have to do it myself. Pinching the smallest amount of plastic I could and still be able to lift the bag, I carried it into the hospital

People bustled by me, not paying any attention to the fact that I carried some poor soul's finger. I tried to get someone to listen to me, but they appeared too busy for the likes of me. I knew time was of the essence. I approached a nurse who sat behind a tall counter.

"Nurse, I have a finger for you." I dangled the bag almost di-rectly over her head.

"Lady, I have a finger for you too. Don't go away." She rolled her chair next to a man, also behind the counter. I only heard parts of her conversation.

". . . looney bin." Her words floated to me. She and the man looked my way.

"No. I mean I have a finger in this bag. It belongs to a man who was just brought in from an accident." Panic filled me. I visualized being placed in a straight jacket and hauled away, never to be heard of again. The scariest thing was, I had no one I could call to verify I wasn't crazy. My body began to twitch and shudder. I must have been a sight to the medical personnel behind the counter.

Suddenly, another woman snatched the finger from my hand. "They're waiting for this in OR." She ran down the hallway.

I practically ran to my car. Once there, I locked all the doors and breathed a sigh of relief. That was too close for comfort.

I have a love-hate relationship with my hair. I fret over it for long periods of time, waiting for it to grow. Then one day I look into the mirror and my auburn curls have reached the exact length needed to look good all day long. Even before I go to bed on my Perfect-do Day, I'm amazed at just how nicely it frames my face, highlights my blinding smile, emphasizes my sparkling eyes, and doesn't detract from my slightly turned-up nose.

When I awake the following morning, my hair is straight, weighted by split-ends, and I have a huge zit on the end of my nose. Turned up right there for everyone to see. I then have to get my hair cut and the process starts all over again.

After the finger thing, most of my week was like waiting for my hair to grow. Slow moving. Wednesday night choir practice had been canceled because Homer King had taken a short hiatus. Everyone, except me, discussed the fact that no one could handle choir members the way he could. I would have loved to have told them I didn't like the way he handled me, but I couldn't find it in my heart to attack the man in his absence.

I missed the time I used to spend with Mary Lou before she became a wife and now spent a lot of her time practicing to be a mother. After Wednesday night service, I followed her home for a cup of coffee. Rex, the heathen, hadn't gone to church. We found him watching a science fiction movie, complete with aliens and busty women. Rex had fake, pointed rubber ears attached to his. At least I think they were fake. Who knows? After all, we were talking about Mary Lou's husband.

"How are you doing, Rex?" My inquiring mind wanted to know.

"Shaba legu nunu." He formed a fist with his thumb pointing up and his pinky pointing down.

"Shave your legs, to you too." I made the same formation with my free hand, then lightly tapped my knuckles to his. I guess that was the handshake used on his planet. He went back to watching his movie.

I followed Mary Lou into the newly-painted nursery. It was beautiful. Pastel colors formed the background for lions and tigers and bears (oh, my) to dance along a flowered border. She already had all the furniture necessary for little Ponder or Petunia, when he or she decided to arrive.

"Look at this." Mary Lou lifted a large doll from the crib. Gently, she placed it on the dressing table. "We've been practicing changing diapers and bathing the baby."

"We? You mean Rex, too?"

"Yeah." She smiled widely. "He really needs practice. He heard Star Trek come on last night, and he drowned the poor thing." Mary Lou appeared truly worried.

"Honey, he'll be a good daddy," I tried to reassure her. "Just don't have the television on during bath time."

On Friday, the doctor rid me of my cast. It felt good to wiggle my fingers and scratch my arm. On the drive back to the garage, I was scratching and wiggling while I waited at a red light. I felt someone staring at me. Carefully glancing to the car on my right, I saw Joe Richardson from Joe's House of Parts waving at me by wiggling his fingers the same way I'd been doing mine. The light changed. I sped to the next intersection only to be caught by the light. Joe screeched to a stop beside me. I looked his way. He winked and made kissy motions in my direction.

I rolled down my passenger window. "You pervert," I hollered.

"Come on Bertie. One drink at the Dew Drop Inn? I'll give you a bigger discount on parts."

I had to laugh at Joe. He really knew how to sweep a gal off her feet. "Go home to Constance, you dirty old man." The light changed. He stuck his arm out the window and waved. I tooted the horn, then made a left-hand turn. Why couldn't I have a younger, single man clamoring for my attention?

Yeah, there was Jeff, but he wasn't making big moves to be with me. I'd seen and heard from him very little lately. Oh, sure, he'd called on Wednesday evening, just as I snuggled between the sheets. He said his company had sent him to Brunswick for an emergency at the paper mill there. He'd been hired to dance at the Patio Lounge in Casper for a bachelorette party on Saturday. So, he wouldn't be back in Sweet Meadow until the first of the week.

In two hours, I'd be free for the whole weekend. Unless I changed my mind about going to the Dew Drop Inn with Joe, I'd have no one to spend my time with.

By five o'clock, I still had no major events scribbled in my Day-Runner, and Joe was out of the question. I rode over to the Bull's Tail barbeque place, ate dinner, then took as many back roads as I could find between Shafer and my street. When I'd killed all the time I could without getting arrested for loitering, I went home.

Arch Fortney stood beside my house, bending at the waist and holding the garden hose over his head. Water poured over his hair and across his bare back. He must have been working in the yard for hours. He'd cut, trimmed, mulched, and weeded the whole area, making it worthy of being next door to Barbie's highly maintained lawn.

I approached him. Apparently he didn't hear me coming. When he straightened, he jumped, flipping the hose in my direction. Water splattered the front of my T-shirt. I sucked in a startled breath.

"I'm sorry." Arch tossed the hose aside and hurried to turn it off. "I didn't know you were here."

Water trickled from his shoulders, down his chest, making a happy trail into his waistband. Did I find that sexy, or had the dampness of my shirt caused me to shiver? Either way, I took a long, hard look at Arch Fortney. The fading sunlight deepened the golden flecks in his dark eyes. His shirtless, medium-framed body bubbled with well-rounded muscles. Nice, comfortable build. Suddenly, I realized Arch was watching me ogling him. Reluctantly, my gaze returned to his face. He sported a bright, toothy smile. Petey had informed me they were his own teeth. At this stage of my life, I'm not sure if that mattered, but somehow I took solace in knowing that.

"I see you got your cast off." Arch took his shirt from a nearby hedge and pulled it over his head. "How does it feel?"

"Good." I wiggled my fingers in the air. "Really good." I looked around the yard. "Everything looks great out here."

"Thanks. I think I've done all I can. Water and Mother Nature will have to take over from here." He appeared to be having trouble keeping his eyes off my wet T-shirt. I glanced down. The white cotton plastered itself to the top of my breasts, which appeared to be shoving their perky selves out of the top of my bra. There wasn't much left for the imagination.

Shyly, I crossed my arms over the medium-sized critters. "Are you through? With the yard, I mean."

Arch cleared his throat. "Yeah. I'd like to do some plaster work inside tomorrow, if it's okay with you."

"Sure. After nine, okay?"

"See you then." Arch took his leave.

Filled with giddy excitement, I hurried into the house. My heart pounded so hard I could barely breathe. Although I didn't have a clue what to do about it, I'd been hit by a thunderbolt named Arch Fortney.

Through the rest of the evening, I analyzed how I could have such strong feelings for a man I hardly knew. Arch and I had a connection because of his father. His father was a nutcase. Arch had a sweet daughter. I knew less about being a mother than Mary Lou. He was a very nice man. So was Jeff. Arch was handsome. Jeff was gorgeous. Arch was handy around the house. Jeff was never around the house. For every plus, there was a negative.

By late in the evening, I'd decided the shock of being doused with cold water had short-circuited my think tank sending sparks in jagged directions. Arch had no interest in me. At thirty-two, it was time I gave up my quest for marriage, home, and hearth.

Locking my determination into place, I decided to quit acting like a dog in heat and to be happy with my occasional dates with Jeff, my Wonder Dancer. Maybe a cold shower would cool me off.

I'd just stepped into the dark bathroom. Before I had time to flip on the light, I heard a thump against the side of my house, right under the shower window. I tiptoed into the hallway and made my way to my bedroom. Slowly, I drew the curtain back. Shrouded in darkness, I peeked out. It was impossible to look down the side of the house without opening the window. Just as I thought I'd have to go to another room, a man passed right in front of me. Fear shot through me. Anger followed close behind.

No one had any business traipsing around my house. I knew that if the man was walking toward the back of the house, I could get to the front door without being seen. Fueled by rage that some-one dared to invade my space, I slipped out of the house into the darkness. Making my way to the side yard, I ducked behind a huge shrub and peeked around it. I could see the outline of a small man making his way in my direction.

At that exact moment, a segment from Oprah flashed through my mind. She'd once interviewed a romance writer who said that heroines who go out into the darkness when they know a killer is on the loose, or in my case, they're being stalked by Jack the Tipper, are too dumb to live. I should run. Run for my life. Too late. The man walked right past me. Like a linebacker, I tackled him. We tumbled to the ground, knocking the air right out of me. I pummeled him around his head. Where was that cast when I needed it?

The man, who was lying on his stomach, covered his head with his arms. All the while, he screamed bloody murder. Straddling his back, I pushed myself to a sitting position.

"Who are you?" I yelled at the bellowing man.

He quit screaming, then talked into my freshly cut grass. "I'm Jack."

"What do you want with me?" I pinched his ear lobe.

"I needed to get more information so I could write you another letter."

I smacked him across the back of his head. "Why? What have I done to you?"

"You humiliated me," he whined into the crook of his arm.

"Humiliated you? I don't even know you." I punched him on his shoulder blade.

"Yes, you do."

I raised my hand to strike him again. He bucked me off. "Quit hitting me."

He jumped to his feet and started to run. I lunged and wrapped my arms around his legs. Down he went with a thud. As I straddled him again, he rolled onto his back. I pinned his arms to the ground.

"I had brothers, buster. So, don't mess with me," I growled at him.

Suddenly, sirens wailed a short distance away. A police cruiser skidded to a halt. Carl Kelly rushed toward us.

"What's going on?" He latched hold of my arm and yanked me into the air. I landed on my feet beside Jack the Tipper. Carl pulled him up too. Once the headlights from the police car lit his face, I couldn't believe my eyes.

"George Bigham, Jr., what are you doing sneaking around my house? You said your name was Jack. You said I humiliated you. When did I do that? Are you nuts?"

"Do you ever shut up?" The man's face turned dark red.

I sucked in a sharp breath. "Why, you little pip squeak, I oughta . . ."

I thrust forward. Carl snatched me back. I heard a crunch and thought my neck might have snapped. I'd stepped on the officer's foot.

"You, sir, tell me what's going on." With his free hand, Carl pointed at George.

"Yeah." I pulled away from my captor. "What's going on with you? And who is your psychiatrist? I'll give him a call."

He looked at Carl. "Can you shoot her, please?"

"Hey, you nitwit." I jumped at him again.

"Knock it off, or I'll run both of you in."

I huffed my response. The officer and I stared at George Bigham, Jr. alias Jack the Tipper.

"She humiliated me in front of my co-workers at the court-house. They haven't had an ounce of respect for me since the day she was there." He curled his upper lip at me.

"They didn't have any respect for you before I got there. That's why they didn't know who you were when I was looking for the person who signed that letter you sent me. You twerp."

"Bertie, could we keep this on an adult level?" Carl asked.

George stuck his tongue out at me. I retaliated by sticking mine out at him.

"Well, it got so bad after that day, I decided to take your advice."

Puzzled, I glared at him. "What advice?"

"You told me to get my own name. You said for me to slather it on a big old name plate. Well, I did just that. Jack. That's me.

Jack. It has a bold ring to it. I'm Jack. Get out of my way. My name's Jack. Wanna make something of it?" With each statement, George/Jack puffed his chest out a little further. He looked like a rooster strutting through the barnyard. At any minute, I expected him to crow.

"It sounds like I did you a favor. Why have you been stalking me? And what the heck did you mean by those stupid tips?"

"I just wanted to scare you like you did me the day you hollered at me. Worked. Didn't it?"

"You're a few feathers short of a hummingbird, aren't you, George?" I asked.

"My name is Jack." He puffed up like Foghorn Leghorn.

I looked at Carl. He and I both were rubbing our temples. "Are you going to take Jack to the chicken coop?"

"Well, he didn't really hurt anybody. He just gave you some tips. Granted, they were the stupidest tips I've ever heard, but relatively harmless."

"I can't believe my ears. He trespassed and wrote some weird things to me. He threatened to fry me like a crispy critter."

"I did not. I warned you not to leave your blow-dryer by the sink. It was friendly advice."

"Add Peeping Tom to that list. He looked in my bathroom window."

"Bertie, I think Mr. Bigham was just a little overwrought. He was exercising his freedom of speech. Don't make me have to do all that paper work just to haul his wimpy carcass in."

"I'm not wimpy," Jack protested.

Carl lifted my arm to feel my muscle. "Did this little lady just take you down, or what?"

Jack dropped his gaze to the ground. I stood toe to toe with the big policeman and shoved my hands to my hips. "What about my rights? I've watched enough Matlock to know that if his exercising his rights strikes fear into my heart, it is harassment and that is an infraction of my rights. Give me the papers, I'll fill them out."

Carl Mirandized Jack, cuffed him, then hauled his whiney butt to the cruiser. By the time the officer got his prisoner into the back seat and walked to the trunk to retrieve the yards of paperwork he'd have to fill out, my adrenalin packed its bags and went to wherever adrenalin comes from to start with. I began feeling sorry for Jack. He did seem a little pathetic.

Down the street, standing under her porch light, I saw Helen Weidemeyer. I felt sure she knew it was her brother I was having arrested. My shoulders slumped.

"Carl." I strolled across the yard toward him. "I've changed my mind."

The officer and his prisoner breathed audible sighs. Carl

nodded and set Jack free.

"If you come back in my yard or bother me in any way, I won't change my mind the next time."

Jack nodded, then skittered down the street like a scared rabbit toward his sister's house. When he got to her porch, dear sweet Helen grabbed her brother by the ear and dragged him inside. That poor guy had taken a beating that night. In my heart, I knew I'd made the right decision.

Chapter 13

Saturday morning, right outside my bedroom window, birds sang their happy tune. As I snuggled deeper under the sheet, their cheerful trill vibrated its way into my heart. *What a great day.* I didn't have a cast to lug around. Jack the Tipper had been captured and rehabilitated in one grand slam, so to speak. My yard looked great, and the deed to Pete Fortney's old house would soon have my name on it.

Roberta Eunice Byrd, Home Owner. Sounded good to me.

Someone knocked on my front door. I glanced at the alarm clock. Red digital lights blinked at me. The electricity must have gone off during the night. I threw back the sheet, swung my feet to the floor, and hurried down the hallway. The battery clock on the kitchen wall read nine-fifteen.

Even though I knew it would be Arch pounding on the door, I peeked out the window. He saw me. I jumped back and glanced down. My long football shirt covered only a minimal part of my bottom. I cracked the door just enough to look out.

"I just woke up. Count to twenty, then come on in. I have to get dressed."

Arch nodded and smiled. "Okay."

Hurriedly, I turned back down the hallway.

"Five-ten-fifteen-twenty." Arch counted. The door squeaked open.

I hadn't quite made it to my room. With the straight view he had from the front to the rear (that was not an intended pun), I'm sure he saw a lot of flesh peeking from under my flapping shirttail.

"Smart aleck," I called over my shoulder. I could hear him chuckling all the way from the living room.

I grabbed my clothes and ran to the shower. In record time, I dressed and joined Arch in the kitchen. He had made coffee and was just buttering toast. Was this what it was like to have a man around the house? Nice.

After we ate, I helped Arch plaster a few nail holes and paint baseboards in the kitchen, living room, hallway, and bathroom.

In the spare bedroom, we moved all the unopened boxes to the center of the room, then worked our way around the walls. By the time we got to my bedroom, it was well after lunch, and we were both hungry.

"I make a killer tuna salad. How 'bout it?" I asked.

"Great." Arch covered the paint cans and gathered the brushes.

When he'd finished cleaning up, I had sandwiches and chips ready. I set the plate in front of him. "Bon appetit."

"Ah. You speak French." Arch smiled.

"Yeah. And you just heard my complete vocabulary."

"You're right. This is a killer tuna sandwich. What's that crunchy stuff in it?" Arch removed the top piece of bread to closely examine the internal workings of my epicurean masterpiece.

"Water chestnuts." I straightened in my seat and inhaled a breath of pride.

"Oh." His face reddened.

"Oh, what?" Fear shoved my pride aside. Something was wrong.

Arch rose from his seat. "Don't panic. I'm highly allergic to water chestnuts." He clutched his throat. His face moved from red to slightly purple. He went out the front door.

When I caught up with him, he was standing halfway between my house and his car, inhaling deep breaths and releasing them slowly.

"What should I do?" My voice squeaked with fright.

"It'll pass." His voice squeaked more than mine, caused by his throat swelling shut.

"My God. I didn't mean to kill you." Tears streamed down my face.

"I didn't eat enough to kill me. It's already passing." Arch hugged me to him. He did sound better, and he'd quit gasping for his last breath. Relaxing, I sank into his embrace and rested my head against his chest. Was that his heart or mine pounding so loudly?

Slowly, I looked up at him. As I watched with eyes wide open, he lowered his lips to mine. The velvety warmth of his kiss flowed through my entire body. My eyes lazily drifted shut. In the darkness behind my closed lids, I saw the prettiest fireworks display anyone had ever seen. I never wanted to move from Arch Fortney's arms.

"Hi there, Bertie. I'm up a tree." At the top of her lungs, Bats-in-the-Belfry Barbie was singing a tune. "I see you and that man k-i-s-s-i-n-g." As if I were going to burst into flames, I jumped away from Arch. With the heat raging through my body, catching on fire could be a possibility. I pressed my hands to my face, hoping to cool my flushed skin.

"Ah. Is that a Dingy Bird I hear warbling from the tree?" Arch laughed.

"Absolutely." At least Barbie gave us a distraction from the awkwardness that usually follows a first kiss. "Are you okay?"

"Couldn't be better." He smiled widely. "Oh, you mean from the water chestnut. Yes, the episode has passed. I know better than to eat without analyzing beforehand, but I never heard of putting them in tuna. For future reference, I'm allergic to pineapple too."

"I'll remember that. Could I fix you something else to eat?"

Before he could answer, Barbie jumped down from her branch. "Thanks, but I already ate lunch," she hollered from under the tree, then walked across her lawn and into her house.

I shook my head. "That is one strange woman."

With his arm around my waist, Arch urged me toward the door. Once there, he stopped. "I think I've done enough today. I'll be back after work Monday to finish the baseboards in the master bedroom. Will that be convenient?"

He was leaving. My head and heart spun at the same rate of speed. "Yes, Monday will be fine." He turned to leave. I felt like tackling him from behind and begging him not to go, but his rapid departure told me he'd kissed me under duress. He thought he was dying. Since that didn't happen, he'd rethought his rash action.

"Look at him," I mumbled under my breath, "he's struggling not to run to his car."

So as not to be forced to watch what Arch must think of as his narrow escape, I went into the house. Maybe the lingering paint fumes would take me away to my tropical isle where I could loll for the rest of the afternoon with Antonio, the cabana boy. There, I could push Arch back into his proper place as my landlord. The heaviness in my heart told me that would be a big job, but I'd give it a try, despite the fireworks.

Around four on Saturday afternoon, I decided I really wanted to see Jeff. Surely, my desire to be with Arch was born out of loneliness. Jeff had said he had to dance at a lounge in Casper, which was two hours away. I called my bestest friend to see if she'd go with me.

"Hi, Rex. Is Mary Lou home?"

"She sure is, and she's crankier than an old pregnant bear. Hang on. I'll get her." Her husband clanged the phone against a hard surface.

In the background I could hear him talking to her. "Snooky, your partner in crime is on the phone."

"Don't touch me, you self-centered baboon."

"I was just trying to help you up."

"If I need help, I'll ask Donna's husband, since you and she seem to be occupying each other's time."

"Snooky, you know that's not true. Your hormones are just running rampant."

Rex must have been standing directly over the phone, because I could hear him loud and clear. I had to strain to hear Mary Lou. And strain I did.

"I'll show you what rampant hormones really mean, Mr. Don Juan." Evidently, Mary Lou had made her way to the phone. I had to move the receiver from my ear to keep from going deaf.

"Hello," she snapped.

"Is this a bad time or would it be okay if I come over and get my head back? You know, the one that you just bit off?"

"Sorry, my rudeness was intended for that doo-doo head I call a husband." Her voice trembled slightly.

"What in the world is going on over there?" I asked.

"It's a long story. Let's change the subject. What are you up to today?"

"Well, I was thinking about driving over to Casper and watching Jeff dance at a bachelorette party. Want to go with me?"

"I'd love to go to a strip joint with you." She spoke loudly for Rex's benefit.

I started to explain the difference between going to see Jeff strip and a strip joint, but suddenly, I couldn't figure out what that would be. "I'll be there in thirty minutes."

In less than twenty minutes, I showered, dressed, and headed out the door. I couldn't wait to hear what Donna had to do with Rex and Mary Lou. When I arrived, he told me that Mary Lou would be ready in a few minutes and for me to make myself at home.

I flopped onto the sofa and waited for him to take his seat in his recliner. "What's she so upset about?"

Rex shook his head. "I ran into Donna at the convenience store this morning. Her kid, Randy, had locked himself in the car outside the store and wouldn't let her in. I took her over to where her husband works to get his key. Before I got back, Millie had called Mary Lou to tell her she'd seen me and Donna riding together in my truck." Rex looked perplexed.

I knew Mary Lou better than anyone in the world. After dating Rex for more than ten years, she and I both knew he'd never have anything to do with Donna, of all people. I chewed my bottom lip to keep from smiling. Mary Lou had an ulterior motive for sizzling Rex with the branding iron. I couldn't wait to hear her side of the story.

"I'm ready." My very pregnant friend entered the room. "Don't wait up for me, Casanova."

I beat her to the door. "You go back there and tell your hubby bye-bye." She started to protest. "Go." I pointed to the man with the sad eyes and rubber pointed ears. Jeeze, couldn't he have waited until we'd gotten out of the house to put those stupid things on? Mary Lou gave him a fleeting kiss on top of his head.

"Love ya, snooky." Rex did have the good sense to wait until we left before he turned on the sci-fi channel.

"Okay, what's the deal? You don't believe for a minute that Rex and Donna have a thing going. Why are you treating him like that?" We were already speeding along the highway headed toward Casper and Jeff, my dancing hunk.

"I read a book that said expectant daddies feel neglected because of all the attention the mothers-to-be get."

"So, you decided to ridicule him so that he feels better about his life when you quit? Is that the method behind your madness?"

"Of course not."

"Of course not. Then, what would be your reasoning, O wise one?"

"He thinks I'm jealous. I wish you could have seen his chest puff up when I told him I'd kill Donna before I let her take him away from me."

"You want him to think you're crazy . . . about him, that is, yet you make his life miserable. What's that all about?" My gaze drifted momentarily to Mary Lou's beaming face, then back to the road.

"Well, if I play up the jealousy thing too much, he might start running around just to get attention, then I'd have to kill him. So

I make him feel important in stages, one of which consists of him groveling and doing major butt kissing. When I get home tonight, I'll tell him that if he promises to never let it happen again, I'll forgive him and bear his children." She glanced at her tummy. "Or, at least, one of them. I'm not making any promises after this one. We'll kiss, have great make-up sex, then live happily . . ."

"Hold it. More than I want to know." I stopped her in the middle of her ever after.

For the rest of the trip, we chatted about anything and everything. Seemed like old times. We zipped through McDonald's and ate as we drove along. At the edge of Casper, I pulled next to a phone booth. While Mary Lou hunted a bathroom, for the third time since we left Sweet Meadow, I looked up the number of the Patio Lounge. I called to get directions.

We were only four miles from the place. We found an empty table in the back near the bathrooms. I couldn't see the dance floor very well, but Mary Lou wouldn't have far to go. When the time came, I could stand on a chair. The cocktail waitress informed us there was a two drink minimum for everyone. Mary Lou ordered two cokes, but was told that didn't count. So, I would have to drink her alcohol in addition to mine. By the time the obvious bride-to-be and her entourage arrived, I had two beers under my belt. The women's laughter shrilled through the bump, bump, bump of loud music. My head could very well have exploded at any minute.

"Excuse me." An attractive blond lady towered above me. She leaned closer to me. "Is this seat taken?" She pointed to an empty chair next to me.

I shook my head and slid the chair toward her. She sat. The waitress slapped a napkin on the table.

"I'll have a Rob Roy," the blonde said, placing her order.

That'll put hair on her chest, I thought, which was almost completely exposed. If she leaned any farther forward, there would be an accident of the Double D size right there on the tiny table. If that woman ran braless, she'd blacken both her eyes. I glanced down at my own chest. *Pathetic.*

I crossed my arms and pretended to watch the dancers on the floor. Mary Lou excused herself for the second time since we'd arrived. She'd just come back to the table when colored lights began dancing around the room. The sound changed from a live band to a pre-recorded drum roll. The dance floor cleared. Everyone gave their undivided attention to the smoke-shrouded silhouette on the bandstand.

A huge fan blew the smoke away. A bright spotlight illuminated a cowboy with boots, hat, holster, no shirt, and cutoff shorts. On the first loud downbeat, he strutted off the stage and began gyrating his major body parts. Deafening whistles and whoops rang out. All that commotion for the cow"boy" I intended to take home and turn into a man.

Jeff danced and sweated his way around the perimeter of the dance floor. He flaunted his wares in the flushed faces of women who probably had husbands and kids waiting at home for them. By this time, everyone had jumped to their feet. Blondie and I were both standing on our chairs. Mary Lou chose to just stay seated.

Suddenly, Jeff looked my way. I could tell he was straining to look past the lights into the darker area where I stood waving at him. Finally, he waved back. My heart pounded with each musical beat. A few seconds later, he blew a kiss in my direction. Blondie reached out in front of me, grabbed my imaginary kiss in her grubby little fist, kissed her knuckles, and tossed it back to Jeff. He grabbed at the air, then tucked his catch into his purple pouch.

Blondie smiled widely, oblivious to the fact that she'd stolen my kiss. Mary Lou had seen what had happened. She handed me my fourth beer. I took a big gulp and handed it back to her.

"Thanks." I yelled above the clamor. She acknowledged me with a slight wave.

When I looked back at Jeff, he was rapidly thrusting his pelvis in my direction. Not the most romantic thing I'd ever seen, but at this point I'd take what I could get. I raised my arms above my head and did a little shimmy. I almost fell off the chair.

The blond Amazon woman with the big boobs however, had great balance. Her gyrations matched Jeff's to a "T" and she didn't even have to hang onto the wall behind her. On top of that, hers and Jeff's gazes were locked as if held together by Super Glue. Wonder how he'd like some glue in his pouch?

I took a deep breath. Jeff made part of his living by exciting women with his almost naked body. If I intended to have a relationship with him, I'd have to accept that fact. I gave him a loving wave and climbed from my chair. From my seat, I had a perfect view of the spectacle Blondie was making of herself. Mary Lou and I exchanged glances, then rolled our eyes in agreement.

The music ended. The woman nodded in Jeff's direction. Because of the people standing in front of me, I couldn't see his response to her. Finally, she climbed down and took her seat next to me.

"The dancer sent this to you." The waitress brought a drink and set it in front of Blondie.

"I think he meant that for me." I pulled it to me.

The woman snatched it back, spilling a lot of it over her hand. "It's for me." She licked the liquid from her skin. She looked like a cat.

I tried to grab it again, but she moved it out of my reach. Mary Lou pulled my arm back.

"Calm down, Bertie. I'm sure it's just a misunderstanding. He'll straighten it out." She nodded toward a back door.

Jeff, dressed in only his G-string, made his way toward me. His smile told me he was glad to see me. Before he could get to me, Blondie wrapped one arm around his neck and let her hand trail down his tight tummy.

I yanked her away from him. "Unless you work for UPS, you better not be checking out his package," I bellowed much louder than necessary since the band had not started playing again.

The woman looked stricken, but for only a brief second. She lashed out and boxed my ears. A ringing sound played over and over again. Mary Lou pulled me back and placed herself between me and the woman.

"She's had a little too much to drink." Mary Lou giggled nervously. "This is her boyfriend and she gets a little out of control when another woman sticks her hand into what little bit of clothing the man has on."

The blonde stepped closer to Mary Lou, almost bumping her tummy. "Well, I'm his wife, and I get a lot out of control when Jeff has a girlfriend."

Dead silence befell the whole lounge. Dead silence that is, except for that infernal ringing in my ears. We all turned to look at Jeff, my wonder dancer. Even in the dimly lit room, you could tell all the blood had drained from his face. His mouth was agape. Was he drooling? Mary Lou snatched up our purses and dragged me toward the parking lot.

"I'll bet he fills that pouch with a rolled wash cloth," Mary Lou said, trying to make me feel better.

"I never got the chance to find out." Mary Lou drove me home. I stared out the window into the lonely, dark Georgia night.

Mary Lou dropped me at my house around eleven thirty. I nuked a cup of leftover coffee and tried to undo the results of the four beers I'd drunk with wild abandon. So much for the plans I'd had to prove my attraction for Arch Fortney was purely from not seeing Jeff in a while.

I'd seen Jeff all right. A couple of hours ago he'd been dancing, for all intents and purposes, butt naked in front of several dozen drooling women. Yet, I foolishly believed him to be my private dancer. I had company in that dream. His wife.

I'd asked him if he was married, and he'd deliberately lied to me. The dirty dog.

Now, I faced a real dilemma. Instead of feeling sadder than Emmett Kelly looked, my mind insisted on focusing on Arch. How I could easily talk to him about anything. The way he made me laugh. Not to mention the fact that he kissed like I imagined Patrick Swayze would. Arch made me see fireworks.

And what was that all about? Just because he thought he was dying didn't give him license to ravish my lips and jumpstart my heart, then run away like I'd given him rabies. He forced me to seek out Jeff, and look where that got me.

Of course, had I not surprised Jeff and found that he'd lied to me, the dirty dog, who knows how long things would have gone on with us. Or, worse yet, how far things would have gone. I could be sitting there at that very moment saying, "I slept with a married man." As it stood now, all I really could say was, "A couple of times, a married man put me to bed with my clothes on."

Actually, I really should thank Arch for that. I glanced at the clock. Ten minutes until twelve. I dialed the number.

"Hello." Arch's husky, sleep-laden voice drifted through the receiver.

"Thank you," I whispered.

"You're welcome."

Gently, I replaced the phone on its cradle, then went to bed and fell into a sound sleep.

The next morning, Mary Lou and Rex picked me up for church. After the services, I went by their house and got my car. I spent the rest of the day feeling out of sorts, torn between being happy that the men in my life had all gone from princes to toads, most with just one kiss, and feeling extremely alone and lonely.

The last few months had been hectic and unpredictable. Maybe I needed a real vacation. Not my usual one where I pretended to be having the time of my life on a tropical isle with Antonio, the cabana boy.

Pop had Linc, who could handle any job that came his way. I hadn't been able to drive the tow truck since I got run over by a plane and my brother Bobby had been there. The trauma of all that was enough to weaken Hercules. That was what had my world in a downward spiral. After a week of rest and relaxation, I'd be good as new.

On Monday morning, I arrived at the garage just before Pop. As I walked across the parking lot, I looked at the old metal sign with the name *Byrd and Sons*. Between the bleaching sun and peeling paint, the words were hard to read. The whole place needed to be spiffed up. When I got back from my R&R, I'd take on the task of giving the garage a facelift.

Thinking of painting reminded me that Arch would be at my house after work to finish the baseboards. While he completed the repairs he insisted on doing, it would be a good thing for me to be out of his way. And him out of my moon-struck sight. Something about the man caused my blood to race through my veins, chomping up my emotions like Pac-Man gobbling dots. Yet, other than one kiss, which he seemed to immediately regret, he'd shown no signs that I caused even the slightest ripple in him.

I let myself into the office. Yes, being away from my house while he finished up would be the best all the way around. I didn't know if I could recover from one more man and, although he appeared to be a kinder, gentler member of that species, he still fell into that category.

A few minutes later, Pop came in. "Good morning, sweetheart."

"Morning, Pop. How's Mom?" I leaned back in my chair.

"I think she's fine. You know your mom, she wouldn't complain if I found her dead." He chuckled. I did too.

"Before you start to work, I'd like to ask you something. I'd like a week's vacation. Do you think you can handle things without me?"

My father looked at me, then tilted his head to the side. I hated it when he did that. He always said he could pick up my thoughts like that. Unfortunately, he could.

"Man trouble again?" He stepped next to me and put his arm around my shoulder. "How bad this time?"

"Not too terrible. But I'm overdue for vacation, and now seems like a perfect time." I leaned against Pop's side. His touch always seemed to absorb some of the lingering effects of the doo-doo in my life.

"Well, don't you worry about it. One day some guy will come along and snatch you away from me. You just haven't found one smart enough yet. Then, I'll get to dance at your wedding." He did a little time step across the room. Pop could always make me smile.

"By the way, where are you going?" he asked.

"Mary Lou and Rex stayed in a cabin in a state park in the northern part of Georgia. I'll get the number from her and call to make a reservation. I'd like to leave in the morning, if that's okay with you."

"Of course it is." He walked back to me and planted a kiss on the top of my head.

I called Mary Lou. She dropped a brochure off for me on her way to work. The cabin looked quaint and very secluded. That's what I needed. Seclusion. Away from everything for a whole week. I made all my arrangements and left work a couple of hours early so I could get packed before Arch got to my house.

Chapter 14

From her yard, Barbie called to me. "Yoo hoo. Bertie."

I really didn't have time for her, but she ran in my direction so swiftly, I didn't have time to escape.

"I'm going to Eaufala, Alabama." This seemed to make her very happy.

"Is that your home?" I asked.

"No, I never heard of it until today. They're having a convention there, and they invited me to go."

"They? They who?" National Dingbat Society popped into my mind.

"The people on the morning news. They said there was still

room for a few more people interested in making money. I'm interested in making money. Are you interested in making money? Want to go with me?"

I glanced at my watch. I needed to get packed, but I couldn't douse her excitement.

"I'm sorry. I'm going on my own vacation in the morning, but that sounds interesting. You have a good time. Tell me all about it when I get back." I hurried into the house.

I'd finished packing and had decided to visit Mary Lou for the rest of the evening, hoping I could miss seeing Arch. Before I could get out of the house, he arrived with his daughter in tow. I guess he felt he needed a buffer between us.

Petey had a board game tucked under her arm. She smiled widely. "Want to play *Clue* with me?" She tapped the box.

"I'm sorry. I have somewhere I have to go." I tucked a stray lock of hair behind her ear. I turned to Arch. "I hope you don't need my help."

"I can manage." He shrugged, then went to my bedroom where we'd left the paint and brushes on Saturday. Petey and I trailed behind.

Inside the room, they both saw my suitcases. Arch looked at me. "Going somewhere?"

Running would be more like it. "I'm going on vacation. I'll be out of your way while you're finishing up. You'll be done by next weekend, won't you?"

His disappointment with my tone played clearly across his face. I didn't mean to sound so edgy about it.

"I'll make a point of it." Abruptly, he plucked a paint can from the floor and turned his back to me.

"Are you going to Disney World?" Petey hopped up and down.

Arch turned to her. "That's not for us to ask. Bertie said she has to leave, so why don't you help me so she can go?" Although he spoke kindly to his daughter, his undertone told me I'd been dismissed.

His name may be on the deed of my house, but I paid the rent. I'd leave when I was darn good and ready. "No, Petey, I'm not going to Disney World. I'm going here." I took the brochure from my dresser and showed her the cute little cabin I'd be staying in.

"It looks like a doll house." The girl looked at the pictures closely and handed the brochure back to me. "You'd have more fun at Disney World."

I couldn't help but smile at the child's reasoning. "Have you ever been there?" I asked.

She shook her head. "No, but Daddy says he'll take me one day."

We both looked at Arch. "I will take her one day. It's hard for a single father to take a child somewhere like that."

"No harder than it would be for a single mother," I countered his feeble excuse.

He shot me a dirty look. "Suddenly, you're an expert on the subject of child rearing?"

"No, but if you need to know about doo-doo heads, I'm your gal." I looked at Petey, who'd been watching her father and me like a fan watching a tennis match. "I've got to run. See you later," I told her.

I picked up my suitcases and carried them into the living room out of Arch's way. In the morning I'd stick them in the trunk of Bobby's car and be on my way. Rushing, I pulled open the door and came face to face with Jeff. Stepping back, I sucked in a sharp breath. "What are you doing here?"

"I have to talk to you." He pushed by me and closed the door.

"Is your wife with you?" I opened the door.

"Of course not." He closed the door.

"What do you want?" I tried to open it again, but he placed his hand against it.

"My wife and I have separated. She came over the other night to try to get back together, but I told her no."

"I don't believe you. Not for one minute. You've lied to me since Day One."

"What have I lied to you about?" Jeff was verbally raising the roof.

"When I asked if you were married, you said your wife had been in a car accident." I matched his volume.

"She had been in an accident, that very morning. She backed into a dumpster. So, you see, that wasn't a lie."

"Oh, of all the unmitigated gall, you have cornered the market." I drilled my index finger into his chest. "Now, listen to me, Mr. Purple Pouch. I want you out of my house and out of my life forever. Don't you ever come back."

"Bertie, you haven't given us a real chance. I think we could make a happy twosome."

"I see you can't count. With your wife, that would make a threesome, and I'm not into that."

Just then he saw my suitcases. "Are you going somewhere?"

"Yes, as a matter of fact, I am. I'm going to a tropical isle with Antonio."

He glanced over my shoulder. His face turned an intriguing shade of purple. "Is that Antonio?" He pointed behind me.

I spun to see Arch standing in the hallway. Embarrassed and furious, I turned back to Jeff. "No. Antonio is my cabana boy. That," I nodded over my shoulder, "is Arch, my handy-man. He does great things with his tools." I opened the door and motioned for Jeff to leave.

He did. I closed the door behind him. Collapsing against it, I thought I might cry. When I opened my eyes, Arch and Petey were watching me with great interest. I couldn't find my voice, but I did find my car keys. I left them standing there, staring. I hoped all the yelling hadn't loosened any of the shingles on the roof. That would delay Arch finishing up and moving on.

I got into the car and leaned to the passenger's seat to get my sunglasses. When I straightened, Barbie was staring in my window. I screamed. She screamed. All we needed was the ice cream. Still struggling not to hyperventilate, I rolled down the window. "What do you want, Barbie?"

"I'm going to Eaufala, Alabama. I'm going to make some money."

"You go, girl. That's a good idea." I started backing out of the driveway. "Have a great time." I waved. She skipped across the lawn. She was singing "Mares Eat Oats and Does Eat Oats and Little Lambs Eat Ivy." Or, it could have been the street song from "Carmen." I wasn't sure.

I spent the evening with Mary Lou. She was so happy, and I was happy for her. Rex watched television and, at one point, fell asleep in his recliner. He snored so loudly that Mary Lou and I moved to the back porch and sipped iced tea through straws.

"While you're gone, I want you to concentrate on getting your karma in line. According to your chart, you're overdue for true love, and it's just waiting for you to pluck it from the vine." Mary Lou knew nothing about charting one's destiny, but she was great at being a friend and giving hope when hope appeared dim.

"Thanks. I'll work on that." We clinked our glasses and toasted to my new karma.

When I pulled into my driveway, I saw two police cars at Barbie's house. I decided I'd better check it out. Maybe Barbie had fallen out of her tree.

Her husband sat on the top step of the porch, his head resting in his hands.

"Rick?" I stood on the bottom step.

He looked up. "Barbie's disappeared. When I got home from work, she was gone."

"Do you live next door?" An officer took his notebook and pen from his pocket.

"Yes."

"Have you seen Mrs. Jamison today?"

"Yes, around five-thirty. She said she was going to Eaufala, Alabama."

Rick jumped to his feet. "Why would she go there?"

I told him about our conversation. "You told her she should go?" Rick barked at me. "Why would you do that?"

"I didn't tell her to go-go. I just agreed that she should if she wanted to. You know." I hoped they did understand, because I didn't like the path this situation had taken.

"How did she go? Did you take her?" Rick stood in front of me.

"No! Of course not." I took a step backwards. "I assumed you were going with her. She said she was going to a convention where she could learn to make money."

"Make money? What does she need money for? Her father owns the third largest nuts and bolts producing company in the United States. She has all the money anyone could ever want. We just choose to live modestly because she's a little different than most socialites."

"Face it, Rickster. She's different than almost everyone." Surely, he realized that without me telling him.

Just then a cab pulled into his driveway. Barbie bounded out, paid her fare, and casually strolled in our direction. Rick hurried to her.

"Where have you been?"

"I started to go to Euafala, Alabama, but the taxi driver couldn't leave the county limits, so we went out to dinner." As the cab drove away, she waved, and he honked the horn.

"You went to dinner with a cab driver?" Rick put his arm around his wife.

"Yeah." She looked up at her husband. "I'm really tired. I'm going to bed." The filthy rich dingbat went into her modest house, leaving her hard-working husband, police officers, and her confused neighbor standing in the middle of her beautiful yard.

You would think that, in light of her father's business, someone could have given Barbie back some of her misplaced nuts and bolts.

"I don't think you should play with Barbie any more," Rick said. "You appear to be a bad influence on her."

I just looked at him, threw up my hands, and walked away.

Inside my house, Arch had left a note on the table telling me he'd be back each evening after work and would definitely be finished with everything by the weekend. If that wasn't okay, I was to leave a note on the front door telling him when he should return. I considered calling him to see if the next five minutes was too soon.

I sat straight up in my bed. Something or someone had awakened me. I wondered if Pete had come back for a visit. The phone rang. My heart leaped to my throat. "Jesus, Joseph, and Mary." The red numbers on the clock read three forty-five. This couldn't be good.

I answered the phone.

"Bertie, honey, you have to get to the hospital right away."

"Oh, my God, Mom. What happened to Pop? Is he . . . ?"

"Not yet. He's had a heart attack. They won't let me see him. I love you. Please, get here soon." She hung up the phone.

I scrambled from the covers. I wish it had only been a visit from Pete. I could handle that. I slipped back into my crumpled clothes which I had piled on the floor next to the bed. Finger combing my hair, I slipped my feet into a pair of sandals and ran to my car. Bobby's car. I wondered if Mom had called him. If not, I could do that after I got to the hospital, which was fifteen minutes away.

Getting to Pop was the most important thing. He couldn't die. What would any of us do without him? Who would walk me down the aisle? Who would dance with me at my wedding? Tears rolled freely down my cheeks.

I found Mom in the waiting room outside the cardiac unit. She looked so small and fragile. Crying had left her skin blotchy and the rims around her eyes red. I rushed into her arms, or she into mine. We clung to each other.

"Have you seen him yet?" I asked.

"Not since they took him in. The doctor was just here, trying to explain what happened. I didn't really understand. He said your dad is flutzing. Again." Mom sucked back a sob.

I drew back to look into her eyes. "Flutzing? Did you ask him what that meant?"

"I was too upset to ask anything. All I really remember is that he said your dad would be fine if he'd leave the stuffed cabbage alone."

I hoped I'd get a chance to talk to the doctor to find out what had happened. A nurse came to the waiting room door. "Mrs. Byrd, you can see your husband now." She motioned for Mom to follow. We both did.

At Pop's door, the nurse turned. "Only one at a time." She stepped aside for Mom to enter.

I paced the hallway in front of his room for what seemed an eternity. Finally, Mom came out. "He's going to be fine." She patted my hand. Her usual sound composure had returned. I took that as a good sign.

"I have to go fill out some insurance papers. They're going to keep him a few hours and run a few more tests. He'll go home in a little while." She gave me a hug. "You go in and keep him company until I get back."

When she'd walked to the elevator, I slowly pushed the door

open. Pop lay flat on his back with an IV in his arm. I stood by the bed staring at his pale face for several seconds before he opened his eyes.

He flinched. "Jesus, Bertie. You scared me to death."

"Oh, Pop. I'm sorry. I guess we're even now because you scared me to death too." I struggled to hold back my tears. "Did they tell you what was wrong with you?'

"Sweetheart, there isn't enough medical information in the world to figure out what's wrong with me. I've been this way all my life." He chuckled.

"Oh, Pop. I'm serious. Mom didn't understand what the doctor said. What happened to your heart?"

"It wasn't my heart. It was a serious case of indigestion."

"What was that Mom said about your flutzing again?"

At first, Pop looked puzzled, then laughed out loud. "The doctor said I had acid re-flux. Re-flux. Not flutzing again. Your mom's a real pip. You know that?"

I knew that and, through my teenage years, I thought both my parents were real pips. Somehow, over the last few years, Mom and Pop had become some of the most normal people I knew. I loved them and needed them in my life.

"I'm glad you're going to be all right. I knew you weren't going to die. You promised to dance at my wedding, and you always keep your promises."

Pop scooted over and patted a place on the bed. I climbed up and stretched out next to him. He cradled me with his arm, and I rested my head on this shoulder. "I'll be there with bells on just as soon as I get an invite."

"That may be a while, Pop. No one's even close to asking."

"Well, here's what I want you to do." He shifted so he could look into my eyes. "You go home, get your things loaded into the car, and go on your vacation. I promise not to eat any more stuffed cabbage while you're gone. When you get back, I'll have a big surprise for you."

"What?" I begged.

"Nope. You have to go away first." Pop kissed me on the forehead.

I snuggled closer to him. "Okay. I'll go."

Mom returned. "Is there room for me in there?" She leaned forward and kissed first me, then Pop on the cheek. "No more cabbage for you, mister. Doctor says it makes you flutz."

Pop chuckled. "It certainly does."

My parents insisted I leave on my planned vacation. Mom maintained I deserved it. Pop agreed and promised that while I was gone he'd let Linc do all the wrecker calls. It had been over two years since I'd had any real time off. Before I left, I hugged Pop and

Mom tighter than I ever remembered, and thanked God Pop would be with us a little longer.

I'd almost made it to the main lobby. "Bertie." From behind me, I heard an all-too-familiar male voice. I turned, knowing full well I'd find Lee Dew coming toward me.

His shoulder-length, mousy brown hair curled from under a Panama hat. His Hawaiian print shirt hung unbuttoned, exposing a strained T-shirt stretched across his beer gut. He wore white socks with his sandals. What had I ever seen in that man? All those years wasted on a beer guzzling, sofa lump. What was I thinking?

"How are you, sweetheart?" He tried to kiss me, but I dodged him.

"Leave me alone, Lee. I don't have the time or the inclination to chat with you right now."

"Oh, Bertie, isn't it time you and I buried the hatchet?"

"Yeah. Where is it? Your head would be a good place to start. What are you doing here anyway?"

"Annie's mom had emergency gallbladder surgery. We've been here all night."

"I'm sorry to hear that. Give her my best." I started to leave. He touched my arm and leaned closer to whisper in my ear. "Let's go to your house, take our clothes off, and rub our bodies together. For old time's sake."

I jerked away from him. The moon must have been perfectly aligned with Venus, because instead of killing the lunatic standing in front of me, I started laughing.

A kaleidoscope of visions swam through my mind: Jeff, dancing for his wife; Runaway Barbie; the shock of almost losing Pop, the joy of still having him; the exciting kiss from Arch, whom I'd mysteriously and all too quickly come to love, yet his reaction to me left me scared to death.

The mismatched sections of my life jarred uncontrollable laughter from deep inside me. Suddenly, I realized Lee was glancing nervously at people who were watching us. The fact that I was embarrassing him made me laugh harder.

Most people have a teeny, tiny bit of evil in them. Mine wormed its way from its hiding place to my lips. "Sorry, Lee." My laughter stopped cold. "I don't have sex with men who wear socks with sandals."

I spun on my heel and marched outside. The last glimpse I had of two-timing Lee Dew, his face had flamed a bright red. I, on the other hand, had finally exacted the revenge I'd plotted since the day he left me for Annie.

I smiled all the way to my car. "Bertie." I'd just opened the door when I heard Lee call my name. Doing him a favor, I looked his way. "At least my sandals match," he yelled across the parking lot.

Dreading what I'd find, I slowly lowered my gaze to my feet. Yep. There they were. Left foot, white shoe. Right foot, pink shoe. The sweet smell of revenge turned rancid. I searched my boundless bank of snappy comebacks. Ah ha!

"These are the shoes I always wear at four in the morning when I think my father's dying, you doo-doo head." I hurried into my car and headed home to get my suitcases. I needed to get out of town as soon as possible.

Before I'd left Sweet Meadow, I'd gone home, showered, left Arch a note on the front door telling him I'd be gone until Saturday. He had free run of the house every night until then. I left him the number where I'd be just in case he needed my opinion on anything having to do with my soon-to-be house. I'd managed to get out of town a little after two.

Around six, I arrived at the cabin in the wilds of north Georgia. Although it wasn't exactly the idyllic setting pictured in the brochure, it did have a certain rustic charm. What I liked most about the place was the fact that the only loons around were the birds down at the lake.

I'd taken my things from my suitcases and distributed them in the chest of drawers in the bedroom section of the one-room-plus-bath log cabin. The wagon-wheel wooden furniture had recently been re upholstered in country blue and green plaid. Matching tie-backs framed the windows. The sofa faced the fireplace which had a television in front of it. In that area, I dumped a bag of romance novels. I intended to read about what my life lacked.

In the tiny kitchen, I unpacked the essential food I'd picked up at the country store fifteen minutes from the cabin. Wine and pop-corn, mostly, with a few TV dinners. Thank heavens the short counter had a microwave. Otherwise, I could starve to death.

I slipped into jogging pants and a football jersey, pulled my hair into a pony tail, and moseyed out to the old rocker on the porch. If I leaned over the banister to the right, I had a clear view of the lake. From the rocker, I could only catch an occasional glimpse of the silvery water through the massive trees.

From somewhere in the distance, I could smell campfire smoke mixed with pine dampened with early evening dew. I sat there until the darkness stole every bit of daylight. Snapping twigs heightened my attention, and I attributed the noise to the small, very small, night creatures scavenging for food. I assumed the hooting came from the two eyes perched at the top of a nearby tree.

I thought of Barbie and wondered if Rick would really keep her away from me. As much as I hated to admit it, I'd grown quite fond of her. My natural curiosity wanted to know about her. What had caused a well-to-do, beautiful socialite to be so off balance? Unless Rick intended to follow through with his threat, I decided to make it my mission to get to know Barbie better.

I'd been sitting on the porch for about an hour. A narrow beam of light from the window spread across the wooden planks and spilled onto the pebbled walkway. Evidently sneaking up on an unaware prey, a red fox crept through the path of light. I held my breath, not wanting to frighten him. A second later, I heard sounds of a struggle and a distressed squeak. I ran into the house and slammed the door behind me. I'd enjoyed enough wildlife for one night.

I turned on the television and flipped through the channels. I found reruns on all the national stations. Infomericals on several others.

Finally, a male voice announced, "We'll return to Tuesday At the Movies after a word from our sponsors."

Great. A movie would be nice. I stretched out on the big sofa and waited for it to come back on. After several commercials, the same man said, "We now return to the Tuesday night movie *Deliverance*, starring Burt Reynolds and Jon Voight."

Not! I switched the channel so rapidly, I made myself dizzy. When my world had stopped spinning, I got up and checked all the doors and windows. Maybe I should get something to eat. Seconds away from the refrigerator, the phone rang. I hoped nothing had gone wrong with Pop. After I'd shoved my heart from my throat, I answered the phone.

"Hi, Bertie. This is Arch."

For a second, I couldn't speak.

"Are you there?"

"Yeah. I'm sorry. Sure, I'm here." *Wish you were too.* Did I think that or say that? My hands were shaking. I believed I was having a nervous breakdown.

"I need to talk to you," Arch said.

"Did you find termites in the house?" What else would make him sound so serious? He didn't know any of my family, so it couldn't be bad news about them.

"I don't know how it happened, but . . . I've fallen in love with you."

I was hallucinating. I'd sucked in too many pine tar fumes. That had to be it. "I think the altitude up here has affected my hearing."

"I'm sure I've shocked you, but I couldn't put this off any longer. It's eating me alive. I know I have no right to hope you feel the same about me, but maybe in time, when you get over the guy who was at your house the other night, maybe you could possibly think about me."

I couldn't possibly think about Arch any more than I already did. In record time, he'd captured my heart and soul. The mere thought of him hampered my breathing. And that kiss! How could I ever forget that star-studded kiss? But something inside me wouldn't let me scream all that into the phone.

"I don't know what to say." I did, but I couldn't. "Can we talk about this the next time we see each other? I need time to think about everything that's happened lately. That's why I'm up here, to sort through a lot of things."

"I hope I haven't made your job harder." Arch's caring tone warmed me to my toes.

"No. Termites would have made my job harder."

His chuckle warmed me even more. "May I call you again to-morrow night?"

"I'd like that. Good night." Arch loved me. He had said those beautiful words to me. With them came a wonderful inner peace. With a sweet feeling of happiness and country quiet, I slept like a baby.

The next morning, I woke up after ten o'clock, rested, and wondering if I'd dreamed Arch's call. After I showered and dressed in another pair of jogging pants and a football jersey, I ate a piece of microwave pizza and went for a walk. In the bright sunlight, smelling the fresh air, I knew for sure Arch's call hadn't been a dream. If I weren't afraid of scaring the animals, I would have broken into a song.

Wet grass covered the ground and moisture formed drops on the foliage. Apparently, it had rained before I woke up. Everything looked and smelled clean and fresh. I slowly made my way down the red clay path toward the lake at the bottom of the hill.

Three rowboats were tied to a small wooden dock, one's nose resting on the end of the walkout. A sign told me the boats were for Fox Run State Park's guests. One of these would be me.

I shoved one aluminum boat, the one with its nose resting on the end of the dock, into the water. I climbed in and began rowing lazily across the lake. Looking back at the shore, I could see the man who had checked me in at the office waving frantically. He motioned for me to come back to shore. I looked around and behind me. Yes, it was definitely me he so badly wanted back at shore.

I started paddling in reverse. Water swirled around my tennis shoes. Where was that coming from? I began rowing in earnest.

Chapter 15

By the time I got to the dock, water soaked the legs of my pants and lapped at my back side. The man grabbed my hand and pulled me to safety. We both stood on the dock. The boat sank out of sight.

"I'm so sorry. Since I'm a guest, I thought it was okay to take the boat." Did I have a sign on my back that said, *Bad Luck Magnet. Send it this way?*

"It's my fault," the man apologized. "I just ran to the office to get a plug for that hole. I should have put a note on it. I hope you're okay."

"I'm fine. I'll just go change out of these wet clothes." I started toward the cabin, then turned back. "Sorry about your boat."

He didn't say anything, just waved. Or, scooted me along.

I looked at the slippery, red clay path I would have to climb to get back to the cabin. Not wanting to look like more of a fool in front of Mr. Boat Man, I walked a little farther along the lake. When I came to a wooded area, I decided the ground looked solid enough to climb the incline to the cabin.

A few yards into the trees, I came to a six-foot embankment. Under normal circumstances I couldn't have climbed it, but luckily, thick roots sprouted from the dirt giving me a place to put my feet. I hoisted my backside to the flat ground above the slope. When I tried to stand, my heel slipped off the ledge. I hit the ground with a thud. It gave way beneath me, sending me sliding down the grade.

One of the roots slid under my blouse and the band of my bra, suspending me in mid air, as if hanging from a hook on a wall. My weight pulled the material of my shirt tight across my arms, keeping me from moving them.

I would guesstimate that my feet were all of three inches off the ground, but nothing I did would set me free from my captor. I heard a snap that sounded like elastic breaking. I prayed it was one of my bones instead. In a flash, my jogging pants, weighted by the heavy, wet legs, fell past my knees. Thank God, I hadn't left home with a hole in my underwear.

There I hung like a rag doll, covered with black dirt and red clay, my football jersey pulled tight under my breast, lifting and separating my boobs like no bra I'd ever owned, and my jogging pants were puddled around my ankles. "Zippity doo da. Zippity day. My, oh my, what a wonderful day." I sang to my heart's content.

I wondered if I should scream for help or just hang there until I starved to death, or I was eaten by a big, bad wolf. I mentally flipped a coin, then called out.

Mr. Boat Man found me. He pulled up my pants, which promptly fell down again.

"Maybe I should get you down first." Obviously embarrassed, he started to lift me by my waist, but when he touched my skin, he drew back as if he'd been burned.

"What's your name?" I asked.

"Buzz, ma'am." He stared at the ground and actually kicked the dirt with his toe.

"Well, Buzz. I need your help and the only way you can do that is to touch me. So, go ahead. You have my permission." I nodded rapidly, hoping to encourage him to get me the heck off my hanger. With every move I made, the root dug deeper into my flesh. Pain radiated through my shoulder blades, yet I had to put Buzz at ease before he'd help me.

He cleared his throat, grabbed my waist, lifted me, and almost threw me to the ground. I pulled my pants up and gathered them around my waist. "Thank you." I breathed a sigh of relief.

"Should you be out here in the woods alone, ma'am?" Buzz stepped out of my way.

Even though I'd been wondering the same thing, I refused to admit it to this man I hardly knew, even if he had seen me in my underwear. "I'll be fine. I've just had a bad morning. Thanks for your help." I started back to the original path.

"Do we have your next of kin listed on your registration card?" Buzz wanted to know.

"I'll be fine. I promise." I hoped that was true.

"There's a first-aid kit in the medicine cabinet. You have blood on the back of your shirt."

"Thanks." I twisted my shoulders. Hopefully, the blood wasn't as bad as the pain indicated.

I climbed the path to the cabin without the slightest slip. Why had it looked so hard earlier? Who knows why my world rotates like it has a flat tire? Thump. Thump. Thump.

For the rest of the day, I stayed close to the cabin. I read for hours and finally dozed off around dusk. The phone woke me around nine o'clock. It was Arch.

"I just finished painting all the rooms. Everything is cake frosting white except for your bedroom. It's Aphrodite blue, just like you wanted."

"Good. I can't wait to see it. Now, can we close on the house?" I asked.

"Sure. I want to put up new gutters and paint the shutters, then we can have it appraised." For a short while, we listened to each other breathe. "How's Petey?" I broke the awkward silence.

"She's bugging me to take her to Disney World, thanks to you." He feigned indignation.

"Maybe you should take her."

"Would you go with us?" He really wanted me to go with them. I heard it in his voice.

"I think I'd like that. By the way, Arch, I'm not nearly as heart-broken as you might think about the guy who was at my house the other night. I'm not sure what I really felt for him."

"Could it have been lust?" I could tell Arch had a hard time asking that question.

"It might have been, but we didn't know each other long enough for me to act on that." I emitted a nervous giggle.

"Just exactly how long does it take you to act on something like that?"

"That would depend on the man. If he made me see fireworks

just by kissing me, and he loved me, I'd probably act pretty quickly."

"When I kissed you, did I make you see fireworks?" Arch asked.

Should I answer that question? Was I letting things go so fast that I would only get hurt? After all, there was the small matter of my bad luck magnet working overtime lately. Oh, heck, besides my heart, what did I have to lose?

"Yes, you made me see fireworks, but then you ran like a scared rabbit."

"I didn't want to leave, but I'd put you in an awkward position by kissing you in front of your neighbor. I thought it best if I just left."

"That woman is the first course in a squirrel's dinner. She roosts in that tree like a vulture waiting on roadkill. I don't know how she can sit up there like that."

"I do." Arch had my attention.

"How?" I asked.

"When I was a lot younger, Dad nailed two tractor seats on one of the big branches. My friends and I used to pretend we were airplane pilots. It's actually quite peaceful and comfortable up there. You should try it some time." He chuckled.

"That takes some of the mystery out of it, but she watches every move I make. Sometimes it unnerves me." I sighed heavily.

"Well, the way you jumped that day, I thought maybe you didn't appreciate my kissing you in front of your neighbor."

"I don't care what she or any of my neighbors think about me. If the time were right, I'd kiss you on the courthouse square."

"I'd rather you kissed me on the lips." We both laughed.

As usual, I was struck by the comfy, cozy feel of our conversation. I hugged a throw pillow to my chest and basked in the best part of my day.

"Are you enjoying your vacation?"

Ugh. I didn't even want to think about that, let alone relate the events of my vacation. "If the rest of it goes like today, I would have been better off staying home and taking my imaginary voyage to my tropical isle with Antonio, my cabana boy," I said, swiftly changing the subject.

"How's the weather there?" I asked. Arch honored my silent request and didn't probe further about my vacation. He answered my mundane questions with enthusiasm.

"Before we hang up, I want to say something." Arch turned somber. "I told you I love you and I do, but I won't say it again until you're ready to hear it. I guess you might say, the ball's in your court. I have all the time in the world."

We hung up. Since I'd napped earlier in the evening, I had no hope of going to sleep any time soon. With it being so late and not a thing on television worth watching, I couldn't keep my mind off

Arch. He loved me. No matter how hard I tried to convince myself that happiness was not in the cards for me, I had to admit I loved him too. Did he have any idea how much jeopardy he placed himself in by being associated with me? Did he know that when I wasn't maiming myself, I was sending out my bad luck vibes to anyone in my path?

With a final, deep sigh, I decided Arch was a grown man. Surely, he knew what he was letting himself in for. I hoped he did, anyway.

I went through the whole next day without incident. Buzz came by to make sure I was still alive. I assured him I was doing just fine, but just in case, I stayed close to the cabin and read and thought about Arch and Petey. I also thought about me some day being Bertie Fortney. Finally, a man who wouldn't give me a stupid name.

That evening, while I waited for Arch to call, my fervor multiplied in its intensity. My heart beat wildly against my chest. I giggled. A lot. By the time the phone rang around seven o'clock, I couldn't contain myself.

Instead of saying hello, I blurted out, "I love you, Arch, more than I ever loved anyone in my life." I waited for his declaration of undying love. Instead, the line went dead. We must have been disconnected. I waited for him to call back. He never did. I sank to the sofa and wondered what I'd done wrong this time.

Around eleven o'clock, just as the movie *Love Story* ended and I had dried my eyes with my shirt tail, someone knocked. I hurried across the room.

"Señorita Bertie." A man with a Spanish accent spoke loudly from the other side of the door. "Estoy Antonio, su cabana boy."

"Who in the world?" I flipped on the porch light and peeked out the kitchen window which gave me a direct view of the porch. There I saw Arch Fortney, dressed in nothing but a skimpy swimsuit. A towel hung over his shoulder and down his bare chest. In his hands he held a bottle of wine and suntan lotion.

I swung the door open and dragged him inside by his Speedo.

On Friday morning, I awoke in a cabin in the back hills of Georgia with the most wonderful man in the world beside me. Arch's rhythmic breathing, laced with only a slight amount of nasalness, draped me with the most pleasant fuzziness I'd ever felt.

When he'd arrived at my door the night before, I couldn't have been happier had it been my long-time dreamboat, Antonio. The surprise overwhelmed me. I'd thrown myself against his bare chest and giggled like a school girl.

I glanced at the clock next to the bed. Ten o'clock. Arch and I hadn't gone to sleep until after four in the morning. I'd learned a lot about him during our talk until the wee hours of the morn. After he'd called me and I'd proclaimed my love for him, he'd made swift arrangements with his next door neighbor to take care of Petey overnight. He threw a few things into a bag, then called the principal of the middle school to tell her she would need to get a substitute for his summer school class on Friday. In less than twenty minutes he was winging his way to "the woman of his dreams." His words, not mine.

I scooted out of bed. I would have loved to have slipped into Arch's shirt like they do in the movies, but he hadn't worn one when he arrived and me in his Speedo wouldn't work at all. I pulled on my jogging pants and football jersey, then padded to the kitchen area which was ten feet from the bed.

As quietly as possible, I put on a pot of coffee. When it was done, I poured a cup and went to the front porch. Sitting there looking at the beautiful greenery and wild flowers, feeling the heat of the summer sun, I knew the winds had changed, bringing me only good luck from this day forward. I felt it in my bones.

Arch left at noon. He had to get home to Petey. We made a date to go to dinner on Saturday night. I had one more day of my vacation, then I would head home the next morning. Even though my hiatus had gotten off to a rocky start, it certainly had perked up. Not wanting to challenge the fates, I stayed close to the cabin and enjoyed the afterglow of Arch.

That evening, I called Mary Lou and told her she'd been right about things changing for me. I filled her in on most of the details.

"So why haven't I met this mystery man you've fallen in love with?" Mary Lou's inquiring mind wanted to know.

"I've thought I loved him for a few weeks now, but you know how things go with me. I really didn't believe it was happening. I was afraid he wouldn't feel the same."

"You always sell yourself short. You're a terrific woman, and any man would be lucky to have you." She moved her mouth away from the receiver. "Wouldn't they, Rex?" I could tell she was shoving the phone at her poor, unsuspecting husband.

"That's right, Bertie, what Mary Lou said," Rex stammered.

"Thanks, Rex. Go back to your television." I appreciated his and Mary Lou's support.

"By the way, Bertie." Mary Lou had taken the phone back. "I need you to do me a favor."

"Sure. What?"

"Before you go home in the morning, will you come to my house? It won't take long, and I can fill you in on the details when you get here. Do you have any idea when that will be?"

What a strange request, even for Mary Lou. "I should be at your house by noon. Will that be soon enough, or is it an emergency?"

"No. Not at all. But it's important you come here before you go home. I have to show you something." Mary Lou giggled.

"What are you up to?" I grilled her.

"Tomorrow, my dear friend. Have a safe trip." She hung up.

Arch called and we whispered and cooed through our phones for a while before we could force ourselves to hang up. Tomorrow couldn't come fast enough.

I got to Mary Lou's house at high noon. Rex let me in and told me she was on the phone and would be right with me. Less than a minute later, she joined us.

"Okay, what's this all about?" I asked.

Mary Lou and Rex looked about to burst. "We want you to follow us somewhere, but we have to wait ten minutes." Mary Lou pointed to the sofa. "Sit down and tell Rex about your night with Arch."

"Mary Lou," I gasped. "I'm not going to tell him anything of the sort."

"Okay, then tell him about your vacation."

As I told him how much I enjoyed the beautiful countryside I'd just left, I tapped my fingernails on the arm of the sofa. As he listened, he tapped his too.

"Come on. Come on. You're driving me crazy. What's going on?" I rose from my seat.

Mary Lou glanced at her watch and shrugged. "Okay, let's go."

I followed them along the familiar route. We appeared to be going to the garage. I hoped nothing was wrong with Pop. Of course not, Mary Lou had been way too jolly for that. My intuition was right. We pulled into the parking lot of the garage.

There were several cars there. The whole place had been re-painted. New awnings covered the windows. There were plastic red, white, and blue flags flying from the top of the building. The scraggly old sign had been replaced with a brand new one. It read *Bertie's Garage and Towing.* Even the new wrecker had been relet-tered with my name on it. Linc rubbed a rag over the writing. He also pointed to tiny letters above the door handle. *Melinda.* Pop had given my wrecker a girl's name. I couldn't believe my eyes.

I scanned the half dozen or so faces staring at me. My parents were standing together. I ran to Pop's open arms and hugged him and Mom at the same time. "I don't know what to say."

Mom rubbed my back in that special way she had of making me feel like her little girl. "Say thank you," she laughed.

I pulled back to look at Pop. "Of course, thank you, but what does this mean?"

"It means it's all yours. You've worked hard for it. You deserve it. And I want to go fishing in the daytime and dancing with your mom at night. I've worked for that. I deserve it."

The whole crowd broke into laughter. Pop looked at someone behind me. "This fellow agrees with me that you can handle the place."

I turned around. Arch, with Petey standing next to him, smiled widely. My heart flipped over. The day couldn't be more perfect. I reached out, took Petey's hand, and pulled them closer.

"I'm so glad you've met my parents, but when did you meet them?" I didn't know if my heart could stand any more surprises.

"About ten minutes ago, when we got here. Mary Lou called this morning to tell me about your surprise and invited us to come. I've been here long enough to introduce myself and agree with your father."

"Ah, you're very smart, agreeing with my family."

Mary Lou joined our circle.

"I didn't think you knew Arch," I said.

"Until I talked to you on the phone last night, I didn't. This morning, I looked up his number in the book and called him." She looked at Arch. "It's nice to meet you." She gave him a hug. "And you too." She hugged Petey.

The little girl looked up at her dad. "You said that if I swallowed a watermelon seed, my belly would blow up." She pointed at Mary Lou. "Is that what hap . . ."

Arch placed his hand over his daughter's mouth. I'm not sure if I laughed harder at Petey's question or at the red flush covering Arch's face. He'd have to get over being so easily embarrassed. Lord knows, it followed me wherever I went.

There are no words to describe the euphoria I felt being surrounded by the most important people in my life, seeing their smiling faces, hearing their words of encouragement and love, and knowing Mom and Pop had placed their lifelong work in my hands. The combination bound my heart with happiness and, at the same time, terrified the stuffings out of me. Evidently, it showed on my face.

Pop hugged me to him like he used to when I was young and something scared me. "You know this business better than I do. You'll do a great job with it," he whispered in my ear. "I love you, and you'll always be my heart."

I would have told him I loved him, too, but the words were lodged in my throat. I'm sure he knew, though, from the sob and whimper I emitted.

Everyone went home, leaving me standing in the parking lot of my own business. "Bertie's Garage and Towing." I said the words aloud, but I had trouble believing them. I thought about the last few days. If I could believe I had a date in about five hours with Arch, who loved me, then surely I could believe I was now an en-tre-pre-neur. Jeeze, if I couldn't say it, how could I believe it?

Chapter 16

I pulled into my driveway and took in the look of my new yard. In my absence, Arch had done more clearing, clipping, and watering. He'd also planted pink and white inpatiens next to my house. My excitement to see the newly-painted inside would have to wait a few minutes. Barbie was walking across her lawn toward her tree. I remembered my promise to myself to get to know her better. Now would be a good time.

"Hi, Barbie. How are you?" I joined her in the shade of the big oak tree.

"I'm fine. I thought I'd take a break and hang out up there for a while." She pointed to a huge limb. For the first time, I looked closely at the branch. Sure enough, there were the two tractor seats Arch had told me about. "Would you like to join me?"

I'd been experiencing such a stellar day, I decided to test the fates and see if I could climb up there and not fall and break my neck. "Sure, why not?"

I followed her around to the back side of the tree. Leaning against the trunk was a ladder. After Barbie had easily climbed to the branch and situated herself in the far seat, I followed her. I gave myself a mental head slap. It hadn't taken any levitating powers to get up there like I'd imagined my dingbat neighbor used to fly to her roost. I could picture Arch and possibly Jack the Tipper playing pilot and co-pilot. I felt like asking the tower for clearance myself.

"This is kinda fun." I smiled.

"You don't think I'd be doing it if it wasn't, do you?"

She had a point. "Of course not."

I told Barbie about the big surprise my parents had just given me and how my brothers had never wanted any part of the family business.

"I never had any brothers or sisters." Barbie's expression saddened. "Maybe if I had, my mother wouldn't have fixated on me so much."

"How did she do that?" Inquiring minds . . .

"I came from a well-to-do family. We had preset standards, and

I had to live up to all of them. Somewhere in my teens, I realized it was my mother who made the rules. I had to wear my hair a certain way, wear only the finest clothes, have no friends that weren't considered the upper crust."

"I guess I wouldn't have been invited to high tea, huh?" I tried to lighten the sullen mood Barbie had moved into.

"No, you wouldn't have. I didn't want to be invited either. There was always a ball, or a party, or a charity function I had to attend, smile, and pretend to like.

"And the boys. Good Lord. To meet my mother's criteria, their ancestors had to have floated over on the Mayflower. And she had ways of finding out these things. Thirty seconds after hearing me mention a boy's name, she could tell you what he had for breakfast that morning and what time he last went to the bathroom." Barbie laughed, but I could tell her statements carried a lot of hurt, and possibly anger.

"How did Rick slip past her?" I hoped that wasn't insulting.

"He didn't. His father worked for the accounting firm that handled my father's affairs. I met him at a fund raiser. We looked at each other and, I swear, lightning bolts flew across the room. Mom must have seen them too." Barbie swung her dangling legs back and forth.

"Why? What happened?"

"Before I went to bed that night, she came to my room. She said I'd made a spectacle of myself with that common trash, and she forbade me to have any further contact with him."

"So, you just ran away with the CPA, you hussy?" I giggled.

She did too. "No, I wouldn't go against my parents' wishes, no matter what. Rick did climb onto my balcony like Romeo a few nights, but I'd never have run off without my parents' knowledge."

"Then, how did all this happen?" I twisted slightly in my seat to face Barbie.

"I like you, Bertie. You've treated me really nice, despite my weird behavior."

"I like you too. I wish I could say you're a diversion from my norm, but unfortunately, I can't say that. Well, tell me. How did you get to marry Romeo?"

"My mother and I were at a tea one afternoon. One of my friends accidently spilled her chocolate cake in her lap. On the way home, my mother ranted and raved. She startled our chauffeur so badly, he ran off the road. Then, she really pitched a fit. She told me that if I ever did anything so stupid, she'd never take me to another function." Barbie started laughing. "Yippee, I thought. Is that all I have to do to get out of going to those stuffy gatherings? Drop cake in my lap?"

"That should have been a piece of cake. Pardon the pun."

"You're pardoned, and it was. The very next time I dropped cake, then the next I laughed at inappropriate times. Once I sang "I've Got a Lovely Bunch of Coconuts" during an afternoon harp recital. My parents took me to several doctors. I was diagnosed with a mental disorder that would make me really nuts if I had to pronounce it."

My new friend placed the back of her hand on her forehead and faked a swoon. "I was unacceptable for society. God only knew what I'd do next to embarrass my wonderful parents. By the way." As if summoning a headwaiter, she snapped her fingers in the air. "Where's that CPA when we need him?"

"So, you were allowed to marry Rick?"

"If I'd go quietly into the dark Georgia night, which was what I wanted to do to start with."

Even though she'd made my mind and my eyes spin, I enjoyed her laughter. She didn't sound nuts at all. "So, you do nutty things to keep up a front?"

"Sometimes. When I think about it."

"But you sit in a tree, Barbie. Isn't that nuts?" I asked.

She motioned toward me.

"I guess your point is well taken. This is a nice, quiet getaway. Maybe I could rent your tree on Tuesdays and Thursdays for myself." I swung my feet too.

"Feel free to borrow it any time, my friend."

I still had a few questions for Not-So-Nuts Barbie. "Why do you sit out here at night?"

"After a hard day at the office with all those checks and balances, Rick likes to unwind in front of the television and watch nature shows. Personally, I can only watch so many monkeys pick bugs off each other and eat them before I have to say there must be something more interesting for me to do.

"So I sit in my tree. When I was a girl, I had our gardener nail a platform in a tree in our western garden. I actually climbed up there two times before Mother found out. She told me it was an unladylike thing to do and I mustn't ever do it again. Now, I do it anytime I please." Rebellious Barbie smiled widely.

Suddenly, sadness filled her eyes. "Mother fired the gardener. I still miss him. He taught me to love flowers and to work in the dirt. Another no-no, according to the rules."

I sat there for a few minutes, taking everything Barbie had just told me into the crevices of my mind. What a sad way to find happiness. I guess the bottom line would be, she did find it.

One more thing bothered me. "You don't really hang out in your attic, do you?"

She looked puzzled.

"You know, like the day you saw the man sneaking around my

house," I explained.

"Oh, no. I happened to be putting some clothes in storage up there that day. It was a fluke, but it helped reinforce my craziness, didn't it?"

"Pretty clever. I gotta get inside. I have a date tonight."

"With Mr. Fortney's son?"

"Yeah. How did you know?"

She placed her hand to her temple and fluttered her lashes. "From my tree, Barbie the Magnificent, sees all and knows all." Our laughter rang from the branches. She twisted in her seat, then swung down to the ground. I joined her. Barbie and I hugged like the sisters we never had, and like the friends I knew we'd always be.

Six weeks later, on a gentle September day, Arch nailed the last shingle onto the roof. After weeks of scraping, priming, painting, new gutters, new carpets, new shutters, and new plumbing, the house was finally ready for the appraiser to set the magical price for me to buy Pete Fortney's house.

Arch climbed down the ladder. While he washed his hands and face under the garden hose, Petey put her father's tools in the trunk of his car. Since that wonderful night we'd spent together, we'd seen each other at least a little while every day. Sunday we always spent with Petey. She came back from the car with a small paint can in her hand.

"Well, all through," Arch said.

"Not quite." She handed him the can. He took it and handed it to me.

"Petey and I want you to have this." I took the new can of golden oak stain, looked at it, shook it. It made no sound. It didn't have anything in it.

"Open it," Arch said.

Petey handed me a screw driver. I pried off the lid. Inside were cotton balls. I removed a few. There, laying on the white fluff, was the prettiest diamond ring I'd ever seen. My hands shook so hard, I couldn't pick it up.

"This is for me?" Tears stung my eyes.

"If you'll marry us." With her green eyes sparkling, Petey looked up at me.

"Oh, yes. Yes. Yes. Yes." I scooped her into my arms and carried both of us into her father's. "A thousand times yes. Besides, it looks like that's the only way I'll ever get my name on the deed to this house."

"I love you." Arch whispered.

"Yes, we love you," my future daughter chimed. My daughter!

I looked at my future husband. My husband! "I love you

both so much."

"Don't make me turn the hose on you guys," Barbie called to us from her tree.

Penelope Tam Fortney
requests the honor of your
presence at the wedding of her father
Archibald Danville Fortney
to Roberta Eunice Byrd, daughter of
Mr. and Mrs. Thomas Mayfield Byrd
At the Sweet Meadow Baptist Church
On Saturday, November 24,
At Two O'Clock in the afternoon.

Reception to follow in
the Banquet Room
at the Dew Drop Inn

My big day had arrived. I rode from my house to the church with Mom and Pop and my attendants. On the ride there, I looked at the town for one last time through single eyes. We had to go right by Bertie's Garage and Towing. I still had a hard time believing I owned it all, lock, stock, and barrel. Of course, Mom and Pop got dividend checks every month. With the way business had been going, it could support all of us.

We passed a billboard which had been put up at the end of summer. A smile played at the corners of my mouth. It read *Elect Jack Bigham, County Commissioner. His Tips Will Serve the Community Well.* Lord, I'd created a monster.

Actually, once I'd checked out his proposals and ideas, I'd voted for him on election day. Two weeks ago, he'd won the race. You go, Jack.

When we arrived at the church, my party slipped through a side door and into a small office off the vestibule. Mom hugged me, then left to enter the church. Mary Lou fussed with my hair. I'd told her to fix it however she wanted. The bigger, the better.

I leaned down to give Petey, my flower girl, a kiss. She wrapped her little arms around my neck. "I love you, Mommy," she said for the very first time.

I squeezed her tight and she left to walk down the aisle. I flapped my hands in front of my face and blinked rapidly. "There goes my mascara."

"Here, do this." Bridesmaid Barbie pinched my nose. "Now, sniff in."

After a few seconds, I asked, "What the heck does that do?"

"It makes you forget about crying." She disappeared through the door to make her trek down the aisle.

Oh, no. My twitch was back. I'd never get through the ceremony without breaking into a blubbering mess.

Mary Lou just took off without a hug or words. We didn't need to say anything. We both knew how the other felt. We loved each other. We were happy for each other. Without saying it, we might salvage our mascaras.

"You look beautiful, sweetheart." Pop's voice cracked.

"Thank you." I pinched my nose really hard.

The wedding march started. We took our places in the vestibule. Millie opened the door and the crowd stood.

For me.

Ahead, Arch stood with his best man and groomsmen, my brothers, Bobby and Billy. I took in several deep breaths, exhaled slowly, and controlled the river of tears trying to escape. I was going to make it.

Pop placed my hand in Arch's, then took a step back. I looked into my soon-to-be husband's eyes. Tears flowed down his cheeks. That was all she wrote for me. Mine trickled down, one behind the other, until I feared I'd drown everyone in the first two pews.

He reached into his breast pocket and pulled out a lady's, embroidered hanky. Leaning close, he whispered, "This was my mom's. Dad would want you to have it. I knew one of us would need it."

Reverend Miller paused for about two minutes for everyone to search the floor for my composure. I had lost it somewhere. Finally, and I really don't know how, we made it through the ceremony that made Arch, Petey, and me a family.

The banquet room at the Dew Drop Inn had been transformed into a magical ballroom, one any charity fund raiser would have been proud of. Barbie had thrown her heart into making our wedding reception a thing to remember. She might not have enjoyed attending those types of functions, but she had been paying attention. I couldn't thank her enough for making it so special.

As Arch and I danced together for the first time as husband and wife, Mary Lou smiled at us from her table. She'd grown to a jumbo mommy-to-be size in the last month. Just two more weeks to go and she'd be a mother.

I searched the room for Petey. Today, I'd become a mother. Pride brightened my heart.

We'd finished the segments of tradition, and would soon be leaving for a four-day weekend in Disney World, along with Petey, of course. Mary Lou gave me the hug she'd withheld before I walked down the aisle.

"When you and your husband were dancing, I took special notice." She raised her eyebrows in that way she did when I should be reading her mind.

I knew exactly what she had been looking for. "And?'

"You're going to be so happy. Your hips are exactly the same height."

In my heart, I knew Arch and I made a good match, but I liked having Mary Lou's theory to back it up.

Just then Mary Lou grimaced, screamed, and clutched her stomach. "I think this is it."

Rex did a hot-coal dance, then decided he should get the car. Arch and I helped her outside.

"We'll follow you," Arch said.

"No, you go on your honeymoon. I'll be fine," Mary Lou tried to reassure us.

"Not on your life, kiddo. I wouldn't miss this for the world," I assured her.

Mom and Pop kept their new granddaughter with them. We would pick her up in a little while to go to Florida. I bundled my wedding dress over my arm and raced Arch to our car. Rex had pulled out of the parking lot onto the highway. We had to wait for oncoming traffic.

A police car pulled along side us. Carl Kelly rolled down his window. "Sorry I couldn't make it to your wedding, but as you can see I had to work. Best wishes to the two of you. If you're half as happy as Karen and I, you'll have a wonderful life." He hooked his thumb toward the back seat. "Gotta go. I have to haul these three shoplifters into juvie." He pulled away.

In the back seat sat Donna's three kids, Pam, Randy, and Jude. I always knew the little twerps would be in jail before they were fifteen.

As we made our way to the hospital where Mary Lou and Rex would soon be parents, I clutched Arch's hand to my heart and gave thanks for my many, many blessings.

Jinxed

Beth Ciotta

Since the day beautiful socialite Afia St. John was born, her life has been plagued with bad luck. After losing her father and two older husbands in "freak" accidents, Afia now discovers her business manager has absconded with her fortune. Vowing not to rely on another man to guide her life, Afia refuses her godfather's help, and jumps at an unexpected job with Leeds Investigations.

With a pregnant, broke, sister, and an investigation agency in the red, control-freak Jake Leeds can't turn down the hefty but secret retainer offered by Afia's godfather for hiring her. Quickly seeing beyond her poor business skills, wacky superstitions, and sensationalized personal history, he realizes Afia is as generous in the heart as she is misunderstood.

But life is never easy for the woman born on Friday the 13th. Will the sexy PI be the good luck charm that puts her on a winning streak, or like everything else in her life, will their relationship wind up Jinxed?

ISBN# 0-9743639-4-4
Contemporary Romance
Available Now

www.bethciotta.com

Charmed

Beth Ciotta

The Princess is in danger . . .

Beloved storyteller to hundreds of children, Lulu Ross champions non-violence.
Just her luck, she's tiara over glass slippers for a man who carries a gun.

Professional bodyguard Colin Murphy is s-e-x-y. Too bad he's delusional. Who
would want to hurt Princess Charming—a low-profile, goody-two-shoes who
performs as a storybook character at children's birthday parties? Surely the sexy gifts
from a secret admirer are meant for her sister, a bombshell wannabe action-star.
Or are they?

Murphy is determined to protect Lulu . . . whether she likes it or not. Perpetually
cheerful and absurdly trusting, the locally famous kiddy-heroine refuses to believe
she's in danger.

Tipped off by the FBI, Murphy knows otherwise, but convincing Lulu that she's
the fantasy target of a mobster's fixation is like trying to hang shades on the sun.
Contending with a woman who favors bubblegum lip gloss and a pink poodle purse
becomes an exercise in fascination and frustration for the world-weary protection
specialist; almost as frustrating as resisting her whimsical charm.

ISBN# 1-932815-04-X
Contemporary Romance
Available Now

www.bethciotta.com

All Keyed Up
by Mary Stella

A MAN WITH A PLAN ...

At home in the Florida Keys on medical leave, undercover agent Jack Benton is on a mission to save his beloved aunt's failing dolphin facility. He's sure he can close a seven-figure deal, until his sassy Aunt Ruby accepts the proposal of a world renowned marine mammal scientist, Dr. Vic Sheffield. Against his better judgment, Jack must cooperate with the project, or break Ruby's heart.

A WOMAN WITH A DREAM ...

More than the temperature in the Florida Keys heats up when Dr. Victoria Sheffield finesses her way into the facility under the guise of her famous father's name, hoping to finally establish herself as a top notch researcher. A lifetime of behavioral observation hasn't prepared her, however, for a suspicious, sexy homo-sapien like Jack Benton. She'll need every last point of her elevated I.Q. to outwit this wily alpha male. He knows she's hiding something, and sooner or later he'll figure it out. And to complicate matters, it's not only his suspicions Victoria is arousing.

When things begin to heat up between the scientist and the undercover agent, a Category Five attraction may cause the biggest storm of the season.

ISBN# 1-932815-08-2
Contemporary Romance
Available Now

www.mary-stella.com

For more information
about these and other
great titles from
Medallion Press, visit
www.medallionpress.com